"No one else
even comes close
to
ROBERT A. HEINLEIN
in
consistently and successfully
fusing scientific thinking
with fictional form."
—*New York Herald Tribune*

REVOLT
IN
2100

By ROBERT A. HEINLEIN

WITH AN INTRODUCTION BY HENRY KUTTNER

A SIGNET BOOK from
NEW AMERICAN LIBRARY
TIMES MIRROR

CONTENTS

DATES	STORIES	CHARACTERS	TECHNICAL
A.D.	( ) Stories-to-be-told		
	Life-Line	Pinero	
	Let There Be Light"	Martin	
	(Word Edgewise)	Douglas / Gaines / Blekinsop	
1975	The Roads Must Roll	Harper	
	Blowups Happen	Erickson / King	
	The Man Who Sold the Moon	Lentz	
	Delilah & the Space Rigger	Harriman	
	Space Jockey	McIntyre	Douglas-Martin sun-power screens
	Requiem	Cummings	
	The Long Watch		
	Gentlemen, Be Seated		
	The Black Pits of Luna	Nehemiah Scudder	
	It's Great to Be Back		Mechanized roads
	We Also Walk Dogs	Wingate / San Jones / Satchel / Rhysling	Commercial rocket travel
2000	Ordeal in Space		Helicopters
	The Green Hills of Earth		
	(Fire Down Below?)		Interplanetary travel
	Logic of Empire		
	(The Sound of His Wings)		artificial radioactives, Uranium 235
	(Eclipse)		atomic artificial radioactives
2025	(The Stone Pillow)	Lazarus Long	
2050		Novak / John Lyle / Zeb Jones / Master Peter / Magedelene	(Hiatus)
	If This Goes On—		Developments in psychometrics and psychodynamics
2075		MacKinnon / "Fader" Randall / Persephone / The "Doctor"	Limited use of telepathy
	Coventry		
2100	Misfit	Ford	Interplanetary travel resumed
	Universe (prologue only)	Libby / McCoy / Rhodes / Doyle	Growth of submolar mechanics, atomic cont.
2125	Methuselah's Children		Static submolar engineering (para statics)
2600	Universe		
	Commonsense		
	(Da Capo)		

DATA	SOCIOLOGICAL	REMARKS
	THE "CRAZY YEARS"	Considerable technical advance during this period, accompanied by a gradual deterioration of mores, orientation and social institutions, terminating in mass psychoses in the sixth decade, and the Interregnum.
Transatlantic rocket flight	Strike of '66 The "FALSE DAWN," 1960-70 First rocket to the Moon, 1978	
Antipodes rocket service		The Interregnum was followed by a period of reconstruction in which the Voorhis financial proposals gave a temporary economic stability and chance for re-orientation. This was ended by the opening of new frontiers and a return to nineteenth-century economy.
	Luna City founded Space Precautionary Act Harriman's Lunar Corporations PERIOD OF IMPERIAL EXPLOITATION, 1970-2020 Revolution in Little America Interplanetary exploration and exploitation American-Australasian anschluss	
Bacteriophage The Travel Unit and the Fighting Unit	Rise of religious fanaticism The "New Crusade" Rebellion and independence of Venusian colonists	Three revolutions ended the short period of interplanetary imperialism: Antarctica, U. S., and Venus. Space travel ceased until 2072.
Commercial stereoptics		
	Religious dictatorship in U. S.	Little research and only minor technical advances during this period. Extreme puritanism. Certain aspects of psychodynamics and psychometrics, mass psychology and social control developed by the priest class.
Booster guns		
Synthetic foods		Re-establishment of civil liberty.
Weather control	THE FIRST HUMAN CIVILIZATION, 2075 et seq.	Renascence of scientific research. Resumption of space travel. Luna City refounded. Science of social relations, based on the negative basic statements of semantics. Rigor of epistemology. The Covenant.
Wave mechanics		
The "Barrier"		
Atomic "tailoring," Elements 98-416 Parastatic engineering.		
		Beginning of the consolidation of the Solar System.
Rigor of colloids Symbiotic research Longevity		First attempt at interstellar exploration. Civil disorder, followed by the end of human adolescence, and beginning of first mature culture.

For Stan and Sophia Mullen

The Innocent Eye: An Introduction

ROBERT A. HEINLEIN is probably the best story-teller in the science-fiction field today. If I were backed into a corner and forced to tell why in one sentence, I'd say, "Heinlein's got a sense of proportion." Well, how does one get a sense of proportion? By experience, I think. And there is only one kind of experience that counts as necessary to a competent writer: experience of mankind.

Literary and scientific techniques are very useful to a writer, but I don't think the study of them is necessary. They are intellectual concepts. Man is also an emotional animal. And a good story must be about man—not man after a lobotomy, but about the irrational part of him as well as the rational. Sentimentality is no substitute; it degrades man instead of treating him with the respect that, God knows, he deserves. Unfortunately, too many science-fiction stories might have been written by robots or spirits.

Now Heinlein does something that is vitally necessary to good writing: he perceives people. He knows how they feel. He has felt that way himself. He has even bridged the difficult gap of realizing that people feel much the same way everywhere, allowing for constitutional differences.

He has accepted membership in the human race.

I don't think you can be a good writer unless you do that. I'm biased, I know; I like good writing, and I have a great deal of respect for it. Good writing is well proportioned. Basically, it treats of man in his environment, and both of those elements must have verisimilitude. That's where Heinlein's sense of proportion comes in. He's eclectic. He follows the principles but not the rules. His stories have verisimilitude because they are about people, and he uses other materials only insofar as they affect those people. And here is the precise point where his sense of proportion appears. The story-elements he uses, technological, sociological, psychological, are chosen according to their natural relation to the center of interest: man. These elements are symbolic of man's values. But it is man, realistically handled, who is the nucleus of each Heinlein story.

If I had to pin a label on Heinlein, I'd call him a romantic humanist. He deals with the relation of man to science. His attitude to science is to my mind a rational one: neither idolatry nor panic, and this may be because he knows something of the social sciences, the link between man and machine.

Man as a dynamic part of a dynamic society is a concept rarely treated in science-fiction. Large faceless masses surge in the background, in an outrageously homogeneous fashion, and against this scene unqualified protagonists perform incredible and unmotivated deeds, through logical processes slightly beyond the utmost bound of human thought. No society has ever been homogeneous, even in Sparta. There will always be Coventries. Heinlein knows this, and is perhaps the only science-fiction writer who has seen the real purpose of creating a temporal frame for stories which by definition deal with the movement of man and society through time. The use of this method of dynamic continuity is one of Heinlein's major contributions to the field of science-fiction.

Imaginative literature ideally reflects and interprets reality. Future "realities" have often been handled by means of what is actually symbolism. That is, of course, one way to do it. It is not the only way; an integrated mirror of a future reality which can be accepted as three-dimensional rather than as a background of "flats" may be achieved by Heinlein's method of dynamic continuity. Once that is achieved, the writer is free to tell a story about the values of men and women which is significant to the men and women who read the story. Since the future societies which Heinlein postulates are workable societies, he can concentrate upon the important problems of human beings in relation to their culture. Those problems may affect the society, but their importance rests in how they affect the individual. And Heinlein understands that the personality is as complex as the society. The same man who wrote Coventry wrote They.

All this, however, does not entirely explain why Heinlein is such an excellent story-teller. C. L. Moore calls Heinlein's work the result of "the innocent eye and the sophisticated mind," which seems to me an accurate analysis. The term, "a sense of wonder," has been too often profaned for me to profane it, but I will go so far as to say that nobody who knows Heinlein could call him blasé. Since I have known him, his attitude has always been, "If this goes on——." And from that, it's only a step to "Once upon a time——."

HENRY KUTTNER

Los Angeles, California

10

"If This Goes On—"

1

IT was cold on the rampart. I slapped my numbed hands together, then stopped hastily for fear of disturbing the
Prophet. My post that night was just outside his personal
apartments—a post that I had won by taking more than usual
care to be neat and smart at guard mount . . . but I had no
wish to call attention to myself now.

I was young then and not too bright—a legate fresh out of
West Point, and a guardsman in the Angels of the Lord, the
personal guard of the Prophet Incarnate. At birth my mother
had consecrated me to the Church and at eighteen my Uncle
Absolom, a senior lay censor, had prayed an appointment to
the Military Academy for me from the Council of Elders.

West Point had suited me. Oh, I had joined in the usual
griping among classmates, the almost ritualistic complaining
common to all military life, but truthfully I enjoyed the
monastic routine—up at five, two hours of prayers and medita-
tion, then classes and lectures in the endless subjects of a military education, strategy and tactics, theology, mob psychology,
basic miracles. In the afternoons we practiced with vortex
guns and blasters, drilled with tanks, and hardened our bodies
with exercise.

I did not stand very high on graduation and had not really
expected to be assigned to the Angels of the Lord, even though
I had put in for it. But I had always gotten top marks in piety
and stood well enough in most of the practical subjects; I was
chosen. It made me almost sinfully proud—the holiest regiment of the Prophet's hosts, even the privates of which were
commissioned officers and whose Colonel-in-Chief was the
Prophet's Sword Triumphant, marshal of all the hosts. The
day I was invested in the shining buckler and spear worn only
by the Angels I vowed to petition to study for the priesthood as
soon as promotion to captain made me eligible.

But this night, months later, though my buckler was still
shining bright, there was a spot of tarnish in my heart. Somehow, life at New Jerusalem was not as I had imagined it while
at West Point. The Palace and Temple were shot through with
intrigue and politics; priests and deacons, ministers of state,
and Palace functionaries all seemed engaged in a scramble
for power and favor at the hand of the Prophet. Even the officers of my own corps seemed corrupted by it. Our proud

motto *"Non Sibi, Sed Dei"* now had a wry flavor in my mouth.

Not that I was without sin myself. While I had not joined in the struggle for worldly preference, I had done something which I knew in my heart to be worse: I had looked with longing on a consecrated female.

Please understand me better than I understood myself. I was a grown man in body, an infant in experience. My own mother was the only woman I had ever known well. As a kid in junior seminary before going to the Point I was almost afraid of girls; my interests were divided between my lessons, my mother, and our parish's troop of Cherubim, in which I was a patrol leader and an assiduous winner of merit badges in everything from woodcraft to memorizing scripture. If there had been a merit badge to be won in the subject of girls —but of course there was not.

At the Military Academy I simply saw no females, nor did I have much to confess in the way of evil thoughts. My human feelings were pretty much still in freeze, and my occasional uneasy dreams I regarded as temptations sent by Old Nick. But New Jerusalem is not West Point and the Angels were neither forbidden to marry nor were we forbidden proper and sedate association with women. True, most of my fellows did n⁻⁺ ask permission to marry, as it would have meant transfer-ᵢₙg to one of the regular regiments and many of them cher-ished ambitions for the military priesthood—but it was not forbidden.

Nor were the lay deaconesses who kept house around the Temple and the Palace forbidden to marry. But most of them were dowdy old creatures who reminded me of my aunts, hardly subjects for romantic thoughts. I used to chat with them occasionally around the corridors, no harm in that. Nor was I attracted especially by any of the few younger sisters—until I met Sister Judith.

I had been on watch in this very spot more than a month earlier. It was the first time I had stood guard outside the Prophet's apartments and, while I was nervous when first posted, at that moment I had been no more than alert against the possibility of the warden-of-the-watch making his rounds.

That night a light had shone briefly far down the inner corridor opposite my post and I had heard a sound of people moving; I had glanced at my wrist chrono—yes, that would be the Virgins ministering to the Prophet . . . no business of mine. Each night at ten o'clock their watch changed—their "guard mount" I called it, though I had never seen the ceremony and never would. All that I actually knew about it was that those coming on duty for the next twenty-four hours drew lots at that time for the privilege of personal attendance in the sacred presence of the Prophet Incarnate.

I had listened briefly and had turned away. Perhaps a quar-

12

ter of an hour later a slight form engulfed in a dark cloak had slipped past me to the parapet, there to stand and look at the stars. I had had my blaster out at once, then had returned it sheepishly, seeing that it was a deaconess.

I had assumed that she was a lay deaconess; I swear that it did not occur to me that she might be a holy deaconess. There was no rule in my order book telling me to forbid them to come outside, but I had never heard of one doing so.

I do not think that she had seen me before I spoke to her. "Peace be unto you, sister."

She had jumped and suppressed a squeal, then had gathered her dignity to answer, "And to you, *little* brother."

It was then that I had seen on her forehead the Seal of Solomon, the mark of the personal family of the Prophet. "Your pardon, Elder Sister. I did not see."

"I am not annoyed." It had seemed to me that she invited conversation. I knew that it was not proper for us to converse privately; her mortal being was dedicated to the Prophet just as her soul was the Lord's, but I was young and lonely—and she was young and very pretty.

"Do you attend the Holy One this night, Elder Sister?"

She had shaken her head at that. "No, the honor passed me by. My lot was not drawn."

"It must be a great and wonderful privilege to serve him directly."

"No doubt, though I cannot say of my own knowledge. My lot has never yet been drawn." She had added impulsively, "I'm a little nervous about it. You see, I haven't been here long."

Even though she was my senior in rank, her display of feminine weakness had touched me. "I am sure that you will deport yourself with credit."

"Thank you."

We had gone on chatting. She had been in New Jerusalem, it developed, even less time than had I. She had been reared on a farm in upper New York State and there she had been sealed to the Prophet at the Albany Seminary. In turn I had told her that I had been born in the middle west, not fifty miles from the Well of Truth, where the First Prophet was incarnated. I then told her that my name was John Lyle and she had answered that she was called Sister Judith.

I had forgotten all about the warden-of-the-watch and his pesky rounds and was ready to chat all night, when my chrono had chimed the quarter hour. "Oh, dear!" Sister Judith had exclaimed. "I should have gone straight back to my cell." She had started to hurry away, then had checked herself. "You wouldn't tell on me. . . . John Lyle?"

"Me? Oh, never!"

I had continued to think about her the rest of the watch.

13

When the warden did make rounds I was a shade less than alert.

A mighty little on which to found a course of folly, eh? A single drink is a great amount to a teetotaler; I was not able to get Sister Judith out of my mind. In the month that followed I saw her half a dozen times. Once I passed her on an escalator; she was going down as I was going up. We did not even speak, but she had recognized me and smiled. I rode that escalator all night that night in my dreams, but I could never get off and speak to her. The other encounters were just as trivial. Another time I heard her voice call out to me quietly, "Hello, John Lyle," and I turned just in time to see a hooded figure go past my elbow through a door. Once I watched her feeding the swans in the moat; I did not dare approach her but I think that she saw me.

The *Temple Herald* printed the duty lists of both my service and hers. I was standing a watch in five; the Virgins drew lots once a week. So it was just over a month later that our watches again matched. I saw her name—and vowed that I would win the guard mount that evening and again be posted at the post of honor before the Prophet's own apartments. I had no reason to think that Judith would seek me out on the rampart—but I was sure in my heart that she would. Never at West Point had I ever expended more spit-and-polish; I could have used my buckler for a shaving mirror.

But here it was nearly half past ten and no sign of Judith, although ʼ ̣ ̣d heard the Virgins gather down the corridor prom ̣ ̣ ̣at ten. All I had to show for my efforts was the poor ̣ ̣ege of standing watch at the coldest post in the Palace.

Probably, I thought glumly, she comes out to flirt with the guardsmen on watch everytime she has a chance. I recalled bitterly that all women were vessels of iniquity and had always been so since the Fall of Man. Who was I to think that she had singled me out for special friendship? She had probably considered the night too cold to bother.

I heard a footstep and my heart leaped with joy. But it was only the warden making his rounds. I brought my pistol to the ready and challenged him; his voice came back, "Watchman, what of the night?"

I answered mechanically, "Peace on Earth," and added, "It is cold, Elder Brother."

"Autumn in the air," he agreed. "Chilly even in the Temple." He passed on by with his pistol and his bandolier of paralysis bombs slapping his armor to his steps. He was a nice old duffer and usually stopped for a few friendly words; tonight he was probably eager to get back to the warmth of the guardroom. I went back to my sour thoughts.

"Good evening, John Lyle."

I almost jumped out of my boots. Standing in the darkness

14

just inside the archway was Sister Judith. I managed to splutter, "Good evening, Sister Judith," as she moved toward me.

"Sssh!" she cautioned me. "Someone might hear us. John . . . John Lyle—it finally happened. My lot was drawn!"

I said, "Huh?" then added lamely, "Felicitations, Elder Sister. May God make his face to shine on your holy service."

"Yes, yes, thanks," she answered quickly, "but John . . . I had intended to steal a few moments to chat with you. Now I can't—I must be at the robing room for indoctrination and prayer almost at once. I must run."

"You'd better hurry," I agreed. I was disappointed that she could not stay, happy for her that she was honored, and exultant that she had not forgotten me. "God go with you."

"But I just had to tell you that I had been chosen." Her eyes were shining with what I took to be holy joy; her next words startled me. "I'm scared, John Lyle."

"Eh? Frightened?" I suddenly recalled how I had felt, how my voice had cracked, the first time I ever drilled a platoon. "Do not be. You will be sustained."

"Oh, I hope so! Pray for me, John." And she was gone, lost in the dark corridor.

I did pray for her and I tried to imagine where she was, what she was doing. But since I knew as little about what went on inside the Prophet's private chambers as a cow knows about courts-martial, I soon gave it up and simply thought about Judith. Later, an hour or more, my revery was broken by a high scream inside the Palace, followed by a commotion, and running footsteps. I dashed down the inner corridor and found a knot of women gathered around the portal to the Prophet's apartments. Two or three others were carrying someone out the portal; they stopped when they reached the corridor and eased their burden to the floor.

"What's the trouble?" I demanded and drew my side arm clear.

An elderly Sister stepped in front of me. "It is nothing. Return to your post, legate."

"I heard a scream."

"No business of yours. One of the Sisters fainted when the Holy One required service of her."

"Who was it?"

"You are rather nosy, little brother." She shrugged. "Sister Judith, if it matters."

I did not stop to think but snapped, "Let me help her!" and started forward. She barred my way.

"Are you out of your mind? Her sisters will return her to her cell. Since when do the Angels minister to nervous Virgins?"

I could easily have pushed her aside with one finger, but she

15

was right. I backed down and went unwillingly back to my post.

For the next few days I could not get Sister Judith out of my mind. Off watch, I prowled the parts of the Palace I was free to visit, hoping to catch sight of her. She might be ill, or she might be confined to her cell for what must certainly have been a major breach of discipline. But I never saw her.

My roommate, Zebadiah Jones, noticed my moodiness and tried to rouse me out of it. Zeb was three classes senior to me and I had been one of his plebes at the Point; now he was my closest friend and my only confidant. "Johnnie old son, you look like a corpse at your own wake. What's eating on you?"

"Huh? Nothing at all. Touch of indigestion, maybe."

"So? Come on, let's go for a walk. The air will do you good."

I let him herd me outside. He said nothing but banalities until we were on the broad terrace surrounding the south turret and free of the danger of eye and ear devices. When we were well away from anyone else he said softly, "Come on. Spill it."

"Shucks, Zeb, I can't burden anybody else with it."

"Why not? What's a friend for?"

"Uh, you'd be shocked."

"I doubt it. The last time I was shocked was when I drew four of a kind to an ace kicker. It restored my faith in miracles and I've been relatively immune ever since. Come on— we'll call this a privileged communication—elder adviser and all that sort of rot."

I let him persuade me. To my surprise Zeb was not shocked to find that I let myself become interested in a holy deaconess. So I told him the whole story and added to it my doubts and troubles, the misgivings that had been growing in me since the day I reported for duty at New Jerusalem.

He nodded casually. "I can see how it would affect you that way, knowing you. See here, you haven't admitted any of this at confession, have you?"

"No," I admitted with embarrassment.

"Then don't. Nurse your own fox. Major Bagby is broad-minded, you wouldn't shock him—but he might find it necessary to pass it on to his superiors. You wouldn't want to face Inquisition even if you were alabaster innocent. In fact, especially since you are innocent—and you *are*, you know; everybody has impious thoughts at times. But the Inquisitor expects to find sin; if he doesn't find it, he keeps on digging."

At the suggestion that I might be put to the Question my stomach almost turned over. I tried not to show it for Zeb went on calmly, "Johnnie my lad, I admire your piety and your innocence, but I don't envy it. Sometimes too much piety is more of a handicap than too little. You find yourself shocked at the idea that it takes politics as well as psalm singing to run a big country. Now take me; I noticed the same things when I

16

was new here, but I hadn't expected anything different and wasn't shocked."

"But—" I shut up. His remarks sounded painfully like heresy; I changed the subject. "Zeb, what do you suppose it could have been that upset Judith so and caused her to faint the night she served the Prophet?"

"Eh? How should I know?" He glanced at me and looked away.

"Well, I just thought you might. You generally have all the gossip around the Palace."

"Well . . . oh, forget it, old son. It's really not important."

"Then you *do* know?"

"I didn't say that. Maybe I could make a close guess, but you don't want guesses. So forget it."

I stopped strolling, stepped in front of him and faced him. "Zeb, anything you know about it—or can guess—I want to hear. It's important to me."

"Easy now! You were afraid of shocking me; it could be that I don't want to shock you."

"What do you mean? Tell me!"

"Easy, I said. We're out strolling, remember, without a care in the world, talking about our butterfly collections and wondering if we'll have stewed beef again for dinner tonight."

Still fuming, I let him take me along with him. He went on more quietly, "John, you obviously aren't the type to learn things just by keeping your ear to the ground—and you've not yet studied any of the Inner Mysteries, now have you?"

"You know I haven't. The psych classification officer hasn't cleared me for the course. I don't know why."

"I should have let you read some of the installments while I was boning it. No, that was before you graduated. Too bad, for they explain things in much more delicate language than I know how to use—and justify every bit of it thoroughly, if you care for the dialectics of religious theory. John, what is your notion of the duties of the Virgins?"

"Why, they wait on him, and cook his food, and so forth."

"They surely do. And so forth. This Sister Judith—an innocent little country girl the way you describe her. Pretty devout, do you think?"

I answered somewhat stiffly that her devoutness had first attracted me to her. Perhaps I believed it.

"Well, it could be that she simply became shocked at overhearing a rather worldly and cynical discussion between the Holy One and, oh, say the High Bursar—taxes and tithes and the best way to squeeze them out of the peasants. It might be something like that, although the scribe for such a conference would hardly be a grass-green Virgin on her first service. No, it was almost certainly the 'And so forth.'"

"Huh? I don't follow you."

Zeb sighed. "You really are one of God's innocents, aren't you? Holy Name, I thought you knew and were just too stubbornly straight-laced to admit it. Why, even the Angels carry on with the Virgins at times, after the Prophet is through with them. Not to mention the priests and the deacons. I remember a time when——" He broke off suddenly, catching sight of my face. "Wipe that look off your face! Do you want somebody to notice us?"

I tried to do so, with terrible thoughts jangling around inside my head. Zeb went on quietly, "It's my guess, if it matters that much to you, that your friend Judith still merits the title 'Virgin' in the purely physical sense as well as the spiritual. She might even stay that way, if the Holy One is as angry with her as he probably was. She is probably as dense as you are and failed to understand the symbolic explanations given her—then blew her top when it came to the point where she couldn't fail to understand, so he kicked her out. Small wonder!"

I stopped again, muttering to myself biblical expressions I hardly thought I knew. Zeb stopped, too, and stood looking at me with a smile of cynical tolerance. "Zeb," I said, almost pleading with him, "these are terrible things. Terrible! Don't tell me that you approve?"

"Approve? Man, it's all part of the Plan. I'm sorry you haven't been cleared for higher study. See here, I'll give you a rough briefing. God wastes not. Right?"

"That's sound doctrine."

"God requires nothing of man beyond his strength. Right?"

"Yes, but—"

"Shut up. God commands man to be fruitful. The Prophet ⸱⸱arnate, being especially holy, is required to be especially fru⸱ful. That's the gist of it; you can pick up the fine points whe⸱ ⸱ou study it. In the meantime, if the Prophet can humble himse⸱ to the flesh in order to do his plain duty, who are you to raise ⸱ ruction? Answer me that."

I coul⸱ not answer, of course, and we continued our walk in silence. ⸱ had to admit the logic of what he had said and that the conclusions were built up from the revealed doctrines. The trouble was that I wanted to eject the conclusions, throw them up as if they had been something poisonous I had swallowed.

Presently I was consoling myself with the thought that Zeb felt sure that Judith had not been harmed. I began to feel better, telling myself that Zeb was right, that it was not my place, most decidedly not my place, to sit in moral judgment on the Holy Prophet Incarnate.

My mind was just getting around to worrying the thought that my relief over Judith arose solely from the fact that I had looked on her sinfully, that there could not possibly be one rule for one holy deaconess, another rule for all the rest, and I was beginning to be unhappy again—when Zeb stopped suddenly. "What was that?"

We hurried to the parapet of the terrace and looked down the wall. The south wall lies close to the city proper. A crowd of fifty or sixty people was charging up the slope that led to the Palace walls. Ahead of them, running with head averted, was a man dressed in a long gabardine. He was headed for the Sanctuary gate.

Zebadiah looked down and answered himself. "That's what the racket is—some of the rabble stoning a pariah. He probably was careless enough to be caught outside the ghetto after five." He stared down and shook his head. "I don't think he is going to make it."

Zeb's prediction was realized at once; a large rock caught the man between the shoulder blades, he stumbled and went down. They were on him at once. He struggled to his knees, was struck by a dozen stones, went down in a heap. He gave a broken high-pitched wail, then drew a fold of the gabardine across his dark eyes and strong Roman nose.

A moment later there was nothing to be seen but a pile of rocks and a protruding slippered foot. It jerked and was still.

I turned away, nauseated. Zebadiah caught my expression.

"Why," I said defensively, "do these pariahs persist in their heresy? They seem such harmless fellows otherwise."

He cocked a brow at me. "Perhaps it's not heresy to them. Didn't you see that fellow resign himself to his God?"

"But that is not the true God."

"He must have thought otherwise."

"But they all know better; we've told them often enough."

He smiled in so irritating a fashion that I blurted out, "I don't understand you, Zeb—blessed if I do! Ten minutes ago you were instructing me in correct doctrine; now you seem to be defending heresy. Reconcile that."

He shrugged. "Oh, I can play the Devil's advocate. I made the debate team at the Point, remember? I'll be a famous theologian someday—if the Grand Inquisitor doesn't get me first."

"Well . . . Look—you *do* think it's right to stone the ungodly? Don't you?"

He changed the subject abruptly. "Did you notice who cast the first stone?" I hadn't and told him so; all I remembered was that it was a man in country clothes, rather than a woman or a child.

"It was Snotty Fassett." Zeb's lip curled.

I recalled Fassett too well; he was two classes senior to me and had made my plebe year something I want to forget. "So that's how it was," I answered slowly. "Zeb, I don't think I could stomach intelligence work."

"Certainly not as an *agent provocateur*," he agreed. "Still,

19

I suppose the Council needs these incidents occasionally. These rumors about the Cabal and all. . . ."

I caught up this last remark. "Zeb, do you really think there is anything to this Cabal? I can't believe that there is any organized disloyalty to the Prophet."

"Well—there has certainly been some trouble out on the West Coast. Oh, forget it; our job is to keep the watch here."

2

BUT we were not allowed to forget it; two days later the inner guard was doubled. I did not see how there could be any real danger, as the Palace was as strong a fortress as ever was built, with its lower recesses immune even to fission bombs. Besides that, a person entering the Palace, even from the Temple grounds, would be challenged and identified a dozen times before he reached the Angel on guard outside the Prophet's own quarters. Nevertheless people in high places were getting jumpy; there must be something to it.

But I was delighted to find that I had been assigned as Zebadiah's partner. Standing twice as many hours of guard was almost offset by having him to talk with—for me at least. As for poor Zeb, I banged his ear endlessly through the long night watches, talking about Judith and how unhappy I was with the way things were at New Jerusalem. Finally he turned on me.

"See here, Mr. Dumbjohn," he snapped, reverting to my plebe year designation, "are you in love with her?"

I tried to hedge. I had not yet admitted to myself that my interest was more than in her welfare. He cut me short.

"You do or you don't. Make up your mind. If you do, we'll talk practical matters. If you don't, then shut up about her."

I took a deep breath and took the plunge. "I guess I do, Zeb. It seems impossible and I know it's a sin, but there it is."

"All of that and folly, too. But there is no talking sense to you. Okay, so you are in love with her. What next?"

"Eh?"

"What do you want to do? Marry her?"

I thought about it with such distress that I covered my face with my hands. "Of course I do," I admitted. "But how can I?"

"Precisely. You can't. You can't marry without transferring away from here; her service can't marry at all. Nor is there any way for her to break her vows, since she is already sealed. But if you can face up to bare facts without blushing, there is plenty you can do. You two could be very cozy—if you could get over being such an infernal bluenose."

A week earlier I would not have understood what he was driving at. But now I knew. I could not even really be angry with him at making such a dishonorable and sinful suggestion; he meant well—and some of the tarnish was now in my own soul. I shook my head. "You shouldn't have said that, Zeb. Judith is not that sort of a woman."

"Okay. Then forget it. And her. And shut up about her."

I sighed wearily. "Don't be rough on me, Zeb. This is more than I know how to manage." I glanced up and down, then took a chance and sat down on the parapet. We were not on watch near the Holy One's quarters but at the east wall; our warden, Captain Peter van Eyck, was too fat to get that far oftener than once a watch, so I took a chance. I was bone tired from not having slept much lately.

"Sorry."

"Don't be angry, Zeb. That sort of thing isn't for me and it certainly isn't for Judith—for Sister Judith." I knew what I wanted for us: a little farm, about a hundred and sixty acres, like the one I had been born on. Pigs and chickens and bare-footed kids with happy dirty faces and Judith to have her face light up when I came in from the fields and then wipe the perspiration from her face with her apron so that I could kiss her . . . no more connection with the Church and the Prophet than Sunday meeting and tithes.

But it could not be, it could never be. I put it out of my mind. "Zeb," I went on, "just as a matter of curiosity—You have intimated that these things go on all the time. How? We live in a goldfish bowl here. It doesn't seem possible."

He grinned at me so cynically that I wanted to slap him, but his voice had no leer in it. "Well, just for example, take your own case—"

"Out of the question!"

"Just for example, I said. Sister Judith isn't available right now; she is confined to her cell. But—"

"Huh? She's been *arrested?*" I thought wildly of the Question and what Zeb had said about the inquisitors.

"No, no, no! She isn't even locked in. She's been told to stay there, that's all, with prayer and bread-and-water as company. They are purifying her heart and instructing her in her spiritual duties. When she sees things in their true light, her lot will be drawn again—and this time she won't faint and make an adolescent fool of herself."

I pushed back my first reaction and tried to think about it calmly. "No," I said. "Judith will never do it. Not if she stays in her cell forever."

"So? I wouldn't be too sure. They can be very persuasive.

21

How would you like to be prayed over in relays? But assume that she does see the light, just so that I can finish my story."

"Zeb, how do you know about this?"

"Sheol, man! I've been here going on three years. Do you think I wouldn't be hooked into the grapevine? You were worried about her—and making yourself a tiresome nuisance if I may say so. So I asked the birdies. But to continue. She sees the light, her lot is drawn, she performs her holy service to the Prophet. After that she is called once a week like the rest and her lot is drawn maybe once a month or less. Inside of a year—unless the Prophet finds some very exceptional beauty in her soul—they stop putting her name among the lots entirely. But it isn't necessary to wait that long, although it is more discreet."

"The whole thing is shameful!"

"Really? I imagine King Solomon had to use some such system; he had even more women on his neck than the Holy One has. Thereafter, if you can come to some mutual understanding with the Virgin involved, it is just a case of following well known customs. There is a present to be made to the Eldest Sister, and to be renewed as circumstances dictate. There are some palms to be brushed—I can tell you which ones. And this great pile of masonry has lots of dark back stairs in it. With all customs duly observed, there is no reason why, almost any night I have the watch and you don't, you should not find something warm and cuddly in your bed."

I was about to explode at the calloused way he put it when my mind went off at a tangent. "Zeb—now I know you are telling an untruth. You were just pulling my leg, admit it. There is an eye and an ear somewhere in our room. Why, even if I tried to find them and cut them out, I'd simply have the security watch banging on the door in three minutes."

"So what? There is an eye and an ear in every room in the place. You ignore them."

I simply let my mouth sag open.

"Ignore them," he went on. "Look, John, a little casual fornication is no threat to the Church—treason and heresy are. It will simply be entered in your dossier and nothing will be said about it—unless they catch you in something really important later, in which case they might use it to hang you instead of preferring the real charges. Old son, they *like* to have such peccadilloes in the files; it increases security. They are probably uneasy about you; you are too perfect; such men are dangerous. Which is probably why you've never been cleared for higher study."

I tried to straighten out in my mind the implied cross purposes, the wheels within wheels, and gave up. "I just don't get it. Look, Zeb, all this doesn't have anything to do with me

22

. . . or with Judith. But I know what I've *got* to do. Somehow I've got to get her out of here."

"Hmm . . . a mighty strait gate, old son."

"I've got to."

"Well . . . I'd like to help you. I suppose I could get a message to her," he added doubtfully.

I caught his arm. "Would you, Zeb?"

He sighed. "I wish you would wait. No, that wouldn't help, seeing the romantic notions in your mind. But it is risky now. Plenty risky, seeing that she is under discipline by order of the Prophet. You'd look funny staring down the table of a court-martial board, looking at your own spear."

"I'll risk even that. Or even the Question."

He did not remind me that he himself was taking even more of a risk than I was; he simply said, "Very well, what is the message?"

I thought for a moment. It would have to be short. "Tell her that the legate she talked to the night her lot was drawn is worried about her."

"Anything else?"

"Yes! Tell her that I am hers to command!"

It seems flamboyant in recollection. No doubt it was—but it was exactly the way I felt.

At luncheon the next day I found a scrap of paper folded into my napkin. I hurried through the meal and slipped out to read it.

I need your help, it read, *and am so very grateful. Will you meet me tonight?* It was unsigned and had been typed in the script of a common voicewriter, used anywhere in the Palace, or out. When Zeb returned to our room, I showed it to him; he glanced at it and remarked in idle tones:

"Let's get some air. I ate too much, I'm about to fall asleep."

Once we hit the open terrace and were free of the hazard of eye and ear he cursed me out in low, dispassionate tones. "You'll never make a conspirator. Half the mess must know that you found something in your napkin. Why in God's name did you gulp your food and rush off? Then to top it off you handed it to me upstairs. For all you know the eye read it and photostated it for evidence. Where in the world were you when they were passing out brains?"

I protested but he cut me off. "Forget it! I know you didn't mean to put both of our necks in a bight—but good intentions are no good when the trial judge-advocate reads the charges. Now get this through your head: the first principle of intrigue is never to be seen doing anything unusual, no matter how harmless it may seem. You wouldn't believe how small a deviation from pattern looks significant to a trained analyst. You should have stayed in the refectory the usual time, hung around

23

and gossiped as usual afterwards, then waited until you were safe to read it. Now where is it?"

"In the pocket of my corselet," I answered humbly. "Don't worry, I'll chew it up and swallow it."

"Not so fast. Wait here." Zeb left and was back in a few minutes. "I have a piece of paper the same size and shape; I'll pass it to you quietly. Swap the two, and then you can eat the real note—but don't be seen making the swap or chewing up the real one."

"All right. But what is the second sheet of paper?"

"Some notes on a system for winning at dice."

"Huh? But that's non-reg, too!"

"Of course, you hammer head. If they catch you with evidence of gambling, they won't suspect you of a much more serious sin. At worst, the skipper will eat you out and fine you a few days pay and a few hours contrition. Get this, John: if you are ever suspected of something, try to make the evidence point to a lesser offense. Never try to prove lily-white innocence. Human nature being what it is, your chances are better."

I gu   Zeb was right; my pockets must have been searched and t evidence photographed right after I changed uniforms for   ade, for half an hour afterwards I was called into the Ex tive Officer's office. He asked me to keep my eyes open fo dications of gambling among the junior officers. It was   n, he said, that he hated to have his younger officers fall   o. He clapped me on the shoulder as I was leaving. "You're   good boy, John Lyle. A word to the wise, eh?"

Zeb and I had the midwatch at the south Palace portal that night. Half the watch passed with no sign of Judith and I was as nervous as a cat in a strange house, though Zeb tried to keep me calmed down by keeping me strictly to routine. At long last there were soft footfalls in the inner corridor and a shape appeared in the doorway. Zebadiah motioned me to remain on tour and went to check. He returned almost at once and motioned me to join him, while putting a finger to his lips. Trembling, I went in. It was not Judith but some woman strange to me who waited there in the darkness. I started to speak but Zeb put his hand over my mouth.

The woman took my arm and urged me down the corridor. I glanced back and saw Zeb silhouetted in the portal, covering our rear. My guide paused and pushed me into an almost pitchblack alcove, then she took from the folds of her robes a small object which I took to be a pocket ferret-scope, from the small d; } that glowed faintly on its side. She ran it up and down and around, snapped it off and returned it to her person. "Now you can talk," she said softly. "It's safe." She slipped away.

I felt a gentle touch at my sleeve. "Judith?" I whispered. "Yes," she answered, so softly that I could hardly hear her.

Then my arms were around her. She gave a little startled cry, then her own arms went around my neck and I could feel her breath against my face. We kissed clumsily but with almost frantic eagerness.

It is no one's business what we talked about then, nor could I give a coherent account if I tried. Call our behavior romantic nonsense, call it delayed puppy love touched off by ignorance and unnatural lives—do puppies hurt less than grown dogs? Call it what you like and laugh at us, but at that moment we were engulfed in that dear madness more precious than rubies and fine gold, more to be desired than sanity. If you have never experienced it and do not know what I am talking about, I am sorry for you.

Presently we quieted down somewhat and talked more reasonably. When she tried to tell me about the night her lot had been drawn she began to cry. I shook her and said, "Stop it, my darling. You don't have to tell me about it. I know."

She gulped and said, "But you don't know. You can't know. I . . . he . . ."

I shook her again. "Stop it. Stop it at once. No more tears. I do know, exactly. And I know what you are in for still—unless we get you out of here. So there is no time for tears or nerves; we have to make plans."

She was dead silent for a long moment, then she said slowly, "You mean for me to . . . desert? I've thought of that. Merciful God, how I've thought about it! But how can I?"

"I don't know—yet. But we will figure out a way. We've got to." We discussed possibilities. Canada was a bare three hundred miles away and she knew the upstate New York country; in fact it was the only area she did know. But the border there was more tightly closed than it was anywhere else, patrol boats and radar walls by water, barbed wire and sentries by land . . . and sentry dogs. I had trained with such dogs; I wouldn't urge my worst enemy to go up against them.

But Mexico was simply impossibly far away. If she headed south she would probably be arrested in twenty-four hours. No one would knowingly give shelter to an unveiled Virgin; under the inexorable rule of associative guilt any such good Samaritan would be as guilty as she of the same personal treason against the Prophet and would die the same death. Going north would be shorter at least, though it meant the same business of traveling by night, hiding by day, stealing food or going hungry. Near Albany lived an aunt of Judith's; she felt sure that her aunt would risk hiding her until some

25

way could be worked out to cross the border. "She'll keep us safe. I know it."

"Us?" I must have sounded stupid. Until she spoke I had had my nose so close to the single problem of how she was to escape that it had not yet occurred to me that she would expect both of us to go.

"Did you mean to send me *alone?*"

"Why . . . I guess I hadn't thought about it any other way."

"No!"

"But—look, Judith, the urgent thing, the thing that must be done at once, is to get you out of here. Two people trying to travel and hide are many times more likely to be spotted than one. It just doesn't make sense to—"

"No! I won't go."

I thought about it, hurriedly. I still hadn't realized that "A" implies "B" and that I myself in urging her to desert her service was as much a deserter in my heart as she was. I said, "We'll get you out first, that's the important thing. You tell me where your aunt lives—then wait for me."

"Not without you."

"But you *must*. The Prophet—"

"Better that than to lose you now!"

I did not then understand women—and I still don't. Two minutes before she had been quietly planning to risk death by ordeal rather than submit her body to the Holy One. Now she was almost casually willing to accept it rather than put up with even a temporary separation. I don't understand women; I sometimes think there is no logic in them at all.

I said, "Look, my dear one, we have not yet even figured out how we are to get you out of the Palace. It's likely to be utterly impossible for us both to escape the same instant. You see that, don't you?"

She answered stubbornly, "Maybe. But I don't like it. Well, how do I get out? And when?"

I had to admit again that I did not know. I intended to consult Zeb as soon as possible, but I had no other notion.

But Judith had a suggestion. "John, you know the Virgin who guided you here? No? Sister Magdalene. I know it is safe to tell her and she *might* be willing to help us. She's very clever."

I started to comment doubtfully but we were interrupted by Sister Magdalene herself. "Quick!" she snapped at me as she slipped in beside us. "Back to the rampart!"

I rushed out and was barely in time to avoid being caught by the warden, making his rounds. He exchanged challenges with Zeb and myself—and then the old fool wanted to chat. He settled himself down on the steps of the portal and started recalling boastfully a picayune fencing victory of the week before. I tried dismally to help Zeb with chit-chat in a fashion normal for a man bored by a night watch.

At last he got to his feet. "I'm past forty and getting a little heavier, maybe. I'll admit frankly it warms me to know that I still have a wrist and eye as fast as you young blades." He straightened his scabbard and added, "I suppose I had better take a turn through the Palace. Can't take too many precautions these days. They do say the Cabal has been active again." He took out his torch light and flashed it down the corridor.

I froze solid. If he inspected that corridor, it was beyond hope that he would miss two women crouching in an alcove.

But Zebadiah spoke up calmly, casually. "Just a moment, Elder Brother. Would you show me that time riposte you used to win that last match? It was too fast for me to follow it."

He took the bait. "Why, glad to, son!" He moved off the steps, came out to where there was room. "Draw your sword. En garde! Cross blades in line of sixte. Disengage and attack me. There! Hold the lunge and I'll demonstrate it slowly. As your point approaches my chest—" (Chest indeed! Captain van Eyck was as pot-bellied as a kangaroo!) "—I catch it with the forte of my blade and force it over yours in riposte seconde. Just like the book, so far. But I do not complete the riposte. Strong as it is, you might parry or counter. Instead, as my point comes down, I beat your blade out of line—" He illustrated and the steel sang. "—and attack you anywhere, from chin to ankle. Come now, try it on me."

Zeb did so and they ran through the phrase; the warden retreated a step. Zeb asked to do it again to get it down pat. They ran through it repeatedly, faster each time, with the warden retreating each time to avoid by a hair Zeb's unbated point. It was strictly against regulations to fence with real swords and without mask and plastron, but the warden really was good . . . a swordsman so precise that he was confident of his own skill not to blind one of Zeb's eyes, not to let Zeb hurt him. In spite of my own galloping jitters I watched it closely; it was a beautiful demonstration of a once-useful military art. Zeb pressed him hard.

They finished up fifty yards away from the portal and that much closer to the guardroom. I could hear the warden puffing from the exercise. "That was fine, Jones," he gasped. "You caught on handsomely." He puffed again and added, "Lucky for me a real bout does not go on as long. I think I'll let you inspect the corridor." He turned away toward the guardroom, adding cheerfully, "God keep you."

"God go with you, sir," Zeb responded properly and brought his hilt to his chin in salute.

As soon as the warden turned the corner Zeb stood by again and I hurried back to the alcove. The women were

27

still there, making themselves small against the back wall. "He's gone," I reassured them. "Nothing to fear for a while."

Judith had told Sister Magdalene of our dilemma and we discussed it in whispers. She advised us strongly not to try to reach any decisions just then. "I'm in charge of Judith's purification; I can stretch it out for another week, perhaps, before she has to draw lots again."

I said, "We've got to act before then!"

Judith seemed over her fears, now that she had laid her troubles in Sister Magdalene's lap. "Don't worry, John," she said softly, "the chances are my lot won't be drawn soon again in any case. We must do what she advises."

Sister Magdalene sniffed contemptuously. "You're wrong about that, Judy, When you are returned to duty, your lot will be drawn, you can be sure ahead of time. Not," she added, "but what you could live through it—the rest of us have. If it seems safer to—" She stopped suddenly and listened. "Sssh! Quiet as death." She slipped silently out of our circle.

A thin pencil of light flashed out and splashed on a figure crouching outside the alcove. I dived and was on him before he could get to his feet. Fast as I had been, Sister Magdalene was just as fast; she landed on his shoulders as he went down. He jerked and was still.

Zebadiah came running in, checked himself at our sides. "John! Maggie!" came his tense whisper. "What is it?"

"We've caught a spy, Zeb," I answered hurriedly. "What'll we do with him?"

Zeb flashed his light. "You've knocked him out?"

"He won't come to," answered Magdalene's calm voice out of the darkness. "I slipped a vibroblade in his ribs."

"Sheol!"

"Zeb, I had to do it. Be glad I didn't use steel and mess up the floor with blood. But what do we do now?"

Zeb cursed her softly, she took it. "Turn him over, John. Let's take a look." I did so and his light flashed again. "Hey, Johnnie—it's Snotty Fassett." He paused and I could almost hear him think. "Well, we'll waste no tears on *him*. John!"

"Yeah, Zeb?"

"Keep the watch outside. If anyone comes, I am inspecting the corridor. I've got to dump this carcass somewhere."

Judith broke the silence. "There's an incinerator chute on the floor above. I'll help you."

"Stout girl. Get going, John."

I wanted to object that it was no work for a woman, but I shut up and turned away. Zeb took his shoulders, the women a leg apiece and managed well enough. They were back in minutes, though it seemed endless to me. No doubt Snotty's body was reduced to atoms before they were back —we might get away with it. It did not seem like murder to me then, and still does not; we did what we had to do, rushed along by events.

Zeb was curt. "This tears it. Our reliefs will be along in ten minutes; we've got to figure this out in less time than that. Well?"

Our suggestions were all impractical to the point of being ridiculous, but Zeb let us make them—then spoke straight to the point. "Listen to me, it's no longer just a case of trying to help Judith and you out of your predicament. As soon as Snotty is missed, we—all four of us—are in mortal danger of the Question. Right?"

"Right," I agreed unwillingly.

"But nobody has a plan?"

None of us answered. Zeb went on, "Then we've got to have help . . . and there is only one place we can get it. The Cabal."

3

"THE Cabal?" I repeated stupidly. Judith gave a horrified gasp.

"Why . . . why, that would mean our immortal souls! They worship Satan!"

Zeb turned to her. "I don't believe so."

She stared at him. "Are *you* a Cabalist?"

"No."

"Then how do you know?"

"And how," I insisted, "can *you* ask them for help?"

Magdalene answered. "I am a member—as Zebadiah knows."

Judith shrank away from her, but Magdalene pressed her with words. "Listen to me, Judith. I know how you feel—and once I was as horrified as you are at the idea of anyone opposing the Church. Then I learned—as you are learning—what really lies behind this sham we were brought up to believe in." She put an arm around the younger girl. "We aren't devil worshipers, dear, nor do we fight against God. We fight only against this self-styled Prophet who pretends to be the voice of God. Come with us, help us fight him—and we will help you. Otherwise we can't risk it."

Judith searched her face by the faint light from the portal. "You swear that this is true? The Cabal fights only against the Prophet and not against the Lord Himself?"

"I swear, Judith."

Judith took a deep shuddering breath. "God guide me," she whispered. "I go with the Cabal."

Magdalene kissed her quickly, then faced us men. "Well?" I answered at once, "I'm in it if Judith is," then whispered to myself, "Dear Lord, forgive me my oath—I must!"

Magdalene was staring at Zeb. He shifted uneasily and said angrily, "I suggested it, didn't I? But we are all damned fools and the Inquisitor will break our bones."

There was no more chance to talk until the next day. I woke from bad dreams of the Question and worse, and heard Zeb's shaver buzzing merrily in the bath. He came in and pulled the covers off me, all the while running off at the mouth with cheerful nonsense. I hate having bed clothes dragged off me even when feeling well and I can't stand cheerfulness before breakfast; I dragged them back and tried to ignore him, but he grabbed my wrist. "Up you come, old son! God's sunshine is wasting. It's a beautiful day. How about two fast laps around the Palace and in for a cold shower?"

I tried to shake his hand loose and called him something that would lower my mark in piety if the ear picked it up. He still hung on and his forefinger was twitching against my wrist in a nervous fashion; I began to wonder if Zeb were cracking under the strain. Then I realized that he was tapping code.

"B-E—N-A-T-U-R-A-L," the dots and dashes said, "S-H-O-W—N-O—S-U-R-P-R-I-S-E—W-E—W-I-L-L — B-E — C-A-L-L-E-D — F-O-R — E-X-A-M-I-N-A-T-I-O-N — D-U-R-I-N-G —T-H-E — R-E-C-R-E-A-T-I-O-N — P-E-R-I-O-D—T-H-I-S—A-F-T-E-R-N-O-O-N"

I hope I showed no surprise. I made surly answers to the stream of silly chatter he had kept up all through it, and got up and went about the mournful tasks of putting the body back in shape for another day. After a bit I found excuse to lay a hand on his shoulder and twitched out an answer: "O-K—I—U-N-D-E-R-S-T-A-N-D"

The day was a misery of nervous monotony. I made a mistake at dress parade, a thing I haven't done since beast barracks. When the day's duty was finally over I went back to our room and found Zeb there with his feet on the air conditioner, working an acrostic in the New York *Times*. "Johnnie my lamb," he asked, looking up, "What is a six-letter word meaning 'Pure in Heart'?"

"You'll never need to know," I grunted and sat down to remove my armor.

"Why, John, don't you think I will reach the Heavenly City?"

"Maybe—after ten thousand years penance."

There came a brisk knock at our door, it was shoved open, and Timothy Klyce, senior legate in the mess and brevet captain, stuck his head in. He sniffed and said in nasal Cape Cod accents, "Hello, you chaps want to take a walk?"

It seemed to me that he could not have picked a worse time. Tim was a hard man to shake and the most punctiliously devout man in the corps. I was still trying to think of an excuse when Zeb spoke up. "Don't mind if we do, provided we walk toward town. I've got some shopping to do."

I was confused by Zeb's answer and still tried to hang back, pleading paper work to do, but Zeb cut me short. "Pfui with paper work. I'll help you with it tonight. Come on." So I went, wondering if he had gotten cold feet about going through with it.

We went out through the lower tunnels. I walked along silently, wondering if possibly Zeb meant to try to shake Klyce in town and then hurry back. We had just entered a little jog in the passageway when Tim raised his hand in a gesture to emphasize some point in what he was saying to Zeb. His hand passed near my face, I felt a slight spray on my eyes—and I was blind.

Before I could cry out, even as I suppressed the impulse to do so, he grasped my upper arm hard, while continuing his sentence without a break. His grip on my arm guided me to the left, whereas my memory of the jog convinced me that the turn should have been to the right. But we did not bump into the wall and after a few moments the blindness wore off. We seemed to be walking in the same tunnel with Tim in the middle and holding each of us by an arm. He did not say anything and neither did we; presently he stopped us in front of a door. Klyce knocked once, then listened.

I could not make out an answer but he replied, "Two pilgrims, duly guided."

The door opened. He led us in, it closed silently behind us, and we were facing a masked and armored guard, with his blast pistol leveled on us. Reaching behind him, he rapped once on an inner door; immediately another man, armed and masked like the first, came out and faced us. He asked Zeb and myself separately:

"Do you seriously declare, upon your honor, that, unbiased by friends and uninfluenced by mercenary motives, you freely and voluntarily offer yourself to the service of this order?"

We each answered, "I do."

"Hoodwink and prepare them."

Leather helmets that covered everything but our mouths and noses were slipped over our heads and fastened under our chins. Then we were ordered to strip off all our clothing. I did so while the goose bumps popped out on me. I was losing my enthusiasm rapidly—there is nothing that makes a man feel as helpless as taking his pants away from him. Then I felt the sharp prick of a hypodermic in my forearm and shortly, though

31

I was awake, things got dreamy and I was no longer jittery.
Something cold was pressed against my ribs on the left side
of my back and I realized that it was almost certainly the hilt
of a vibroblade, needing only the touch of the stud to make
me as dead as Snotty Fassett—but it did not alarm me. Then
there were questions, many questions, which I answered automatically, unable to lie or hedge if I had wanted to. I remember them in snatches:

"—of your own free will and accord?" "—conform to the
ancient established usages—" "—a man, free born, of good
repute, and well recommended."

Then, for a long time I stood shivering on the cold tile floor
while a spirited discussion went on around me; it had to do
with my motives in seeking admission. I could hear it all and
I knew that my life hung on it, with only a word needed to
cause a blade of cold energy to spring into my heart. And I
knew that the argument was going against me.

Then a contralto voice joined the debate. I recognized Sister
Magdalene and knew that she was vouching for me, but doped
as I was I did not care; I simply welcomed her voice as a
friendly sound. But presently the hilt relaxed from my ribs and
I again felt the prick of a hypodermic. It brought me quickly
out of my dazed state and I heard a strong bass voice intoning
a prayer:

"Vouchsafe thine aid, Almighty Father of the Universe.
. . . love, relief, and truth to the honor of Thy Holy Name.
Amen."

And the answering chorus, "So mote it be!"

Then I was conducted around the room, still hoodwinked,
while questions were again put to me. They were symbolic in
nature and were answered for me by my guide. Then I was
stopped and was asked if I were willing to take a solemn oath
pertaining to this degree, being assured that it would in no
material way interfere with duty that I owed to God, myself,
family, country, or neighbor.

I answered, "I am."

I was then required to kneel on my left knee, with my left
hand supporting the Book, my right hand steadying certain
instruments thereon.

The oath and charge was enough to freeze the blood of anyone foolish enough to take it under false pretenses. Then I was
asked what, in my present condition, I most desired. I answered
as I had been coached to answer: "Light!"

And the hoodwink was stripped from my head.

It is not necessary and not proper to record the rest of my
instruction as a newly entered brother. It was long and of
solemn beauty and there was nowhere in it any trace of the
blasphemy or devil worship that common gossip attributed
to us; quite the contrary it was filled with reverence for God,

brotherly love, and uprightness, and it included instruction in the principles of an ancient and honorable profession and the symbolic meaning of the working tools thereof.

But I must mention one detail that surprised me almost out of the shoes I was not wearing. When they took the hoodwink off me, the first man I saw, standing in front of me dressed in the symbols of his office and wearing an expression of almost inhuman dignity, was Captain Peter van Eyck, the fat ubiquitous warden of my watch—*Master* of this lodge!

The ritual was long and time was short. When the lodge was closed we gathered in a council of war. I was told that the senior brethren had already decided not to admit Judith to the sister order of our lodge at this time even though the lodge would reach out to protect her. She was to be spirited away to Mexico and it was better, that being the case, for her not to know any secrets she did not need to know. But Zeb and I, being of the Palace guard, could be of real use; therefore we were admitted.

Judith had already been given hypnotic instructions which —it was hoped—would enable her to keep from telling what little she already knew if she should be put to the Question. I was told to wait and not to worry; the senior brothers would arrange to get Judith out of danger before she next was required to draw lots. I had to be satisfied with that.

For three days running Zebadiah and I reported during the afternoon recreation period for instruction, each time being taken by a different route and with different precautions. It was clear that the architect who had designed the Palace had been one of us; the enormous building had hidden in it traps and passages and doors which certainly did not appear in the official plans.

At the end of the third day we were fully accredited senior brethren, qualified with a speed possible only in time of crisis. The effort almost sprained my brain; I had to bone harder than I ever had needed to in school. Utter letter-perfection was required and there was an amazing lot to memorize—which was perhaps just as well, for it helped to keep me from worrying. We had not heard so much as a rumor of a kickback from the disappearance of Snotty Fassett, a fact much more ominous than would have been a formal investigation.

A security officer can't just drop out of sight without his passing being noticed. It was remotely possible that Snotty had been on a roving assignment and was not expected to check in daily with his boss, but it was much more likely that he had been where we had found him and killed him because some one of us was suspected and he had been ordered to shadow. If that was the case, the calm silence could only mean that the chief security officer was letting us have more rope, while his psychotechnicians analyzed our behavior—in which case the absence of Zeb and myself from any known location during our free time for several days running was almost certainly a datum entered on a chart. If the entire regiment started out equally suspect, then our personal indices each gained a fractional point each of those days.

I never boned savvy in such matters and would undoubtedly have simply felt relieved as the days passed with no overt trouble had it not been that the matter was discussed and worried over in the lodge room. I did not even know the name of the Guardian of Morals, nor even the location of his security office—we weren't supposed to know. I knew that he existed and that he reported to the Grand Inquisitor and perhaps to the Prophet himself, but that was all. I discovered that my lodge brothers, despite the almost incredible penetration of the Cabal throughout the Temple and Palace, knew hardly more than I did—for the reason that we had no brothers, not one, in the staff of the Guardian of Morals. The reason was simple; the Cabal was every bit as careful in evaluating the character, *persona*, and psychological potentialities of a prospective brother as the service was in measuring a prospective intelligence officer—and the two types were as unlike as geese and goats. The Guardian would never accept the type of personality who would be attracted by the ideals of the Cabal; my brothers would never pass a—well, a man like Fassett.

I understand that, in the days before psychological measurement had become a mathematical science, an espionage apparatus could break down through a change in heart on the part of a key man and, the Guardian of Morals had no such worry; his men never suffered a change in heart. I understand, too, that our fraternity, in the early days when it was being purged and tempered for the ordeal to come, many times had blood on the floors of lodge rooms—I don't know; such records were destroyed.

On the fourth day we were not scheduled to go to the lodge room, having been told to show our faces where they would be noticed to offset our unwonted absences. I was spending my free time in the lounge off the mess room, leafing through magazines, when Timothy Klyce came in. He glanced at me, nodded, then started thumbing through a stack of magazines himself. Presently he said, "These antiques belong in a dentist's office. Have any of you chaps seen this week's TIME?"

His complaint was addressed to the room as a whole; no one answered. But he turned to me. "Jack, I think you are sitting on it. Raise up a minute."

I grunted and did so. As he reached for the magazine his head came close to mine and he whispered, "Report to the Master."

I had learned a little at least so I went on reading. After a bit I put my magazine aside, stretched and yawned, then got up

34

and ambled out toward the washroom. But I walked on past and a few minutes later entered the lodge room. I found that Zeb was already there, as were several other brothers; they were gathered around Master Peter and Magdalene. I could feel the tension in the room.

I said, "You sent for me, Worshipful Master?"

He glanced at me, looked back at Magdalene. She said slowly, "Judith has been arrested."

I felt my knees go soft and I had trouble standing. I am not unusually timid and physical bravery is certainly common-place, but if you hit a man through his family or his loved ones you almost always get him where he is unprotected. "The Inquisition?" I managed to gasp.

Her eyes were soft with pity. "We think so. They took her away this morning and she has been incommunicado ever since."

"Has any charge been filed?" asked Zeb.

"Not publicly."

"Hm-m-m— That looks bad."

"And good as well," Master Peter disagreed. "If it is the matter we think it is—Fassett, I mean—and had they had any evidence pointing to the rest of you, all four of you would have been arrested at once. At least, that is in ac-cordance with their methods."

"But what can we *do?*" I demanded.

Van Eyck did not answer. Magdalene said so⸺ngly, "There is nothing for you to do, John. You coul⸺ get within several guarded doors of her."

"But we can't just do nothing!"

The lodge Master said, "Easy, son. Maggie is the ⸺ one of us with access to that part of the inner Palace. ⸺ must leave it in her hands."

I turned again to her; she sighed and said, "Yes, but there is probably little I can do." Then she left.

We waited. Zeb suggested that he and I should leave the lodge room and continue with being seen in our usual haunts; to my relief van Eyck vetoed it. "No. We can't be sure that Sister Judith's hypnotic protection is enough to see her through the ordeal. Fortunately you two and Sister Magdalene are the only ones she can jeopardize—but I want you here, safe, until Magdalene finds out what she can. Or fails to return," he added thoughtfully.

I blurted out, "Oh, Judith will never betray us!"

He shook his head sadly. "Son, *anyone* will betray *any-thing* under the Question—unless adequately guarded by hypno compulsion. We'll see."

I had paid no attention to Zeb, being busy with my own very self-centered thoughts. He now surprised me by say-ing angrily, "Master, you are keeping us here like pet hens

—but you have just sent Maggie back to stick her head in a trap. Suppose Judith *has* cracked? They'll grab Maggie at once."

Van Eyck nodded. "Of course. That is the chance we must take since she is the only spy we have. But don't you worry about her. They'll never arrest her—she'll suicide first."

The statement did not shock me; I was too numbed by the danger to Judith. But Zeb burst out with, "The swine! Master, you shouldn't have sent her."

Van Eyck answered mildly, "Discipline, son. Control yourself. This is war and she is a soldier." He turned away.

So we waited . . . and waited . . . and waited. It is hard to tell anyone who has not lived in the shadow of the Inquisition how we felt about it. We knew no details but we sometimes saw those unlucky enough to live through it. Even if the inquisitors did not require the auto da fé, the mind of the victim was usually damaged, often shattered.

Presently Master Peter mercifully ordered the Junior Warden to examine both of us as to our progress in memorizing ritual. Zeb and I sullenly did as we were told and were forced with relentless kindness to concentrate on the intricate rhetoric. Somehow nearly two hours passed.

At last came three raps at the door and the Tyler admitted Magdalene. I jumped out of my chair and rushed to her. "Well?" I demanded. "Well?"

"Peace, John," she answered wearily. "I've seen her."

"How is she? Is she all right?"

"Better than we have any right to expect. Her mind is still intact and she hasn't betrayed us, apparently. As for the rest, she may keep a scar or two—but she's young and healthy; she'll recover."

I started to demand more facts but the Master cut me off. "Then they've already put her to the Question. In that case, how did you get in to see her?"

"Oh, that!" Magdalene shrugged it off as something hardly worth mentioning. "The inquisitor prosecuting her case proved to be an old acquaintance of mine; we arranged an exchange of favors."

Zeb started to interrupt; the Master snapped, "Quiet!" then added sharply, "The Grand Inquisitor isn't handling it himself? In that case I take it they don't suspect that it could be a Cabal matter?"

Maggie frowned. "I don't know. Apparently Judith fainted rather early in the proceedings; they may not have had time to dig into that possibility. In any case I begged a respite for her until tomorrow. The excuse is to let her recover strength for more questioning, of course. They will start in on her again early tomorrow morning."

36

Van Eyck pounded a fist into a palm. "They must not start again—we can't risk it! Senior Warden, attend me! The rest of you get out! Except you, Maggie."

I left with something unsaid. I had wanted to tell Maggie that she could have my hide for a door mat any time she lifted her finger.

Dinner that night was a trial. After the chaplain droned through his blessing I tried to eat and join in the chatter but there seemed to be a hard ring in my throat that kept me from swallowing. Seated next to me was Grace-of-God Bearpaw, half Scottish, half Cherokee. Grace was a classmate but no friend of mine; we hardly ever talked and tonight he was as taciturn as ever.

During the meal he rested his boot on mine; I impatiently moved my foot away. But shortly his foot was touching mine again and he started to tap against my boot:

"—hold still, you idiot—" he spelled out. "You have been chosen—it will be on your watch tonight—details later—eat and start talking—take a strip of adhesive tape on watch with you—six inches by a foot—repeat message back."

I managed somehow to tap out my confirmation while continuing to pretend to eat.

4

WE relieved the watch at midnight. As soon as the watch section had marched away from our post I told Zeb what Grace had passed on to me at chow and asked him if he had the rest of my instructions. He had not. I wanted to talk but he cut me short; he seemed even more edgy than I was.

So I walked my post and tried to look alert. We were posted that night at the north end of the west rampart; our tour covered one of the Palace entrances. About an hour had passed when I heard a hiss from the dark doorway. I approached cautiously and made out a female form. She was too short to be Magdalene and I never knew who she was, for she shoved a piece of paper in my hand and faded back into the dark corridor.

I rejoined Zeb. "What shall I do? Read it with my flash? That seems risky."

"Open it up."

I did and found that it was covered with fine script that glowed in the darkness. I could read it but it was too dim to be picked up by any electronic eye. I read it:

At the middle of the watch exactly on the bell you will enter

*the Palace by the door where you received this. Forty paces
inside, take the stair on your left; climb two flights. Proceed
north fifty paces. The lighted doorway on your right leads to
the Virgins' quarters; there will be a guard at this door. He
will not resist you but you must use a paralysis bomb on him
to give him an alibi. The cell you seek is at the far end of the
central east & west corridor of the quarters. There will be a
light over the door and a Virgin on guard. She is not one of us.
You must disable her completely but you are forbidden to
injure or kill her. Use the adhesive tape as gag and blindfold
and tie her up with her clothes. Take her keys, enter the cell,
and remove Sister Judith. She will probably be unconscious.
Bring her to your post and hand her over to the warden of your
watch.*

*You must make all haste from the time you paralyze the
guard, as an eye may see you when you pass the lighted doorway and the alarm may sound at once.*

*Do not swallow this note; the ink is poisonous. Drop it in
the incinerator chute at the head of the stairs.*

Go with God.

Zeb read it over my shoulder. "All you need," he said grim-
ly, "is the ability to pass miracles at will. Scared?"

"Yes."

"Want me to go along?"

"No. I guess we had better carry out ___ ___ders as given."

"Yes, we had—if I know the Lodg ___ ___r. Besides, it jus
might happen that I might need to ___ ___mebody rather suddenly while you are gone. I'll b ___ ___ng your rear."

"I suppose so."

"Now let's shut up and bon ___ ___ilitary." We went back to
walking our post.

At the two muted strokes of the middle of the watch I
propped my spear against the wall, took off my sword and
corselet and helmet and the rest of the ceremonial junk we
were required to carry but which would hamper me on this
job. Zeb shoved a gauntleted hand in mine and squeezed. Then
I was off.

Two—four—six—forty paces. I groped in the dark along
the left wall and found the opening, felt around with my foot.
Ah, there were the steps! I was already in a part of the Palace I
had never been in; I moved by dead reckoning in the dark
and hoped the person who had written my orders understood
that. One flight, two flights—I almost fell on my face when I
stepped on a 'top' step that wasn't there.

Where was the refuse chute? It should be at hand level
and the instructions said "head of the stairs." I was debating
frantically whether to show a light or chance keeping it when
my left hand touched its latch; with a sigh of relief I chucked
away the evidence that could have incriminated so many

38

others. I started to turn away, then was immediately filled with panic. Was that really an incinerator chute? Could it have been the panel for a delivery lift instead? I groped for it in the dark again, opened it and shoved my hand in.

My hand was scorched even through my gauntlet; I jerked it back with relief and decided to trust my instructions, have no more doubts. But forty paces north the passageway jogged and that was not mentioned in my orders; I stopped and reconnoitered very cautiously, peering around the jog at floor level.

Twenty-five feet away was the guard and the doorway. He was supposed to be one of us but I took no chances. I slipped a bomb from my belt, set it by touch to minimum intensity, pulled the primer and counted off five seconds to allow for point blank range. Then I threw it and ducked back into the jog to protect myself from the rays.

I waited another five seconds and stuck my head around. The guard was slumped down on the floor, with his forehead bleeding slightly where it had struck a fragment of the bomb case. I hurried out and stepped over him, trying to run and keep quiet at the same time. The central passage of the Virgins' quarters was dim, with only blue night lights burning, but I could see and I reached the end of the passage quickly —then jammed on the brakes. The female guard at the cell there, instead of walking a post, was seated on the floor with her back to the door.

Probably she was dozing, for she did not look up at once. Then she did so, saw me, and I had no time to make plans; I dove for her. My left hand muffled her scream; with the edge of my left hand I chopped the side of her neck—not a killing stroke but I had no time to be gentle; she went limp.

Half the tape across her mouth first, then the other half across her eyes, then tear clothing from her to bind her—and hurry, hurry, hurry all the way, for a security man might already have monitored the eye that was certainly at the main doorway and have seen the unconscious guard. I found her keys on a chain around her waist and straightened up with a silent apology for what I had done to her. Her little body was almost childlike; she seemed even more helpless than Judith.

But I had no time for soft misgivings; I found the right key, got the door open—and then my darling was in my arms.

She was deep in a troubled sleep and probably drugged. She moaned as I picked her up but did not wake. But her gown slipped and I saw some of what they had done to her—I made a life vow, even as I ran, to pay it back seven times, if the man who did it could live that long.

The guard was still where I had left him. I thought I had gotten away with it without being monitored or waking anyone and was just stepping over him, when I heard a gasp

39

from the corridor behind me. Why are women restless at night? If this woman hadn't gotten out of bed, no doubt to attend to something she should have taken care of before retiring, I might never have been seen at all.

It was too late to silence her, I simply ran. Once around the jog I was in welcome darkness but I overran the stair head, had to come back, and feel for it—then had to grope my way down step by step. I could hear shouts and high-pitched voices somewhere behind me.

Just as I reached ground level, turned and saw the portal outlined against the night sky before me, all the lights came on and the alarms began to clang. I ran the last few paces headlong and almost fell into the arms of Captain van Eyck. He scooped her out of my arms without a word and trotted away toward the corner of the building.

I stood staring after them half-wittedly when Zeb brought me to my senses by picking up my corselet and shoving it out for me to put in my arms. "Snap out of it, man!" he hissed. "That general alarm is for *us*. You're supposed to be on guard duty."

He strapped on my sword as I buckled the corselet, then slapped my helmet on my head and shoved my spear into my left hand. Then we stood back to back in front of the portal, pistols drawn, safeties off, in drill-manual full alert. Pending further orders, we were not expected nor permitted to do ~ything else, since the alarm had not taken place o_
o ~.

~ stood like statues for several minutes. We could hea_
~ds of running feet and of challenges. The Officer o_
~e Day ran past us into the Palace, buckling his corsele_
over his night clothes as he ran. I almost blasted him out of existence before he answered my challenge. Then th_
relief watch section swung past at double time with the relief warden at its head.

Gradually the excitement died away; the lights remained on but someone thought to shut off the alarm. Zeb ventured a whisper. "What in Sheol happened? Did you muff it?"

"Yes and no." I told him about the restless Sister.

"Hmmph! Well, son, this ought to teach you not to fool around with women when you are on duty."

"Confound it, I wasn't fooling with her. She just popped out of her cell."

"I didn't mean tonight," he said bleakly.

I shut up.

About half an hour later, long before the end of the watch, the relief section tramped back. Their warden halted them, our two reliefs fell out and we fell in the empty places. We marched back to the guardroom, stopping twice more on the way to drop reliefs and pick up men from our own section.

5

WE were halted in the inner parade facing the guardroom door and left at attention. There we stood for fifty mortal minutes while the Officer of the Day strolled around and looked us over. Once a man in the rear rank shifted his weight. It would have gone unnoticed at dress parade, even in the presence of the Prophet, but tonight the Officer of the Day bawled him out at once and Captain van Eyck noted down his name.

Master Peter looked just as angry as his superior undoubtedly was. He passed out several more gigs, even stopped in front of me and told the guardroom orderly to put me down for "boots not properly shined"—which was a libel, unless I had scuffed them in my efforts. I dared not look down to see but stared him in the eye and said nothing, while he stared back coldly.

But his manner recalled to me Zeb's lecture about intrigue. Van Eyck's manner was perfectly that of a subordinate officer let down and shamed by his own men; how should I feel if I were in fact new-born innocent?

Angry, I decided—angry and self-righteous. Interested and stimulated by the excitement at first, then angry at being kept standing at attention like a plebe. They were trying to soften us up by the strained wait; how would I have felt about it, say two months ago? Smugly sure of my own virtue, it would have offended me and humiliated me—to be kept standing like a pariah waiting to whine for the privilege of a ration card— to be placed on the report like a cadet with soup on his jacket.

By the time the Commander of the Guard arrived almost an hour later I was white-lipped with anger. The process was synthetic but the emotion was real. I had never really liked our Commander anyway. He was a short, supercilious little man with a cold eye and a way of looking through his junior officers instead of at them. Now he stood in front of us with his priest's robes thrown back over his shoulders and his thumbs caught in his sword belt.

He glared at us. "Heaven help me, Angels of the Lord indeed," he said softly into the dead silence—then barked, "Well?"

No one answered.

"Speak up!" he shouted. "Some one of you knows about this. Answer me! Or would you all rather face the Question?"

A murmur ran down our ranks—but no one spoke.

He ran his eyes over us again. His eye caught mine and I stared back truculently. "Lyle!"

"Yes, reverend sir?"

"What do you know of this?"

"I know that I would like to sit down, reverend sir!"

He scowled at me, then his eye got a gleam of cold amusement. "Better to stand before me, my son, than to sit before the Inquisitor." But he passed on and heckled the man next to me.

He badgered us endlessly, but Zeb and I seemed to receive neither more nor less attention than the others. At last he seemed to give up and directed the Officer of the Day to dismiss us. I was not fooled; it was a certainty that every word spoken had been recorded, every expression cinemographed, and that analysts were plotting the data against each of our past behavior patterns before we reached our quarters.

But Zeb is a wonder. He was gossiping about the night's events, speculating innocently about what could have caused the hurrah, even before we reached our room. I tried to answer in what I had decided was my own "proper" reaction and groused about the way we had been treated. "We're officers and gentlemen," I complained. "If he thinks we are guilty of something, he should prefer formal charges."

I went to bed still griping, then lay awake and worried. I tried to tell myself that Judith must have reached a safe place, or else the brass would not be in the dark about it. But I d‸ off to sleep still fretting.

‸t someone touch me and I woke instantly. Then I re‸d when I realized that my hand was being gripped in the ‸cognition grip of the lodge. "Quiet," a voice I did not recognize whispered in my ear. "I must give you certain treatment to protect you." I felt the bite of a hypodermic in my arm; in a few seconds I was relaxed and dreamy. The voice whispered, "You saw nothing unusual on watch tonight. Until the alarm was sounded your watch was quite without incident—" I don't know how long the voiced droned on.

I was awakened a second time by someone shaking me roughly. I burrowed into my pillow and said, "Go 'way! I'm going to skip breakfast."

Somebody struck me between my shoulder blades; I turned and sat up, blinking. There were four armed men in the room, blasters drawn and pointed at me. "Come along!" ordered the one nearest to me.

They were wearing the uniform of Angels but without unit insignia. Each head was covered by a black mask that exposed only the eyes—and by these masks I knew them: proctors of the Grand Inquisitor.

I hadn't really believed it could happen to me. Not to *me* . . . not to Johnnie Lyle who had always behaved himself, been a credit to his parish and a pride to his mother. No! The Inquisition was a bogieman, but a bogieman for sinners—not for John Lyle.

But I knew with sick horror when I saw those masks that I was already a dead man, that my time had come and here at last was the nightmare that I could not wake up from.

But I was not dead yet. From somewhere I got the courage to pretend anger. "What are *you* doing here?"

"Come along," the faceless voice repeated.

"Show me your order. You can't just drag an officer out of his bed any time you feel—"

The leader gestured with his pistol; two of them grabbed my arms and hustled me toward the door, while the fourth fell in behind. But I am fairly strong; I made it hard for them while protesting, "You've got to let me get dressed, at least. You've no right to haul me away half naked, no matter what the emergency is. I've a right to appear in the uniform of my rank."

Surprisingly the appeal worked. The leader stopped. "Okay. But snap into it!"

I stalled as much as I dared while going through the motions of hurrying—jamming a zipper on my boot, fumbling clumsily with all my dressing. How could I leave some sort of a message for Zeb? Any sort of a sign that would show the brethren what had happened to me?

At last I got a notion, not a good one but the best I could manage. I dragged clothing out of my wardrobe, some that I would need, some that I did not, and with the bunch a sweater. In the course of picking out what I must wear I managed to arrange the sleeves of the sweater in the position taken by a lodge brother in giving the Grand Hailing Sign of Distress. Then I picked up loose clothing and started to put some of it back in the wardrobe; the leader immediately shoved his blaster in my ribs and said, "Never mind that. You're dressed."

I gave in, dropping the meaningless clothing on the floor. The sweater remained spread out as a symbol to him who could read it. As they led me away I prayed that our room servant would not arrive and "tidy" it out of meaning before Zeb spotted it.

They blindfolded me as soon as we reached the inner Palace. We went down six flights, four below ground level as I figured it, and reached a compartment filled with the breathless silence of a vault. The hoodwink was stripped from my eyes. I blinked.

"Sit down, my boy, sit down and make yourself comfortable." I found myself looking into the face of the Grand Inquisitor himself, saw his warm friendly smile and his collie-dog eyes.

His gentle voice continued, "I'm sorry to get you so rudely

out of a warm bed, but there is certain information needed by our Holy Church. Tell me, my son, do you fear the Lord? Oh, of course you do; your piety is well known. So you won't mind helping me with this little matter even though it makes you late for breakfast. It's to the greater glory of God." He turned to his masked and black-robed assistant questioner, hovering behind him. "Make him ready—and pray be gentle."

I was handled quickly and roughly, but not painfully. They touched me as if they regarded me as so much lifeless matter to be manipulated as impersonally as machinery. They stripped me to the waist and fastened things to me, a rubber bandage tight around my right arm, electrodes in my fists which they taped closed, another pair of electrodes to my wrists, a third pair at my temples, a tiny mirror to the pulse in my throat. At a control board on the left wall one of them made some adjustments, then threw a switch and on the opposite wall a shadow show of my inner workings sprang into being.

A little light danced to my heart beat, a wiggly line on an iconoscope display showed my blood pressure's rise and fall, another like it moved with my breathing, and there were several others that I did not understand. I turned my head away and concentrated on remembering the natural logarithms from one to ten.

"You see our methods, son. Efficiency and kindness, those are our watch words. Now tell me—*Where did you put her?*"

I broke off with the logarithm of eight. "Put who?"

"Why did you do it?"

"I am sorry, Most Reverend Sir. I don't know what it is I am supposed to have done."

Someone slapped me hard, from behind. The lights on the wall jiggled and the Inquisitor studied them thoughtfully, then spoke to an assistant. "Inject him."

Again my skin was pricked by a hypodermic. They let me rest while the drug took hold; I spent the time continuing with the effort of recalling logarithms. But that soon became too difficult; I grew drowsy and lackadaisical, nothing seemed to matter. I felt a mild and childish curiosity about my surroundings but no fear. Then the soft voice of the Inquisitor broke into my reverie with a question. I can't remember what it was but I am sure I answered with the first thing that came into my head.

I have no way of telling how long this went on. In time they brought me back to sharp reality with another injection. The Inquisitor was examining a slight bruise and a little purple dot on my right forearm. He glanced up. "What caused this, my boy?"

"I don't know, Most Reverend Sir." At the instant it was truth.

He shook his head regretfully. "Don't be naive, my son—

and don't assume that I am. Let me explain something to you. What you sinners never realize is that the Lord always prevails. Always. Our methods are based in loving-kindness but they proceed with the absolute certainty of a falling stone, and with the result equally preordained.

"First we ask the sinner to surrender himself to the Lord and answer from the goodness that remains in his heart. When that loving appeal fails—as it did with you—then we use the skills God has given us to open the unconscious mind. That is usually as far as the Question need go—unless some agent of Satan has been there before us and has tampered with the sacred tabernacle of the mind.

"Now, my son, I have just returned from a walk through your mind. I found much there that was commendable, but I found also, in murky darkness, a wall that had been erected by some other sinner, and what I want—what the Church needs—is behind that wall."

Perhaps I showed a trace of sat faction or perhaps the lights gave me away, for he smiled sad and added, "No wall of Satan can stop the Lord. When we d such an obstacle, there are two things to do: given time enough I could remove that wall gently, delicately, stone by stone, without any damage to your mind. I wish I had time to, I really do, for you are a good boy at heart, John Lyle, and you do not belong with the sinners.

"But while eternity is long, time is short; there is the second way. We can disregard the false barrier in the unconscious mind and make a straightforward assault on the conscious mind, with the Lord's banners leading us." He glanced away from me. "Prepare him."

His faceless crew strapped a metal helmet on my head, some other arrangements were made at the control board. "Now look here, John Lyle." He pointed to a diagram on the wall. "No doubt you know that the human nervous system is partly electrical in nature. There is a schematic representation of a brain, that lower part is the thalamus; covering it is the cortex. Each of the sensory centers is marked as you can see. Your own electrodynamic characteristics have been analyzed; I am sorry to say that it will now be necessary to heterodyne your normal senses."

He started to turn away, turned back. "By the way, John Lyle, I have taken the trouble to minister to you myself because, at this stage, my assistants through less experience in the Lord's work than my humble self sometimes mistake zeal for skill and transport the sinner unexpectedly to his reward. I don't want that to happen to you. You are merely a strayed lamb and I purpose saving you."

I said, "Thank you, Most Reverend Sir."

"Don't thank me, thank the Lord I serve. However," he

went on, frowning slightly, "this frontal assault on the mind, while necessary, is unavoidably painful. You will forgive me?"

I hesitated only an instant. "I forgive you, holy sir."

He glanced at the lights and said wryly, "A falsehood. But you are forgiven that falsehood; it was well intended." He nodded at his silent helpers. "Commence."

A light blinded me, an explosion crashed in my ears. My right leg jerked with pain, then knotted in an endless cramp. My throat contracted; I choked and tried to throw up. Something struck me in the solar plexus; I doubled up and could not catch my breath. "Where did you put her?" A noise started low and soft, climbed higher and higher, increasing in pitch and decibels, until it was a thousand dull saws, a million squeaking slate pencils, then wavered in a screeching ululation that tore at the thin wall of reason. "Who helped you?" Agonizing heat was at my crotch; I could not get away from it. "Why did you do it?" I itched all over, intolerably, and tried to tear at my skin—but my arms would not work. The itching was worse than pain; I would have welcomed pain in lieu of scratching. "Where is she?"

Light . . . sound . . . pain . . . heat . . . convulsions . . . cold . . . falling . . . light and pain . . . cold and falling . . . nausea and sound. "Do you love the Lord?" Searing heat and shocking cold . . . pain and a pounding in my head that made me scream—"Where did you take her? Who else was in it? Give up and save your immortal soul." Pain and an endless nakedness to the outer darkness.

I suppose I fainted.

Some one was slapping me across the mouth. "Wake up, John Lyle, and confess! Zebadiah Jones has given you away."

I blinked and said nothing. It was not necessary to simulate a dazed condition, nor could I have managed it. But the words had been a tremendous shock and my brain was racing, trying to get into gear. Zeb? Old Zeb? Poor old Zeb! Hadn't they had time to give him hypnotic treatment, too? It did not occur to me even then to suspect that Zeb had broken under torture alone; I simply assumed that they had been able to tap his unconscious mind. I wondered if he were already dead and remembered that I had gotten him into this, against his good sense. I prayed for his soul and prayed that he would forgive me.

My head jerked to another roundhouse slap. "Wake up! You can hear me—Jones has revealed your sins."

"Revealed what?" I mumbled.

The Grand Inquisitor motioned his assistants aside and leaned over me, his kindly face full of concern. "Please, my son, do this for the Lord—and for me. You have been brave in trying to protect your fellow sinners from the fruits of their folly, but they failed you and your stiff-necked courage no longer means anything. But don't go to judgment with this on your soul. Confess, and let death come with your sins forgiven."

"So you mean to kill me?"

He looked faintly annoyed. "I did not say that. I know that you do not fear death. What you should fear is to meet your Maker with your sins still on your soul. Open your heart and confess."

"Most Reverend Sir, I have nothing to confess."

He turned away from me and gave orders in low, gentle tones. "Continue. The mechanicals this time; I don't wish to burn out his brain."

There is no point in describing what he meant by "the mechanicals" and no sense in making this account needlessly grisly. His methods differed in no important way from torture techniques used in the Middle Ages and even more recently—except that his knowledge of the human nervous system was incomparably greater and his knowledge of behavior psychology made his operations more adroit. In addition, he and his assistants behaved as if they were completely free of any sadistic pleasure in their work; it made them cooly efficient.

But let's skip the details.

I have no notion of how long it took. I must have passed out repeatedly, for my clearest memory is of catching a bucket of ice water in the face not once but over and over again, like a repeating nightmare—each time followed by the inevitable hypo. I don't think I told them anything of any importance while I was awake and the hypno instructions to my unconscious may have protected me while I was out of my head. I seem to remember trying to make up a lie about sins I had never committed; I don't remember what came of it.

I recall vaguely coming semi-awake once and hearing a voice say, "He can take more. His heart is strong."

I was pleasantly dead for a long time, but finally woke up as if from a long sleep. I was stiff and when I tried to shift in bed my side hurt me. I opened my eyes and looked around; I was in bed in a small, windowless but cheerful room. A sweet-faced young woman in a nurse's uniform came quickly to my side and felt my pulse.

"Hello."

"Hello," she answered. "How are we now? Better?"

"What happened?" I asked. "Is it over? Or is this just a rest?"

"Quiet," she admonished. "You are still too weak to talk. But it's over—you are safe among the brethren."

"I was rescued?"

"Yes. Now be quiet." She held up my head and gave me something to drink. I went back to sleep.

It took me days to convalesce and catch up with events.

47

The infirmary in which I woke up was part of a series of subbasements under the basement proper of a department store in New Jerusalem; there was some sort of underground connection between it and the lodge room under the Palace—just where and how I could not say; I was never in it. While conscious, I mean.

Zeb came to see me as soon as I was allowed to have visitors. I tried to raise up in bed. "Zeb! Zeb boy—I thought you were dead!"

"Who? Me?" He came over and shook my left hand. "What made you think that?"

I told him about the dodge the Inquisitor had tried to pull on me. He shook his head. "I wasn't even arrested. Thanks to you, pal. Johnnie, I'll never call you stupid again. If you hadn't had that flash of genius to rig your sweater so that I could read the sign in it, they might have pulled us both in and neither one of us have gotten out of it alive. As it was, I went straight to Captain van Eyck. He told me to lie doggo in the lodge room and then planned your rescue."

I wanted to ask how that had been pulled off but my mind jumped to a more important subject. "Zeb, where is Judith? Can't you find her and bring her to see me? My nurse just smiles and tells me to rest."

He looked surprised. "Didn't they tell you?"

"Tell me what? No, I haven't seen anybody but the nurse and the doctor and they treat me like an idiot. Don't keep me in suspense, Zeb. Did anything go wrong? She's all right—isn't she?"

"Oh, sure! But she's in Mexico by now—we got a report by sensitive circuit two days ago."

In my physical weakness I almost wept. "Gone! Why, what a dirty, scabby trick! Why couldn't they have waited until I was well enough to tell her good-by?"

Zeb said quickly, "Hey, look, stupid—no, forget that 'stupid'; you aren't. Look, old man, your calendar is mixed up. She was on her way before you were rescued, before we were even sure you could be rescued. You don't think the brethren could bring her back just to let you two bill and coo, do you?"

I thought about it and calmed down. It made sense, even though I was bitterly disappointed. He changed the subject. "How do you feel?"

"Oh, pretty good."

"They tell me you get that cast off your leg tomorrow."

"So? They haven't told me." I twisted, trying to get comfortable. "I'm almost more anxious to get shut of this corset, but the doc says I'll have to wear it for several weeks yet."

"How about your hand? Can you bend your fingers?"

I tried it. "Fairly well. I may have to write left-handed for a while."

48

"All in all, it looks like you're too mean to die, old son. By the way, if it's any consolation to you, the laddy boy who worked on Judith got slightly dead in the raid in which you were rescued."

"He was? Well, I'm sorry. I had planned to save him for myself."

"No doubt, but you would have had to take your place in line, if he had lived. Lots of people wanted him. Me, for example."

"But I had thought of something special for him—I was going to make him bite his nails."

"Bite his nails?" Zeb looked puzzled.

"Until he reached his elbows. Follow me?"

"Oh." Zeb grinned sourly. "Not nearly imaginative enough, boy. But he's dead, we can't touch him."

"He's infernally lucky. Zeb, why didn't you arrange to get him yourself? Or did you, and things were just too hurried to let you do a proper job?"

"Me? Why, I wasn't on the rescue raid. I haven't been back in the Palace at all."

"Huh?"

"You didn't think I was still on duty, did you?"

"I haven't had time to think about it."

"Well, naturally I couldn't go back after I ducked out to avoid arrest; I was through. No, my fine fellow, you and I are both deserters from the United States Army—with every cop and every postmaster in the country anxious to earn a deserter's reward by turning us in."

I whistled softly and let the implications of his remark sink in.

6

I HAD joined the Cabal on impulse. Certainly, under the stress of falling in love with Judith and in the excitement of the events that had come rushing over me as a result of meeting her, I had no time for calm consideration. I had not broken with the Church as a result of philosophical decision.

Of course I had known logically that to join the Cabal was to break with all my past ties, but it had not yet hit me emotionally. What was it going to be like never again to wear the uniform of an officer and a gentleman? I had been proud to walk down the street, to enter a public place, aware that all eyes were on me.

I put it out of my mind. The share was in the furrow, my

hand was on the plow; there could be no turning back. I was in this until we won or until we were burned for treason.

I found Zeb looking at me quizzically. "Cold feet, Johnnie?"

"No. But I'm still getting adjusted. Things have moved fast."

"I know. Well, we can forget about retired pay, and our class numbers at the Point no longer matter." He took off his Academy ring, chucked it in the air, caught it and shoved it into his pocket. "But there is work to be done, old lad, and you will find that this is a military outfit, too—a real one. Personally, I've had my fill of spit-and-polish and I don't care if I never again hear that 'Sound off' and 'Officers, center!' and 'Watchman, what of the night?' manure again. The brethern will make full use of our best talents—and the fight really matters."

Master Peter van Eyck came to see me a couple of days later. He sat on the edge of my bed and folded his hands over his paunch and looked at me. "Feeling better, son?"

"I could get up if the doctor would let me."

"Good. We're shorthanded; the less time a trained officer spends on the sick list the better." He paused and chewed his lip. "But, son, I don't know just what to do with you."

"Eh? Sir?"

"Frankly, you should never have been admitted to the Order in the first place—a military command should not mess around with affairs of the heart. It confuses motivations, causes false decisions. Twice, because we took you in, we have had to show our strength in sorties that—from a strictly military standpoint—should never have happened."

I did not answer, there was no answer—he was right. My face was hot with embarrassment.

"Don't blush about it," he added kindly. "Contrariwise, it is good for the morale of the brethern to strike back occasionally. The point is, what to do with you? You are a stout fellow, you stood up well—but do you really understand the ideals of freedom and human dignity we are fighting for?"

I barely hesistated. "Master—I may not be much of a brain, and the Lord knows it's true that I've never thought much about politics. But I know which side I'm on!"

He nodded. "That's enough. We can't expect each man to be his own Tom Paine."

"His own what?"

"Thomas Paine. But then you've never heard of him, of course. Look him up in our library when you get a chance. Very inspiring stuff. Now about your assignment. It would be easy enough to put you on a desk job here—your friend Zebadiah has been working sixteen hours a day trying to straighten out our filing system. But I can't waste you two on clerical jobs. What is your savvy subject, your specialty?"

"Why, I haven't had any P.G. work yet, sir."

"I know. But what did you stand high in? How were you in applied miracles, and mob psychology?"

"I was fairly good in miracles, but I guess I'm too wooden for psychodynamics. Ballistics was my best subject."

"Well, we can't have everything. I could use a technician in morale and propaganda, but if you can't, you can't."

"Zeb stood one in his class in mob psychology, Master. The Commandant urged him to aim for the priesthood."

"I know and we'll use him, but not here. He is too much interested in Sister Magdalene; I don't believe in letting couples work together. It might distort their judgments in a pinch. Now about you. I wonder if you wouldn't make a good assassin?"

He asked the question seriously but almost casually; I had trouble believing it. I had been taught—I had always taken it for granted that assassination was one of the unspeakable sins, like incest, or blasphemy. I blurted out, "The brethern use *assassination?*"

"Eh? Why not?" Van Eyck studied my face. "I keep forgetting. John, would you kill the Grand Inquisitor if you got a chance?"

"Well—yes, of course. But I'd want to do it in a fair fight."

"Do you think you will ever be given that chance? Now let's suppose we are back at the day Sister Judith was arrested by him. Suppose you could stop him by killing him—but only by poisoning him, or knifing him in the back. What would you do?"

I answered savagely, "I would have killed him!"

"Would you have felt any shame, any guilt?"

"None!"

"So. But he is only one of many in this foulness. The man who eats meat cannot sneer at the butcher—and every bishop, every minister of state, every man who benefits from this tyranny, right up to the Prophet himself, is an accomplice before the fact in every murder committed by the inquisitors. The man who condones a sin because he enjoys the result of the sin is equally guilty of the sin. Do you see that?"

Oddly enough, I did see it, for it was orthodox doctrine as I had learned it. I had choked over its new application. But Master Peter was still talking: "But we don't indulge in vengeance—vengeance still belongs to the Lord. I would never send *you* against the Inquisitor because you might be tempted to exult in it personally. We don't tempt a man with sin as a bait. What we do do, what we are doing, is engaging in a calculated military operation in a war already commenced. One key man is often worth a regiment; we pick out that key man and kill him. The bishop in one diocese may be such a man; the bishop in the next state may be just a bungler, propped up by the system. We kill the first, let the second stay where he is. Gradually we are eliminating their best brains. Now—" He leaned toward me. "—do you want a job picking off those key men? It's very important work."

It seemed to me that, in this business, someone was continually making me face up to facts, instead of letting me dodge unpleasant facts the way most people manage to do throughout their lives. Could I stomach such an assignment? Could I refuse it—since Master Peter had implied at least that assassins were volunteers—refuse it and try to ignore in my heart that it was going on and that I was condoning it?

Master Peter was right; the man who buys the meat is brother to the butcher. It was squeamishness, not morals . . . like the man who favors capital punishment but is himself too "good" to fit the noose or swing the axe. Like the person who regards war as inevitable and in some circumstances moral, but who avoids military service because he doesn't like the thought of killing.

Emotional infants, ethical morons—the left hand *must* know what the right hand doeth, and the heart is responsible for both. I answered almost at once, "Master Peter, I am ready to serve . . . that way or whatever the brethern decide I can do best."

"Good man!" He relaxed a bit and went on, "Between ourselves, it's the job I offer to every new recruit when I'm not sure that he understands that this is not a ball game, but a cause to which he must commit himself without any reservation—his life, his fortune, his sacred honor. We have no place for the man who wants to give orders but who won't clean the privy."

I felt relieved. "Then you weren't seriously picking me out for assassination work?"

"Eh? Usually I am not; few men are fitted for it. But in your case I am quite serious, because we already know that you have an indispensable and not very common qualification."

I tried to think what was so special about me and could not. "Sir?"

"Well, you'll get caught eventually, of course. Three point seven accomplished missions per assassin is what we are running now—a good score, but we ought to do better as suitable men are so scarce. But with you we know already that when they do catch you and put you to the Question, you won't crack."

My face must have shown my feelings. The Question? Again? I was still half dead from the first time. Master Peter said kindly, "Of course you won't have to go up against it again to the fullest. We always protect assassins; we fix it so that they can suicide easily. You don't need to worry."

Believe me, having once suffered the Question, his assurance to me did not seem calloused; it was a real comfort. "How, sir?"

"Eh? A dozen different ways. Our surgeons can booby-trap

you so that you can die at will in the tightest bonds anyone can put on you. There is the old hollow tooth, of course, with cyanide or such—but the proctors are getting wise to that; sometimes they gag a man's mouth open. But there are many ways. For example—" He stretched his arms wide and bent them back, but not far. "—if I were to cramp my arms backward in a position a man never assumes without very considerable conscious effort, a little capsule between my shoulder blades would rupture and I would make my last report. Yet you could pound me on the back all day and never break it."

"Uh . . . were you an assassin, sir?"

"Me? How could I be, in my job? But all of our people in positions of maximum exposure are loaded—it's the least we can do for them. Besides that, I've got a bomb in my belly—" He patted his paunch. "—that will take a roomful of people with me if it seems desirable."

"I could have used one of those last week," I said emphatically.

"You're here, aren't you? Don't despise your luck. If you need one, you'll have one." He stood up and prepared to leave. "In the meantime, don't give any special thought to being selected as an executioner. The psychological evaluation group will still have to pass on you and they are hard men to convince."

Despite his words, I did think about it, of course, though it ceased to worry me. I was put on light duty shortly thereafter and spent several days reading proof on the *Iconoclast*, a smug, mildly critical, little reform-from-within paper which the Cabal used to pave the way for its field missionaries. It was a "Yes, but—" paper, overtly loyal to the Prophet but just the sort of thing to arouse doubt in the minds of the stiff-necked and intolerant. Its acid lay in how a thing was said, not what was said. I had even seen copies of it around the Palace.

I also acquainted with some of the ramifications of the amazing underground headquarters at New Jerusalem. The department store above us was owned by a Past Grand Master and was an extremely important means of liaison with the outside world. The shelves of the store fed us and clothed us; through taps into the visiphone circuits serving the store commercially we had connection with the outside and could even put in transcontinental calls if the message could be phrased or coded to allow for the likelihood that it would be monitored. The owner's delivery trucks could be used to spirit fugitives to or from our clandestine quarters—I learned that Judith started her flight that way, with a bill of lading that described her as gum boots. The store's manifold commercial operations were a complete and plausible blind for our extensive operations.

Successful revolution is Big Business—make no mistake about that. In a modern, complex, and highly industrialized state, revolution is not accomplished by a handful of conspirators whispering around a guttering candle in a deserted ruin. It requires countless personnel, supplies, modern machinery and modern weapons. And to handle these factors successfully there must be loyalty, secrecy, and superlative staff organization.

I was kept busy but my work was fill-in work, since I was awaiting assignment. I had time to dig into the library and I looked up Tom Paine, which led me to Patrick Henry and Thomas Jefferson and others—a whole new world was opened up to me. I had trouble at first in admitting the possibility of what I read; I think perhaps of all the things a police state can do to its citizens, distorting history is possibly the most pernicious. For example, I learned for the first time that the United States had not been ruled by a bloodthirsty emissary of Satan before the First Prophet arose in his wrath and cast him out— but had been a community of free men, deciding their own affairs by peaceful consent. I don't mean that the first republic had been a scriptural paradise, but it hadn't been anything like what I had learned in school.

For the first time in my life I was reading things which had not been approved by the Prophet's censors, and the impact on my mind was devastating. Sometimes I would glance over my shoulder to see who was watching me, frightened in spite of myself. I began to sense faintly that secrecy is the keystone of all tyranny. Not force, but secrecy . . . censorship. When any government, or any church for that matter, undertakes to say to its subjects, "This you may not read, this you must not see, this you are forbidden to know," the end result is tyranny and oppression, no matter how holy the motives. Mighty little force is needed to control a man whose mind has been hoodwinked; contrariwise, no amount of force can control a free man, a man whose mind is free. No, not the rack, not fission bombs, not anything—you can't conquer a free man; the most you can do is kill him.

My thoughts did not then fall into syllogisms; my head was filled with an inchoate spate of new ideas, each more exciting than the last. I discovered that travel between the planets, almost a myth in my world, had not stopped because the First Prophet had forbidden it as a sin against the omnipotence of God; it had ceased because it had gone into the red financially and the Prophet's government would not subsidize it. There was even an implied statement that the "infidels" (I still used that word in my mind) still sent out an occasional research ship and that there were human beings even now on Mars and Venus.

I grew so excited at that notion that I almost forgot the plight we were all in. If I had not been chosen for the Angels of the Lord, I would probably have gone into rocketry. I was good at anything of that sort, the things that called for quick reflexes combined with knowledge of the mathematical and mechanical arts. Maybe someday the United States would have space ships again. Perhaps I . . .

But the thought was crowded out by a dozen new ones. Foreign newspapers—why, I had not even been sure the infidels could read and write. The London *Times* made unbelievable and exciting reading. I gradually got it through my head that the Britishers apparently did not now eat human flesh, if indeed they ever had. They seemed remarkably like us, except that they were shockingly prone to do as they pleased—there were even letters in the *Times* criticizing the government. And there was another letter signed by a bishop of their infidel church, criticizing the people for not attending services. I don't know which one puzzled me the more; both of them seemed to indicate a situation of open anarchy.

Master Peter informed me that the psych board had turned me down for assassination duty. I found myself both relieved and indignant. What was wrong with me that they would not trust me with the job? It seemed like a slur on my character—by then.

"Take it easy," van Eyck advised dryly. "They made a dummy run based on your personality profile and it figured almost an even chance that you would be caught your first time out. We don't like to expend men that fast."

"But—"

"Peace, lad. I'm sending you out to General Headquarters for assignment."

"General Headquarters? Where is that?"

"You'll know when you get there. Report to the staff metamorphist."

Dr. Mueller was the staff face-changer; I asked him what he had in mind for me. "How do I know until I find out what you are?" He had me measured and photographed, recorded my voice, analyzed my walk, and had a punched card made up of my physical characteristics. "Now we'll find your twin brother." I watched the card sorter go through several thousand cards and I was beginning to think I was a unique individual, resembling no one else sufficiently to permit me to be disguised successfully, when two cards popped out almost together. Before the machine whirred to a stop there were five cards in the basket.

"A nice assortment," Dr. Mueller mused as he looked them over, "one synthetic, two live ones, a deader, and one female. We can't use the woman for this job, but we'll keep it in mind; it might come in very handy someday to know that there is a female citizen you could impersonate successfully."

"What's a synthetic?" I enquired.

"Eh? Oh, it's a composite personality, very carefully built

55

from faked records and faked backgrounds. A risky business—it involves tampering with the national archives. I don't like to use a synthetic, for there really isn't any way to fill in completely the background of a man who doesn't exist. I'd much rather patch into the real background of a real person."

"Then why use synthetics at all?"

"Sometimes we have to. When we have to move a refugee in a hurry, for example, and there is no real person we can match him with. So we try to keep a fairly broad assortment of synthetics built up. Now let me see," he added, shuffling the cards, "we have two to choose from—"

"Just a second, Doctor," I interrupted, "why do you keep dead men in the file?"

"Oh, they aren't legally dead. When one of the brethern dies and it is possible to conceal the fact, we maintain his public personality for possible future use. Now then," he continued, "can you sing?"

"Not very well."

"This one is out, then. He's a concert baritone. I can make a lot of changes in you, but I can't make a trained singer of you. It's Hobson's choice. How would you like to be Adam Reeves, commercial traveler in textiles?" He held up a card.

"Do you think I could get away with it?"

"Certainly—when I get through with you."

A fortnight later my own mother wouldn't have known me. Nor, I believe, could Reeves' mother have told me from her son. The second week Reeves himself was available to work with me. I grew to like him very much while I was studying him. He was a mild, quiet man with a retiring disposition, which always made me think of him as small although he was, of course, my height, weight, and bony structure. We resembled each other only superficially in the face.

At first, that is. A simple operation made my ears stand out a little more than nature intended; at the same time they trimmed my ear lobes. Reeves' nose was slightly aquiline; a little wax under the skin at the bridge caused mine to match. It was necessary to cap several of my teeth to make mine match his dental repair work; that was the only part I really minded. My complexion had to be bleached a shade or two; Reeves' work did not take him out into the sun much.

But the most difficult part of the physical match was artificial fingerprints. An opaque, flesh-colored flexible plastic was painted on my finger pads, then my fingers were sealed into molds made from Reeves' fingertips. It was touchy work; one finger was done over seven times before Dr. Mueller would pass it.

That was only the beginning; now I had to learn to act like Reeves—his walk, his gestures, the way he laughed, his table manners. I doubt if I could ever make a living as an actor—my coach certainly agreed and said so.

"Confound it, Lyle, won't you ever get it? Your life will depend on it. You've *got* to learn!"

"But I thought I was acting just like Reeves," I objected feebly.

"Acting! That's just the trouble—you were *acting* like Reeves. And it was as phony as a false leg. You've got to *be* Reeves. Try it. Worry about your sales record, think about your last trip, think about commissions and discounts and quotas. Go on. Try it."

Every spare minute I studied the current details of Reeves' business affairs, for I would actually have to sell textiles in his place. I had to learn a whole trade and I discovered that there was more to it than carrying around samples and letting a retailer make his choice—and I didn't know a denier from a continuous fibre. Before I finished I acquired a new respect for business men. I had always thought that buying and selling was simple; I was wrong again. I had to use the old phonographic tutor stunt and wear earphones to bed. I never sleep well that way and would wake up each morning with a splitting head and with my ears, still tender from the operations, sore as two boils.

But it worked, all of it. In two short weeks I *was* Adam Reeves, commercial traveler, right down to my thoughts.

7

"LYLE," Master Peter van Eyck said to me, "Reeves is due to catch the *Comet* for Cincinnati this afternoon. Are you ready?"

"Yes, sir."

"Good. Repeat your orders."

"Sir, I am to carry out my—I mean his—selling schedule from here to the coast. I check in at the San Francisco office of United Textiles, then proceed on his vacation. In Phoenix, Arizona, I am to attend church services at the South Side Tabernacle. I am to hang around afterwards and thank the priest for the inspiration of his sermon; in the course of which I am to reveal myself to him by means of the accustomed usages of our order. He will enable me to reach General Headquarters."

"All correct. In addition to transferring you for duty, I am going to make use of you as a messenger. Report to the psychodynamics laboratory at once. The chief technician will instruct you."

"Very well, sir."

The lodge Master got up and came around his desk to me. "Good-by, John. Watch yourself, and may the Great Architect help you."

"Thank you, sir. Uh, is this message I am to carry important?"

"Quite important."

He let it go at that and I was a bit irked; it seemed silly to be mysterious about it when I would find out just what it was in a few minutes. But I was mistaken. At the laboratory I was told to sit down, relax, and prepare myself for hypnosis.

I came out of it with the pleasant glow that usually follows hypnosis. "That's all," I was told. "Carry out your orders."

"But how about the message I was to carry?"

"You have it."

"Hypnotically? But if I'm arrested, I'll be at the mercy of any psycho-investigator who examines me!"

"No, you won't. It's keyed to a pair of signal words; you can't possibly remember until they are spoken to you. The chance that an examiner would hit on both words and in the right order is negligible. You can't give the message away, awake or asleep."

I had rather expected to be "loaded" for suicide, if I was to carry an important message—though I hadn't seen how they could do it at the last minute, other than supplying me with a pill, I mean, a method almost useless if the policeman knows his business. But if I couldn't give away the message I carried, then I preferred to take my chances; I didn't ask for poison. I'm not the suiciding type anyhow—when Satan comes for me, he'll have to drag me . . .

The rocket port serving New Jerusalem is easier to get to than is the case at most of the older cities. There was a tube station right across from the department store that hid our headquarters. I simply walked out of the store, took the bridge across the street, found the tube stall marked "Rocket Port," waited for an empty cartridge, and strapped myself and my luggage in. The attendant sealed me and almost at once I was at the port.

I bought my ticket and took my place at the end of the queue outside the port police station. I'll admit I was nervous; while I didn't anticipate having any trouble getting my travel pass validated, the police officers who must handle it were no doubt on the lookout for John Lyle, renegade army officer. But they were always looking for someone and I hoped the list of wanted faces was too long to make the search for me anything other than routine.

The line moved slowly and that looked like a bad sign—especially so when I noticed that several people had been thumbed out of line and sent to wait behind the station railing. I got downright jittery. But the wait itself gave me time to get myself in hand. I shoved my papers at the sergeant, glanced at my chrono, up at the station clock, and back at my wrist.

The sergeant had been going through my papers in a leisurely, thorough manner. He looked up. "Don't worry about catching your ship," he said not unkindly. "They can't leave until we clear their passenger list." He pushed a pad across the counter. "Your fingerprints, please."

I gave them without comment. He compared them with the prints on my travel pass and then with the prints Reeves had left there on his arrival a week earlier. "That's all, Mr. Reeves. A pleasant trip."

I thanked him and left.

The *Comet* was not too crowded. I picked a seat by a window, well forward, and had just settled down and was unfolding a late-afternoon copy of the *Holy City*, when I felt a touch on my arm.

It was a policeman.

"Will you step outside, please?"

I was herded outside with four other male passengers. The sergeant was quite decent about it. "I'm afraid I'll have to ask you four to return to the station for further identification. I'll order your baggage removed and have the passenger list changed. Your tickets will be honored on the next flight."

I let out a yelp. "But I've got to be in Cincinnati tonight!"

"I'm sorry." He turned to me. "You're Reeves, aren't you? Hmm . . . you are the right size and build. Still . . . let me see your pass again. Didn't you arrive in town just last week?"

"That's right."

He went through my papers again. "Uh, yes, I remember now; you came in Tuesday morning on the *Pilgrim*. Well, you can't be in two places at once, so I guess that clears you." He handed my papers back to me. "Go aboard again. Sorry we bothered you. The rest of you come along."

I returned to my seat and picked up my newspaper. A few minutes later the first heavy surge of the rockets threw us to the west. I continued reading the paper to cover up my agitation and relief, but soon got interested. I had been reading a Toronto paper only that morning, underground; the contrast was startling. I was back in a world for which the outside world hardly existed; the "foreign affairs" news, if you could call it that, consisted of glowing reports of our foreign missions and some accounts of atrocities among the infidels. I began to wonder where all that money went that was contributed each year for missionary work; the rest of the world, if you could believe *their* newspapers, didn't seem much aware that our missions existed.

Then I began going through the paper, picking out items

that I knew to be false. By the time I was through we were down out of the ionosphere and gliding into Cincy. We had overtaken the sun and had sunset all over again.

There must be a peddler's pack in my family tree. I not only covered Reeves' territory in Cincinnati, but bettered his quota. I found that I got as much pleasure out of persuading some hard-boiled retailer that he should increase his line of yard goods as I ever had from military work. I stopped worrying about my disguise and thought only about textiles. Selling isn't just a way to eat; it's a game, it's fun.

I left for Kansas City on schedule and had no trouble with the police in getting a visa for my travel pass. I decided that New Jerusalem had been the only ticklish check point; from here west nobody would expect to pick up John Lyle, formerly officer and gentleman; he would be one of thousands of wanted men, lost in the files.

The rocket to K.C. was well filled; I had to sit beside another passenger, a well-built chap in his middle thirties. We looked each other over as I sat down, then each busied himself with his own affairs. I called for a lap table and started straightening out the order blanks and other papers I had accumulated during busy, useful days in Cincinnati. He lounged back and watched the news broadcast in the TV tank at the forward end of the car.

I felt a nudge about ten minutes later and looked around. My seatmate flicked a thumb toward the television tank; in it there was displayed a large public square filled with a mob. It was surging toward the steps of a massive temple, over which floated the Prophet's gold-and-crimson banner and the pennant of a bishopric. As I watched, the first wave of the crowd broke against the temple steps.

A squad of temple guards trotted out a side door near the giant front doors and set up their tripods on the terrace at the head of the wide stairs. The scene cut to another viewpoint; we were looking down right into the faces of the mob hurrying toward us—apparently from a telephoto pick-up somewhere on the temple roof.

What followed made me ashamed of the uniform I had once worn. Instead of killing them quickly, the guards aimed low and burned off their legs. One instant the first wave was running toward me up the steps—then they fell, the cauterized stumps of their legs jerking convulsively. I had been watching a youngish couple right in the center of the pick-up; they had been running hand in hand. As the beam swept across them they went down together.

She stayed down. He managed to lift himself on what had been his knees, took two awkward dying steps toward her and fell across her. He pulled her head to his, then the scene cut away from them to the wide view of the square.

I snatched the earphones hanging on the back of the seat in front of me and listened: "—apolis, Minnesota. The situation is well in hand and no additional troops will be needed. Bishop Jennings has declared martial law while the agents of Satan are rounded up and order restored. A period of prayer and fasting will commence at once.

"The Minnesota ghettos have been closed and all local pariahs will be relocated in the reservations in Wyoming and Montana in order to prevent future outbreaks. Let this be a warning to the ungodly everywhere who might presume to dispute the divine rule of the Prophet Incarnate.

"This on-the-spot cast by the No-Sparrow-Shall-Fall News Service is coming to you under the sponsorship of the Associated Merchants of the Kingdom, dealers in the finest of household aids toward grace. Be the first in your parish to possess a statuette of the Prophet that miraculously *glows in the dark!* Send one dollar, care of this station—"

I switched off the phones and hung them up. Why blame the pariahs? That mob wasn't made up of pariahs.

But I kept my lip zipped and let my companion speak first—which he did, with vehemence. "Serves them right, the bloody fools! Imagine charging against a fortified position with your bare hands." He kept his voice down and spoke almost in my ear.

"I wonder why they rioted?" was all that I answered.

"Eh? No accounting for the actions of an heretic. They aren't sane."

"You can sing that in church," I agreed firmly. "Besides, even a sane heretic—if there could be such a thing, I mean—could see that the government is doing a good job of running the country. Business is good." I patted my brief case happily. "For me, at least, praise the Lord."

We talked business conditions and the like for some time. As we talked I looked him over. He seemed to be the usual leading-citizen type, conventional and conservative, yet something about him made me uneasy. Was it just my guilty nerves? Or some sixth sense of the hunted?

My eyes came back to his hands and I had a vague feeling that I should be noticing something. But there was nothing unusual about them. Then I finally noticed a very minor thing, a calloused ridge on the bottom joint of the third finger of his left hand, the sort of a mark left by wearing a heavy ring for years and just the sort I carried myself from wearing my West Point class ring. It meant nothing, of course, since lots of men wear heavy seal rings on that finger. I was wearing one myself—not my West Point ring naturally, but one belonging to Reeves.

But why would this conventional-minded oaf wear such a ring habitually, then stop? A trifling thing, but it worried me;

a hunted animal lives by noticing trifles. At the Point I had never been considered bright in psychology; I had missed cadet chevrons on that issue alone. But now seemed a good time to use what little I had learned . . . so I ran over in my mind all I had noticed about him.

The first thing he had noticed, the one thing he had commented on, was the foolhardiness of charging into a fortified position. That smacked of military orientation in his thinking. But that did not prove he was a Pointer. On the contrary, an Academy man wears his ring at all times, even into his grave, even on leave and wearing mufti . . . unless for some good reason he does not wish to be recognized.

We were still chatting sociably and I was worrying over how to evaluate insufficient data when the stewardess served tea. The ship was just beginning to bite air as we came down out of the fringes of space and entered the long glide into Kansas City; it was somewhat bumpy and she slopped a little hot tea on his thigh. He yelped and uttered an expletive under his breath. I doubt if she caught what he said.

But I did catch it—and I thought about it furiously while I dabbed at him with a handkerchief. "B. J. idiot!" was the term he used and it was strictly West Point slang.

Ergo, the ring callous was no coincidence; he was a West Pointer, an army officer, pretending to be a civilian. Corollary: he was almost certainly on a secret service assignment. Was I his assignment?

Oh, come now, John! His ring might be at a jeweller's, being repaired; he might be going home on thirty days. But in the course of a long talk he had let me think that he was a business man. No, he was an undercover agent.

But even if he was not after *me*, he had made two bad breaks in my presence. But even the clumsiest tyro (like myself, say) does not make two such slips in maintaining an assumed identity—and the army secret service was not clumsy; it was run by some of the most subtle brains in the country. Very well, then—they were not accidental slips but calculated acts; I was intended to notice them and *think* that they were accidents. Why?

It could not be simply that he was not sure I was the man he wanted. In such case, under the old and tested principle that a man was sinful until proved innocent, he would simply have arrested me and I would have been put to the Question.

Then *why?*

It could only be that they wanted me to run free for a while yet—but to be scared out of my wits and run for cover . . . and thereby lead them to my fellow conspirators. It was a far-fetched hypothesis, but the only one that seemed to cover all the facts.

When I first concluded that my companion must be an

agent on my trail I was filled with that cold, stomach-twisting fear that can be compared only with seasickness. But when I thought I had figured out their motives I calmed down. What would Zebadiah do? "The first principle of intrigue is not to be stampeded into any unusual act—" Sit tight and play dumb. If this cop wanted to follow me, I'd lead him into every department store in K.C.—and let him watch while I peddled yard goods.

Nevertheless my stomach felt tight as we got off the ship in Kansas City. I expected that gentle touch on the shoulder which is more frightening than a fist in the face. But nothing happened. He tossed me a perfunctory God-keep-you, pushed ahead of me, and headed for the lift to the taxicab platform while I was still getting my pass stamped. It did not reassure me, as he could have pointed me out half a dozen ways to a relief. But I went on over to the New Muehlbach by tube as casually as I could manage.

I had a fair week in K.C., met my quota and picked up one new account of pretty good size. I tried to spot any shadow that might have been placed on me, but I don't know to this day whether or not I was being trailed. If I was, somebody spent an awfully dull week. But, although I had about concluded that the incident had been nothing but imagination and my jumpy nerves, I was happy at last to be aboard the ship for Denver and to note that my companion of the week before was not a passenger.

We landed at the new field just east of Aurora, many miles from downtown Denver. The police checked my papers and fingerprinted me in the routine fashion and I was about to shove my wallet back into my pocket when the desk sergeant said, "Bare your left arm, please, Mr. Reeves."

I rolled up my sleeve while trying to show the right amount of fretful annoyance. A white-coated orderly took a blood sample. "Just a normal precaution," the sergeant explained. "The Department of Public Health is trying to stamp out spotted fever."

It was a thin excuse, as I knew from my own training in P.H.—but Reeves, textiles salesman, might not realize it. But the excuse got thinner yet when I was asked to wait in a side room of the station while my blood sample was run. I sat there fretting, trying to figure out what harm they could do me with ten c.c. of my blood—and what I could do about it even if I did know.

I had plenty of time to think. The situation looked anything but bright. My time was probably running out as I sat there— yet the excuse on which they were holding me was just plausible enough that I didn't dare cut and run; that might be what they wanted. So I sat tight and sweated.

The building was a temporary structure and the wall between

me and the sergeant's office was a thin laminate; I could hear voices through it without being able to make out the words. I did not dare press my ear to it for fear of being caught doing so. On the other hand I felt that I just had to do it. So I moved my chair over to the wall, sat down again, leaned back on two legs of the chair so that my shoulders and the back of my neck were against the wall. Then I held a newspaper I had found there up in front of my face and pressed my ear against the wall.

I could hear every word then. The sergeant told a story to his clerk which would have fetched him a month's penance if a morals proctor had been listening—still, I had heard the same story, only slightly cleaned up, right in the Palace, so I wasn't really shocked, nor was I in any mood to worry about other people's morals. I listened to several routine reports and an inquiry from some semi-moron who couldn't find the men's washroom, but not a word about myself. I got a crick in my neck from the position.

Just opposite me was an open window looking out over the rocket field. A small ship appeared in the sky, braked with nose units, and came in to a beautiful landing about a quarter of a mile away. The pilot taxied toward the administration building and parked outside the window, not twenty-five yards away.

It was the courier version of the *Sparrow Hawk*, ram jet with rocket take-off and booster, as sweet a little ship as was ever built. I knew her well; I had pushed one just like her, playing number-two position for Army in sky polo—that was the year we had licked both Navy and Princeton.

The pilot got out and walked away. I eyed the distance to the ship. If the ignition were not locked—Sheol! what if it was? Maybe I could short around it, I looked at the open window. It might be equipped with vibrobolts; if so, I would never know what hit me. But I could not spot any power leads or trigger connections and the flimsy construction of the building would make it hard to hide them. Probably there was nothing but contact alarms; there might not be so much as a selenium circuit.

While I was thinking about it I again heard voices next door; I flattened my ear and strained to listen.

"What's the blood type?"

"Type one, sergeant."

"Does it check?"

"No, Reeves is type three."

"Oho! Phone the main lab. We'll take him into town for a retinal."

I was caught cold and knew it. They knew positively that I wasn't Reeves. Once they photographed the pattern of blood vessels in the retina of either eye they would know just as certainly who I really was, in no longer time than it took to radio the picture to the Bureau of Morals & Investigation—less,

64

if copies had been sent out to Denver and elsewhere with the tab on me.

I dove out the window.

I lit on my hands, rolled over in a ball, was flung to my feet as I unwound. If I set off an alarm I was too busy to hear it. The ship's door was open and the ignition was not locked—there was help indeed for the Son of a Widow! I didn't bother to taxi clear, but blasted at once, not caring if my rocket flame scorched my pursuers. We bounced along the ground, the little darling and I, then I lifted her nose by gyro and scooted away to the west.

8

I LET her reach for the sky, seeking altitude and speed where the ram jets would work properly. I felt exalted to have a good ship under me and those cops far behind. But I snapped out of that silly optimism as I leveled off for jet flight.

If a cat escapes up a tree, he must stay there until the dog goes away. That was the fix I was in and in my case the dog would not go away, nor could I stay up indefinitely. The alarm would be out by now; behind me, on all sides of me, police pilots would be raising ship in a matter of minutes, even seconds. I was being tracked, that was sure, and the blip of my craft on several screens was being fed as data into a computer that would vector them in on me no matter where I turned. After that—well, it was land on command or be shot down.

The miracle of my escape began to seem a little less miraculous. Or *too* miraculous, perhaps? Since when were the police so sloppy that they would leave a prisoner in a room with an unguarded window? Wasn't it just a little too much of a coincidence that a ship I knew how to herd should come to that window and be left there—with the ignition unlocked—just as the sergeant said loudly the one thing that would be sure to make me try for it?

Maybe this was a second, and successful, attempt to panic me. Maybe somebody else knew my liking for the *Sparrow Hawk* courier, knew it because he had my dossier spread out in front of him and was as familiar with my sky polo record as I was. In which case they might not shoot me down just yet; they might be counting on me to lead them straight to my comrades.

Or perhaps, just possibly, it was a real escape—if I could exploit it. Either way, I was neither ready to be caught again, nor to lead them to my brethren—nor to die. I had an important

65

message (I told myself); I was too busy to oblige them by dying just now.

I flipped the ship's commer to the police & traffic frequency and listened. There was some argument going on between the Denver port and a transport in the air but no one as yet was shouting for me to ground or get my pants shot off. Later perhaps—I left it switched on and thought.

The dead-reckoner showed me some seventy-five miles from Denver and headed north of west; I was surprised to see that I had been in the air less than ten minutes . . . so hopped up with adrenalin, no doubt, that my time sense was distorted. The ram-jet tanks were nearly full; I had nearly ten hours and six thousand miles at economy cruising—but of course at that speed they could almost throw rocks at me.

A plan, silly and perhaps impossible and certainly born of desperation but even so better than no plan at all, was beginning to form in my brain. I consulted the great-circle indicator and set a course for the Republic of Hawaii; my baby nosed herself slightly south of west. Then I turned to the fuel-speed-distance gnomograph and roughed a problem—3100 miles about, at around 800 mph, ending with dry tanks and depending on rocket juice and the nose units to cushion a cold-jet landing. Risky.

Not that I cared. Somewhere below me, shortly after I set the autopilot on the indicated course and speed, analyzers in the cybernetwork would be telling their human operators that I was attempting to escape to the Free State of Hawaii, on such a course, such an altitude, and at max speed for that range . . . and that I would pass over the Pacific coast between San Francisco and Monterey in sixty-odd minutes unless intercepted. But interception was certain. Even if they were still playing with me, cat and mouse, ground-to-air snarlers would rise up from the Sacramento Valley. If they missed (most unlikely!), manned ships as fast or faster than my baby, with full tanks and no need to conserve radius, would be waiting at altitude at the coast. I had no hope of running that gauntlet.

Nor did I intend to. I *wanted* them to destroy the little honey I was pushing, destroy her completely and in the air—because I had no intention of being aboard when it happened.

Operation Chucklehead, phase two: how to get out of the durn thing! Leaving a jet plane in powered flight has all been figured out by careful engineers; you slap the jetison lever and pray; the rest is done for you. The survival capsule closes down on you and seals, then the capsule with you in it is shot clear of the ship. In due course, at proper pressure and terminal air speed, the drogue is fired; it pulls your chute open, and there you are, floating comfortably toward God's good earth, with your emergency oxygen bottle for company.

There is only one hitch: both the capsule and the abandoned

66

ship start sending out radio signals, dots for the capsule, dashes for the ship, and, for good measure, the capsule has a built-in radar-beacon.

The whole thing is about as inconspicuous as a cow in church.

I sat there chewing my thumb and staring out ahead. It seemed to me that the yonder was looking even wilder and bluer than usual—my own mood, no doubt, for I knew that thirteen ground miles were slipping out from under me each minute and that it was high time for me to find my hat and go home. Of course, there was a door right alongside me; I could strap on a chute and leave. But you can't open a door in a ram-jet plane in powered flight; nor do you jettison it—to do so will cause the plane to behave like a kicked pup. Nor is an eight-hundred mile-an-hour breeze to be ignored even at 60,000 feet; I'd be sliced like butter on the door frame.

The answer depended on how good an autopilot this buggy had. The better robopilots could do everything but sing hymns; some of the cheaper ones could hold course, speed, and altitude but there their talents ended. In particular I wanted to know whether or not this autopilot had an emergency circuit to deal with a case of "fire out," for I intended to stop the ship, step out, and let the ship continue on in the direction of Hawaii by itself—if it could.

A ram jet won't operate at all except at high speed; that's why ram ships have rocket power as well, else they could never take off. If you drop below the critical speed of your jet engines your fire goes out, then you must start it again, either by rocket power or by diving to gain speed. It is a touchy business and a number of ram-jet pilots have been gathered to their heavenly reward through an unexpected case of "fire out."

My earlier experience with the courier *Sparrow Hawk* told me nothing, as you don't use autopilots in sky polo. Believe me, you don't. So I looked for the instruction manual in the glove compartment, failed to find it, then looked over the pilot itself. The data plate failed to say. No doubt, with a screw driver and plenty of time, I could have opened it, worried out the circuits and determined the fact—say in about a day and a half; those autopilots are a mass of transistors and spaghetti.

So I pulled the personal chute out of its breakaway clips and started shrugging my way into it while sighing, "Pal, I *hope* you have the necessary gimmick built into your circuits." The autopilot didn't answer, though I wouldn't have been much surprised if it had. Then I squeezed back into place and proceeded to override the autopilot manually. I didn't have too much time; I was already over the Deseret basin and I could see the setting sun glinting on the waters of the Great Salt Lake ahead and to the right.

First I took her down some, because 60,000 feet is thin and

chilly—too little partial pressure of oxygen for the human lung. Then I started up in a gentle curving climb that would neither tear her wings off nor gee me into a blackout. I had to take her fairly high, because I intended to cut out the rocket motors entirely and force my best girl to light her stovepipes by diving for speed, it being my intention to go into a vertical stall, which would create "fire out"—and get off in a hurry at that point. For obvious reasons I did not want the rocket motors to cut loose just as I was trying to say good-by.

I kept curving her up until I was lying on my back with the earth behind me and sky ahead. I nursed it along, throttling her down, with the intention of stalling with the fire dead at thirty thousand feet—still thin but within jumping distance of breathable air and still high enough to give my lady a chance to go into her dive without cracking up on the Utah plateau. At about 28,000 I got that silly, helpless feeling you get when the controls go mushy and won't bite. Suddenly a light flashed red on the instrument board and both fires were out. It was time to leave.

I almost forgot the seat bottle. I was still stuffing the mouthpiece between my teeth and snapping the nosepiece over my nose while I was trying with the other hand to get the door open—all of this greatly impeded by the fact that the ship and I together were effectively in free fall; the slight air drag at the top of the stall trajectory made me weigh a few ounces, no more.

The door would not open. I finally remembered to slap the spill valve, then it came open and I was almost snatched outside. I hung there for a second or two, while the ground spun crazily overhead, then the door slammed shut and latched—and I shoved myself away from the plane. I didn't jump—we were falling together, I shoved.

I may have banged my head against a wing. In any case there is a short blank in my memory before I found myself sitting on space about twenty-five yards from the ship. She was spinning slowly and earth and sky were revolving lazily around me. There was a thin cold wind as I fell but I was not yet aware of the cold. We stayed pretty well together for a few moments—or hours; time had stopped—then the ship straightened out into a dive and pulled away from me.

I tried to follow her down by eye and became aware of the icy wind of my fall. My eyes hurt and I remembered something I had read about frozen eyeballs; I covered them with both hands. It helped a lot.

Suddenly I became frightened, panicky at the thought that I had delayed the jump too long and was about to smash into the desert floor. I uncovered my eyes and sneaked a look.

No, the ground was still a long way off, two or three miles perhaps. My guess was not worth much as it was already dark

68

down there. I tried to catch sight of the ship, could not see it, then suddenly spotted it as her fires came on. I risked frozen eyes and watched, exaltation in my heart. The autopilot did indeed have built into it the emergency circuit for "fire out" and everything was proceeding according to plan. The little sweetheart leveled off, headed west on course, and began to climb for the altitude she had been told to use. I sent a prayer after her that she would win through and end up in the clean Pacific, rather than be shot down.

I watched her glowing tailpipes out of sight while I continued to fall.

The triumph of my little ship had made me forget to be scared. I had known when I bailed out that it would have to be a delayed jump. My own body, in leaving the ship, would make a secondary blip on the screen of anything tracking the ship; my only hope of convincing the trackers that what they had witnessed was a real emergency—"fire out"—lay in getting away from the ship quickly and then in not being spotted on the way down. That meant that I must fall rapidly right out of the picture and not pull the rip cord until I was close to the ground, in visual darkness and in ground radar shadow.

But I had never made a delayed jump before; in fact I had jumped only twice, the two easy practice jumps under a jump-master which are required of every cadet in order to graduate. I wasn't especially uncomfortable as long as I kept my eyes closed, but I began to get a truly overpowering urge to pull that rip cord. My hand went to the handle and gripped it. I told myself to let go but I couldn't make myself do it. I was still much too high, dead sure to be spotted if I broke out that great conspicuous bumbershoot and floated down the rest of the way.

I had intended to rip the chute out somewhere between one thousand and five hundred feet above ground, but my nerve played out and I couldn't wait that long. There was a large town almost under me—Provo, Utah, by what I remembered of the situation from higher up. I convinced myself that I had to pull the rip cord to keep from landing right in the city.

I remembered just in time to remove the oxygen face piece, thereby avoiding a mouthful of broken teeth most likely, for I had never gotten around to strapping the bottle to me; I had been holding it in my left hand all the way down. I suppose I could have taken time even then to secure it, but what I did was to throw it in the general direction of a farm, hoping that it would land on plowed ground rather than on some honest citizen's skull. Then I pulled the handle.

For the horrible split second I thought that I had a faultily-packed chute. Then it opened and knocked me out—or I fainted with fright. I came to, hanging in the harness with the ground swinging and turning slowly beneath me. I was still too high up and I seemed to be floating toward the lights of Provo.

So I took a deep breath—real air tasted good after the canned stuff—gathered a double handful of shrouds and spilled some wind.

I came down fast then and managed to let go just in time to get full support for the landing. I couldn't see the ground well in the evening darkness but I knew it was close; I gathered up my knees just as it says in the manual, then took it rather unexpectedly, stumbling, falling, and getting tangled in the chute. It is supposed to be equal to a fourteen-foot free jump; all I can say is it seems like more.

Then I was sitting on my tail in a field of sugar beets, and rubbing my left ankle.

Spies always bury their parachutes so I suppose I should have buried mine. But I didn't feel up to it and I didn't have any tools; I stuffed it into a culvert I found running under the road that edged the field, then started slogging that road toward the lights of Provo. My nose and right ear had been bleeding and the blood was dry on my face; I was covered with dirt, I had split my trousers, my hat was the Lord knows where—Denver, maybe, or over Nevada—, my left ankle seemed slightly sprained, my right hand was badly skinned, and I had had a childish accident. I felt swell.

I could hardly keep from whistling as I walked, I felt so good. Sure, I was still hunted, but the Prophet's proctors thought I was still high in the sky and headed for Hawaii. At least I hoped they believed that and, in any case, I was still free, alive, and reasonably intact. If one has to be hunted, Utah was a better place for it than most; it had been a center of heresy and schism ever since the suppression of the Mormon church, back in the days of the First Prophet. If I could keep out of the direct sight of the Prophet's police, it was unlikely that any of the natives would turn me in.

Nevertheless I lay flat in the ditch every time a truck or a ground car came along and I left the road and took to the fields again before it entered the city proper. I swung wide and entered by a dimly lighted side street. It lacked two hours of curfew; I needed to carry out the first part of my plan before the night patrol took to the streets.

I wandered around dark residential streets and avoided any direct encounters with people for most of an hour before finding what I wanted—some sort of a flier I could steal. It turned out to be a Ford family skycar, parked in a vacant lot. The house next to it was dark.

I sneaked up to it, keeping to the shadows, and broke my penknife jimming the door—but I got it open. The ignition was locked, but I had not expected that sort of luck twice. I had had an extremely practical education at taxpayers' expense which included detailed knowledge of I.C. engines, and this time there was no hurry; it took me twenty minutes, working in the dark, to short around the lock.

After a quick reconnoitre of the street I got in and started the electric auxiliary and glided quietly into the street, then rounded a corner before turning on the car's lights. Then I drove away as openly as a farmer returning from prayer meeting in town. Nevertheless I was afraid of running into a police check point at the city limits, so as soon as the houses thinned out I ran the car into the first open field and went on well away from the road—then unexpectedly dropped a front wheel into an irrigation ditch. That determined my take-off point.

The main engine coughed and took hold; the rotor unfolded its airfoils with a loud creak. She was sloppy on the take-off, being canted over into the ditch, but she made it. The ground dropped away.

9

THE car I had stolen was a jalopy, old, not properly kept up, a bad valve knock in the engine, and a vibration in the rotor that I didn't like at all. But she would run and she had better than half a tank of fuel, enough to get me to Phoenix. I couldn't complain.

Worst was a complete lack of any navigating equipment other than an old-style uncompensated Sperry robot and a bundle of last year's strip maps of the sort the major oil companies give away. There was radio, but it was out of order.

Well, Columbus got by with less. Phoenix was almost due south and almost five hundred miles away. I estimated my drift by crossing my eyes and praying, set the robot on course and set her to hold real altitude of five hundred feet. Any more might get me into the cybernetwork; any less might get some local constable annoyed with me. I decided that running lights were safer than no running lights, this being no time to pick up a ticket, so I switched them on to "dim." After that I took a look around.

No sign of pursuit to the north—apparently my latest theft had not been noticed as yet. As for my first—well, the sweet darling was either shot down by now or far out over the Pacific. It occurred to me that I was hanging up quite a record for a mother's boy—accessory before and after the fact in murder, perjury before the Grand Inquisitor, treason, impersonation, grand larceny twice. There was still arson, and barratry, whatever that was, and rape. I decided I could avoid rape,

71

out barratry I might manage, if I could find out what it meant. I still felt swell even though my nose was bleeding again.

It occurred to me that marrying a holy deaconess might be considered statutory rape under the law and that made me feel better; by then I didn't want to miss anything.

I stayed at the controls, overriding the pilot and avoiding towns, until we were better than a hundred miles south of Provo. From there south, past the Grand Canyon and almost to the ruins of the old "66" roadcity, people are awfully scarce; I decided that I could risk some sleep. So I set the pilot on eight hundred feet, ground altitude, told it firmly to watch out for trees and bluffs, went back to the after passenger bench and went at once to sleep.

I dreamt that the Grand Inquisitor was trying to break my nerve by eating juicy roast beef in my presence. "Confess!" he said, as he stabbed a bite and chewed. "Make it easy on yourself. Will you have some rare, or the slice off the end?" I was about to confess, too, when I woke up.

It was bright moonlight and we were just approaching the Grand Canyon. I went quickly to the controls and overrode the order about altitude—I was afraid that the simple little robot might have a nervous breakdown and start shedding capacitances in lieu of tears if it tried to hold the ship just eight hundred feet away from that Gargantuan series of ups and downs and pinnacles.

In the meantime I was enjoying the view so much that I forgot that I was starving. If a person hasn't seen the Canyon, there is no point in describing it—but I strongly recommend seeing it by moonlight from the air.

We sliced across it in about twenty minutes and I turned the ship back to automatic and started to forage, rummaging through the instrument panel compartment and the lockers. I turned up a chocolate almond bar and a few peanuts, which was a feast as I was ready for raw skunk. . . . I had eaten last in Kansas City. I polished them off and went back to sleep.

I don't recall setting the pilot alarm but must have done so for it woke me up just before dawn. Dawn over the desert was another high-priced tourist item but I had navigating to do and could not spare it more than a glance. I turned the crate at right angles for a few minutes to check drift and speed made good over ground to south, then figured a bit on the edge of a strip map. With luck and assuming that my guesses about wind were about right, Phoenix should show up in about half an hour.

My luck held. I passed over some mighty rough country, then suddenly, spread out to the right, was a wide flat desert valley, green with irrigated crops and with a large city in it— the Valley of the Sun and Phoenix. I made a poor landing in a boxed-in, little dry arroyo leading into the Salt River Canyon;

I tore off one wheel and smashed the rotor but I didn't care—the important thing was that it wasn't likely to be found there very soon, it and my fingerprints . . . Reeves' prints, I mean. Half an hour later, after picking my way around enormous cacti and still bigger red boulders, I came out on the highway that leads down the canyon and into Phoenix.

It was going to be a long walk into Phoenix, especially with one sore ankle, but I decided not to risk hitching a ride. Traffic was light and I managed to get off the road and hide each time for the first hour. Then I was caught on a straight up-and-down piece by a freighter; there was nothing to do but give the driver a casual wave as I flattened myself to the rock wall and pretend to be nonchalant. He brought his heavy vehicle to a quick, smooth stop. "Want a lift, bud?"

I made up my mind in a hurry. "Yes, thanks!"

He swung a dural ladder down over the wide tread and I climbed into the cab. He looked me over. "Brother!" he said admiringly. "Was it a mountain lion, or a bear?"

I had forgotten how I looked. I glanced down at myself. "Both," I answered solemnly. "Strangled one in each hand."

"I believe it."

"Fact is," I added, "I was riding a unicycle and bounced it off the road. On the high side, luckily, but I wrecked it."

"A unicycle? On this road? Not all the way from Globe?"

"Well, I had to get off and push at times. It was the down grade that got me, though."

He shook his head. "Let's go back to the lion-and-bear theory. I like it better." He didn't question me further, which suited me. I was beginning to realize that off-hand fictions led to unsuspected ramifications; I had never been over the road from Globe.

Nor had I ever been inside a big freighter before and I was interested to see how much it resembled, inside, the control room of an Army surface cruiser—the same port and starboard universal oleo speed gears controlling the traction treads, much the same instrument board giving engine speed, port and starboard motor speeds, torque ratios, and so forth. I could have herded it myself.

Instead I played dumb and encouraged him to talk. "I've never been in one of these big babies before. Tell me how it works, will you?"

That set him off and I listened with half an ear while thinking about how I should tackle Phoenix. He demonstrated how he applied both power and steering to the treads simply by tilting the two speed bars, one in each fist, and then discussed the economy of letting the diesel run at constant speed while he fed power as needed to the two sides. I let him talk—my first need was a bath and a shave and a change of clothes, that was sure; else I'd be picked up on sight for suspected vagrancy.

73

Presently I realized he had asked a question. "I think I see," I answered. "The Waterburies drive the treads."

"Yes and no," he went on. "It's a diesel-electric hook up. The Waterburies just act like a gear system, although there aren't any gears in them; they're hydraulic. Follow me?"

I said I thought so (I could have sketched them)—and filed away in my mind the idea that, if the Cabal should ever need cruiser pilots in a hurry, freighter jacks could be trained for the job in short order.

We were going downhill slightly even after we left the canyon; the miles flowed past. My host pulled off the road and ground to a stop by a roadside restaurant and oil station. "All out," he grunted. "Breakfast for us and go-juice for the go-buggy."

"Sounds good." We each consumed a tall stack with eggs and bacon and big, sweet Arizona grapefruit. He wouldn't let me pay for his and tried to pay for mine. As we went back to the freighter he stopped at the ladder and looked me over.

"The police gate is about three-quarters of a mile on in," he said softly. "I suppose that's as good a spot to check in as any." He looked at me and glanced away.

"Mmm . . ." I said. "I think I could stand to walk the rest of the way, to settle my breakfast. Thanks a lot for the lift."

"Don't mention it. Uh, there's a side road about two hundred yards back. It swings south and then west again, into town. Better for walking. Less traffic."

"Uh, thanks."

I walked back to the side road, wondering if my criminal career was that plain to everyone. One thing sure, I *had* to improve my appearance before tackling the city. The side road led through ranches and I passed several ranch houses without having the nerve to stop. But I came presently to a little house occupied by a Spanish-Indian family with the usual assortment of children and dogs. I took a chance; many of these people were clandestine Catholics, I knew, and probably hated the proctors as much as I did.

The Señora was home. She was fat and kindly and mostly Indian by her appearance. We couldn't talk much as my Spanish is strictly classroom quality, but I could ask for *agua*, and *agua* I got, both to drink and to wash myself. She sewed up the rip in my trousers while I stood foolishly in my shorts with the children making comments; she brushed me off and she even let me use her husband's razor. She protested over letting me pay her but I was firm about it. I left there looking passable.

The road swung back into town as the freighter jack had said—and without benefit of police. Eventually I found a neighborhood shopping center and in it a little tailor shop. There I waited while the rest of my transformation back to respectability was completed. With my clothes freshly pressed, the spots removed, a brand-new shirt and hat I was then able to walk down the street and exchange a blessing with any proctor I might meet while looking him calmly in the eye. A phone book gave me the address of the South Side Tabernacle; a map on the wall of the tailor shop got me oriented without asking questions. It was within walking distance.

I hurried down the street and reached the church just as eleven o'clock services were starting. Sighing with relief I slipped into a back pew and actually enjoyed the services, just as I had as a boy, before I had learned what was back of them. I felt peaceful and secure; in spite of everything I had made it safely. I let the familiar music soak into my soul while I looked forward to revealing myself to the priest afterwards and then let him do the worrying for a while.

To tell the truth I went to sleep during the sermon. But I woke up in time and I doubt if anyone noticed. Afterwards I hung around, waited for a chance to speak to the priest, and told him how much I had enjoyed his sermon. He shook hands and I gave him the recognition grip of the brethren.

But he did not return it. I was so upset by that that I almost missed what he was saying. "Thank you, my boy. It's always good news to a new pastor to hear that his ministrations are appreciated."

I guess my face gave me away. He added, "Something wrong?"

I stammered, "Oh, no, reverend sir. You see, I'm a stranger myself. Then you aren't the Reverend Baird?" I was in cold panic. Baird was my only contact with the brethren short of New Jerusalem; without someone to hide me I would be picked up in a matter of hours. Even as I answered I was making wild plans to steal another ship that night and then try to run the border patrol into Mexico.

His voice cut into my thoughts as if from a great distance. "No, I'm afraid not, my son. Did you wish to see the Reverend Baird?"

"Well, it wasn't terribly important, sir. He is an old friend of my uncle. I was to look him up while I was here and pay my respects." Maybe that nice Indian woman would hide me until dark?

"That won't be difficult. He's here in town. I'm just supplying his pulpit while he is laid up."

My heart made a full turn at about twelve gee; I tried to keep it out of my face. "Perhaps if he is sick I had better not disturb him."

"Oh, not at all. A broken bone in his foot—he'll enjoy a bit of company. Here." The priest fumbled under his robes, found a piece of paper and a pencil and wrote out the address. "Two streets over and half a block down. You can't miss it."

Of course I did miss it, but I doubled back and found it, an

75

old vine-grown house with a suggestion of New England about it. It was set well back in a large, untidy garden—eucalyptus, palms, shrubs, and flowers, all in pleasant confusion. I pressed the announcer and heard the whine of an old-style scanner; a speaker inquired: "Yes?"

"A visitor to see the Reverend Baird, if he so pleases."

There was a short silence while he looked me over, then: "You'll have to let yourself in. My housekeeper has gone to the market. Straight through and out into the back garden." The door clicked and swung itself open.

I blinked at the darkness, then went down a central hallway and out through the back door. An old man was lying in a swing there, with one foot propped up on pillows. He lowered his book and peered at me over his glasses.

"What do you want of me, son?"

"Light."

An hour later I was washing down the last of some superb enchiladas with cold, sweet milk. As I reached for a cluster of muscatel grapes Father Baird concluded his instructions to me. "Nothing to do until dark, then. Any questions?"

"I don't think so, sir. Sanchez takes me out of town and delivers me to certain others of the brethren who will see to it that I get to General Headquarters. My end of it is simple enough."

"True. You won't be comfortable however."

I left Phoenix concealed in a false bottom of a little vegetable truck. I was stowed like cargo, with my nose pressed against the floor boards. We were stopped at a police gate at the edge of town; I could hear brusque voices with that note of authority, and Sanchez' impassioned Spanish in reply. Someone rummaged around over my head and the cracks in the false bottom gleamed with light.

Finally a voice said, "It's okay, Ezra. That's Father Baird's handyman. Makes a trip out to the Father's ranch every night or so."

"Well, why didn't he say so?"

"He gets excited and loses his English. Okay. Get going, chico. Vaya usted con Dios."

"Gracias, senores. Buenas noches."

At the Reverend Baird's ranch I was transferred to a helicopter, no rickety heap this time, but a new job, silent and well equipped. She was manned by a crew of two, who exchanged pass grips with me but said nothing other than to tell me to get into the passenger compartment and stay there. We took off at once.

The windows of the passenger space had been covered; I don't know which way we went, nor how far. It was a rough ride, as the pilot seemed dead set on clipping daisies the whole way. It was a reasonable precaution to avoid being spotted in a scope, but I hoped he knew what he was doing—I wouldn't want to herd a heli that way in broad daylight. He must have scared a lot of coyotes—I know he frightened me.

At last I heard the squeal of a landing beam. We slid along it, hovered, and bumped gently to a stop. When I got out I found myself staring into the maw of a tripod-mounted blaster backed up by two alert and suspicious men.

But my escort gave the password, each of the guards questioned me separately, and we exchanged recognition signals. I got the impression that they were a little disappointed that they couldn't let me have it; they seemed awfully eager. When they were satisfied, a hoodwink was slipped over my head and I was led away. We went through a door, walked maybe fifty yards, and crowded into a compartment. The floor dropped away.

My stomach caught up with me and I groused to myself because I hadn't been warned that it was an elevator, but I kept my mouth shut. We left the lift, walked a way, and I was nudged onto a platform of some sort, told to sit down and hang on—whereupon we lurched away at breakneck speed. It felt like a rollercoaster—not a good thing to ride blindfolded. Up to then I hadn't really been scared. I began to think that the hazing was intentional, for they could have warned me.

We made another elevator descent, walked several hundred paces, and my hoodwink was removed. I caught my first sight of General Headquarters.

I didn't recognize it as such; I simply let out a gasp. One of my guards smiled. "They all do that," he said dryly.

It was a limestone cavern so big that one felt outdoors rather than underground and so magnificently lavish in its formations as to make one think of fairyland, or the Gnome King's palace. I had assumed that we were underground from the descents we had made, but nothing had prepared me for what I saw.

I have seen photographs of what the Carlsbad Caverns used to be, before the earthquake of '96 destroyed them; General Headquarters was something like that, although I can't believe that the Carlsbad Caverns were as big or half as magnificent. I could not at first grasp the immensity of the room I was in; underground there is nothing to judge size by and the built-in rangefinder of a human's two-eyed vision is worthless beyond about fifty feet without something in the distance to give him scale—a house, a man, a tree, even the horizon itself. Since a natural cave contains nothing at all that is well known, customary, the human eye can't size it.

So, while I realized that the room I stood in was big, I could not guess just how big; my brain scaled it down to fit my prejudices. We were standing higher than the main floor and at one end of the room; the whole thing was softly floodlighted. I got through craning my neck and *oh*ing and *ah*ing, looked down and saw a toy village some distance away below us. The little buildings seemed to be about a foot high.

Then I saw tiny people walking around among the buildings —and the whole thing suddenly snapped into scale. The toy village was at least a quarter of a mile away; the whole room was not less than a mile long and many hundreds of feet high. Instead of the fear of being shut in that people normally experience in caves I was suddenly hit by the other fear, the fear of open spaces, agoraphobia. I wanted to slink along close to the walls, like a timid mouse.

The guide who had spoken touched my arm. "You'll have plenty of time for rubbernecking later. Let's get going." They led me down a path which meandered between stalagmites, from baby-finger size to Egyptian pyramids, around black pools of water with lilypads of living stone growing on them, past dark wet domes that were old when man was new, under creamy translucent curtains of onyx and sharp rosy-red and dark green stalactites. My capacity to wonder began to be overloaded and presently I quit trying.

We came out on a fairly level floor of bat droppings and made good time to the village. The buildings, I saw as I got closer, were not buildings in the outdoors sense, but were mere partitions of that honeycomb plastic used for sound-deadening—space separators for efficiency and convenience. Most of them were not roofed. We stopped in front of the largest of these pens; the sign over its door read ADMINIS-TRATION. We entered and I was taken into the personnel office. This room almost made me homesick, so matter of fact, so professionally military was it in its ugly, efficient appointments. There was even the elderly staff clerk with the nervous sniff who seems to be general issue for such an office since the time of Caesar. The sign on his desk described him as Warrant Officer R. E. Giles and he had quite evidently come back to his office after working hours to check me in.

"Pleased to meet you, Mr. Lyle," he said, shaking hands and exchanging recognition. Then he scratched his nose and sniffed. "You're a week or so early and your quarters aren't ready. Suppose we billet you tonight with a blanket roll in the lounge of B.O.Q. and get you squared away in the morning?"

I said that would be perfectly satisfactory and he seemed relieved.

10

I GUESS I had been expecting to be treated as some sort of a conquering hero on my arrival—you know, my new comrades hanging breathlessly on every word of my modest account of my adventures and hairbreadth escapes and giving thanks to the Great Architect that I had been allowed to win through with my all-important message.

I was wrong. The personnel adjutant sent for me before I had properly finished breakfast, but I didn't even see him; I saw Mr. Giles. I was a trifle miffed and interrupted him to ask how soon it would be convenient for me to pay my formal call on the commanding officer.

He sniffed. "Oh, yes. Well, Mr. Lyle, the C.G. sends his compliments to you and asks you to consider that courtesy calls have been made, not only on him but on department heads. We're rather pushed for time right now. He'll send for you the first spare moment he has."

I knew quite well that the general had not sent me any such message and that the personnel clerk was simply following a previously established doctrine. It didn't make me feel better.

But there was nothing I could do about it; the system took me in hand. By noon I had been permanently billeted, had had my chest thumped and so forth, and had made my reports. Yes, I got a chance to tell my story—to a recording machine. Flesh-and-blood men did receive the message I carried, but I got no fun out of that; I was under hypnosis at the time, just as I had been when it was given to me.

This was too much for me; I asked the psychotechnician who operated me what the message was I carried. He answered stiffly, "We aren't permitted to tell couriers what they carry." His manner suggested that my question was highly improper.

I lost my temper a bit. I didn't know whether he was senior to me or not as he was not in uniform, but I didn't care. "For pity's sake! What is this? Don't the brethren *trust* me? Here I risk my neck—"

He cut in on me in a much more conciliatory manner. "No, no, it's not that at all. It's for your protection."

"Huh?"

"Doctrine. The less you know that you don't need to know the less you can spill if you are ever captured—and the safer it is for you and for everybody. For example, do you know where you are now? Could you point it out on a map?"

"No."

"Neither do I. We don't need to know so we weren't told. However," he went on, "I don't mind telling you, in a general way, what you were carrying—just routine reports, confirming stuff we already had by sensitive circuits mostly. You were coming this way, so they dumped a lot of such stuff into you. I took three spools from you."

"Just routine stuff? Why, the Lodge Master told me I was carrying a message of vital importance. That fat old joker!"

The technician grudged a smile. "I'm afraid he was pulling—Oh!"

"Eh?"

"I know what he meant. You were carrying a message of vital importance—to you. You carried your own credentials hypnotically. If you had not been, you would never have been allowed to wake up."

I had nothing to say. I left quietly.

My rounds of the medical office, psych office, quartermaster, and so forth had begun to give me a notion of the size of the place. The "toy village" I had first seen was merely the administrative group. The power plant, a packaged pile, was in a separate cavern with many yards of rock wall as secondary shielding. Married couples were quartered where they pleased—about a third of us were female—and usually chose to set up their houses (or pens) well away from the central grouping. The armory and ammo dump were located in a side passage, a safe distance from offices and quarters.

There was fresh water in abundance, though quite hard, and the same passages that carried the underground streams appeared to supply ventilation—at least the air was never stale. It stayed at a temperature of 69.6 Fahrenheit and a relative humidity of 32%, winter and summer, night and day.

By lunchtime I was hooked into the organization, and found myself already hard at work at a temporary job immediately after lunch—in the armory, repairing and adjusting blasters, pistols, squad guns, and assault guns. I could have been annoyed at being asked, or ordered, to do what was really gunnery sergeant work, but the whole place seemed to be run with a minimum of protocol—we cleared our own dishes away at mess, for example. And truthfully it felt good to sit at a bench in the armory, safe and snug, and handle calipers and feather gauges and drifts again—good, useful work.

Just before dinner that first day I wandered into the B.O.Q. lounge and looked around for an unoccupied chair. I heard a familiar baritone voice behind me: "Johnnie! John Lyle!" I whirled around and there, hurrying toward me, was Zebadiah Jones—good old Zeb, large as life and his ugly face split with a grin.

We pounded each other on the back and swapped insults. "When did you get here?" I finally asked him.

"Oh, about two weeks ago."

"You did? You were still at New Jerusalem when I left. How did you do it?"

"Nothing to it. I was shipped as a corpse—in a deep trance. Sealed up in a coffin and marked 'contagious'."

I told him about my own mixed-up trip and Zeb seemed impressed, which helped my morale. Then I asked him what he was doing.

"I'm in the Psych & Propaganda Bureau," he told me, "under Colonel Novak. Just now I'm writing a series of oh-so-respectful articles about the private life of the Prophet and his acolytes and attending priests, how many servants they have, how much it costs to run the Palace, all about the fancy ceremonies and rituals, and such junk. All of it perfectly true, of course, and told with unctuous approval. But I lay it on a shade too thick. The emphasis is on the jewels and the solid gold trappings and how much it all costs, and I keep telling the yokels what a privilege it is for them to be permitted to pay for such frippery and how flattered they should feel that God's representative on earth lets them take care of him."

"I guess I don't get it," I said, frowning. "People like that circusy stuff. Look at the way the tourists to New Jerusalem scramble for tickets to a Temple ceremony."

"Sure, sure—but we don't peddle this stuff to people on a holiday to New Jerusalem; we syndicate it to little local papers in poor farming communities in the Mississippi Valley, and in the Deep South, and in the back country of New England. That is to say, we spread it among some of the poorest and most puritanical elements of the population, people who are emotionally convinced that poverty and virtue are the same thing. It grates on their nerves; in time it should soften them up and make doubters of them."

"Do you seriously expect to start a rebellion with picayune stuff like that?"

"It's not picayune stuff, because it acts directly on their emotions, below the logical level. You can sway a thousand men by appealing to their prejudices quicker than you can convince one man by logic. It doesn't have to be a prejudice about an important matter either. Johnnie, you savvy how to use connotation indices, don't you?"

"Well, yes and no. I know what they are; they are supposed to measure the emotional effects of words."

"That's true, as far as it goes. But the index of a word isn't fixed like the twelve inches in a foot; it is a complex variable function depending on context, age and sex and occupation of the listener, the locale and a dozen other things. An index is a particular solution of the variable that tells you whether a particular word used in a particular fashion to a particular

81

reader or type of reader will affect that person favorably, unfavorably, or simply leave him cold. Given proper measurements of the group addressed it can be as mathematically exact as any branch of engineering. We never have all the data we need so it remains an art—but a very precise art, especially as we employ 'feedback' through field sampling. Each article I do is a little more annoying than the last—and the reader never knows why."

"It sounds good, but I don't see quite how it's done."

"I'll give you a gross case. Which would you rather have? A nice, thick, juicy, tender steak—or a segment of muscle tissue from the corpse of an immature castrated bull?"

I grinned at him. "You can't upset me. I'll take it by either name . . . not too well done. I wish they would announce chow around here; I'm starved."

"You think you aren't affected because you were braced for it. But how long would a restaurant stay in business if it used that sort of terminology? Take another gross case, the Anglo-Saxon monosyllables that naughty little boys write on fences. You can't use them in polite company without offending, yet there are circumlocutions or synonyms for every one of them which may be used in any company."

I nodded agreement. "I suppose so. I certainly see how it could work on other people. But personally, I guess I'm immune to it. Those taboo words don't mean a thing to me—except that I'm reasonably careful not to offend other people. I'm an educated man, Zeb—'Sticks and stones may break my bones, et cetera.' But I see how you could work on the ignorant."

Now I should know better than to drop my guard with Zeb. The good Lord knows he's tripped me up enough times. He smiled at me quietly and made a short statement involving some of those taboo words.

"You leave my mother out of this!"

I was the one doing the shouting and I came up out of my chair like a dog charging into battle. Zeb must have anticipated me exactly and shifted his weight before he spoke, for, instead of hanging one on his chin, I found my wrist seized in his fist and his other arm around me, holding me in a clinch that stopped the fight before it started. "Easy, Johnnie," he breathed in my ear. "I apologize. I most humbly apologize and ask your forgiveness. Believe me, I wasn't insulting you."

"So you say!"

"So I say, most humbly. Forgive me?"

As I simmered down I realized that my outbreak had been very conspicuous. Although we had picked a quiet corner to talk, there were already a dozen or more others in the lounge, waiting for dinner to be announced. I could feel the dead silence and sense the question in the minds of others as to

82

whether or not it was going to be necessary to intervene. I started to turn red with embarrassment rather than anger. "Okay. Let me go."

He did so and we sat down again. I was still sore and not at all inclined to forget Zeb's unpardonable breach of good manners, but the crisis was past. But he spoke quietly, "Johnnie, believe me, I was not insulting you nor any member of your family. That was a scientific demonstration of the dynamics of connotational indices, and that is all it was."

"Well—you didn't have to make it so personal."

"Ah, but I did have to. We were speaking of the psychodynamics of emotion . . . and emotions are personal, subjective things which must be experienced to be understood. You were of the belief that you, as an educated man, were immune to this form of attack—so I ran a lab test to show you that no one is immune. Now just what did I say to you?"

"You said— Never mind. Okay, so it was a test. But I don't care to repeat it. You've made your point: I don't like it."

"But what did I say? All I said, in fact, was that you were the legitimate offspring of a legal marriage. Right? What is insulting about that?"

"But—" I stopped and ran over in my mind the infuriating, insulting, and degrading things he had said—and, do you know, that is absolutely all they added up to. I grinned sheepishly. "It was the *way* you said it."

"Exactly, exactly! To put it technically, I selected terms with high negative indices, for this situation and for this listener. Which is precisely what we do with this propaganda, except that the emotional indices are lesser quantitatively to avoid arousing suspicion and to evade the censors—slow poison, rather than a kick in the belly. The stuff we write is all about the Prophet, lauding him to the skies . . . so the irritation produced in the reader is transferred to him. The method cuts below the reader's conscious thought and acts on the taboos and fetishes that infest his subconscious."

I remembered sourly my own unreasoned anger. "I'm convinced. It sounds like heap big medicine."

"It is, chum, it is. There is magic in words, black magic—if you know how to invoke it."

After dinner Zeb and I went to his cubicle and continued to bat the breeze. I felt warm and comfortable and very, very contented. The fact that we were part of a revolutionary plot, a project most unlikely to succeed and which would most probably end with us both dead in battle or burned for treason, affected me not at all. Good old Zeb! What if he did get under my guard and hit me where it hurt? He was my "family"— all the family that I had. To be with him now made me feel the way I used to feel when my mother would sit me down in the kitchen and feed me cookies and milk.

We talked about this and that, in the course of which I learned more about the organization and discovered—was very surprised to discover—that not all of our comrades were brethren. Lodge Brothers, I mean. "But isn't that dangerous?"

"What isn't? And what did you expect, old son? Some of our most valuable comrades can't join the Lodge; their own religious faith forbids it. But we don't have any monopoly on hating tyranny and loving freedom and we need all the help we can get. Anybody going our direction is a fellow traveler. Anybody."

I thought it over. The idea was logical, though somehow vaguely distasteful. I decided to gulp it down quickly. "I suppose so. I imagine even the pariahs will be of some use to us, when it comes to the fighting, even if they aren't eligible for membership."

Zeb gave me a look I knew too well. "Oh, for Pete's sake, John! When are you going to give up wearing diapers?"

"Huh?"

"Haven't you gotten it through your head yet that the whole 'pariah' notion is this tyranny's scapegoat mechanism that every tyranny requires?"

"Yes, but—"

"Shut up. Take sex away from people. Make it forbidden, evil, limit it to ritualistic breeding. Force it to back up into suppressed sadism. Then hand the people a scapegoat to hate. Let them kill a scapegoat occasionally for cathartic release. The mechanism is ages old. Tyrants used it centuries before the word 'psychology' was ever invented. It works, too. Look at yourself."

"Look, Zeb, I don't have anything against the pariahs."

"You had better not have. You'll find a few dozen of them in the Grand Lodge here. And by the way, forget that word 'pariah.' It has, shall we say, a very high negative index."

He shut up and so did I; again I needed time to get my thoughts straight. Please understand me—it is easy to be free when you have been brought up in freedom; it is *not* easy otherwise. A zoo tiger, escaped, will often slink back into the peace and security of his bars. If he can't get back, they tell me he will pace back and forth within the limits of bars that are no longer there. I suppose I was still pacing in my conditioned pattern.

The human mind is a tremendously complex thing; it has compartments in it that its owner himself does not suspect. I had thought that I had given my mind a thorough housecleaning already and had rid it of all the dirty superstitions I had been brought up to believe. I was learning that the "housecleaning" had been no more than a matter of sweeping the dirt under the rugs—it would be years before the cleansing would be complete, before the clean air of reason blew through every room.

All right, I told myself, if I meet one of these par— no, "comrades," I'll exchange recognition with him and be polite —as long as he is polite to me! At the time I saw nothing hypocritical in the mental reservation.

Zeb lay back, smoking, and let me stew. I knew that he smoked and he knew that I disapproved. But it was a minor sin and, when we were rooming together in the Palace barracks, I would never have thought of reporting him. I even knew which room servant was his bootlegger. "Who is sneaking your smokes in now?" I asked, wishing to change the subject.

"Eh? Why, you buy them at the P.X., of course." He held the dirty thing out and looked at it. "These Mexican cigarettes are stronger than I like. I suspect that they use real tobacco in them, instead of the bridge sweepings I'm used to. Want one?"

"Huh? Oh, no, thanks!"

He grinned wryly. "Go ahead, give me your usual lecture. It'll make you feel better."

"Now look here, Zeb, I wasn't criticizing. I suppose it's just one of the many things I've been wrong about."

"Oh, no. It's a dirty, filthy habit that ruins my wind and stains my teeth and may eventually kill me off with lung cancer." He took a deep inhalation, let the smoke trickle out of the corners of his mouth, and looked profoundly contented. "But it just happens that I *like* dirty, filthy habits."

He took another puff. "But it's not a sin and my punishment for it is here and now, in the way my mouth tastes each morning. The Great Architect doesn't give a shout in Sheol about it. Catch on, old son? He isn't even watching."

"There is no need to be sacrilegious."

"I wasn't being so."

"You weren't, eh? You were scoffing at one of the most fundamental—perhaps the one fundamental—proposition in religion: the certainty that God is watching!"

"*Who* told *you?*"

For a moment all I could do was to sputter. "Why, it isn't necessary. It's an axiomatic certainty. It's—"

"I repeat, *who* told *you?* See here, I retract what I said. Perhaps the Almighty is watching me smoke. Perhaps it is a mortal sin and I will burn for it for eons. Perhaps. But who told *you?* Johnnie, you've reached the point where you are willing to kick the Prophet out and hang him to a tall, tall tree. Yet you are willing to assert your own religious convictions and to use them as a touchstone to judge my conduct. So I repeat: who told you? What hill were you standing on when the lightning came down from Heaven and illuminated you? Which archangel carried the message?"

I did not answer at once. I could not. When I did it was with a feeling of shock and cold loneliness. "Zeb . . . I think I understand you at last. You are an—atheist. Aren't you?"

Zeb looked at me bleakly. "Don't call me an atheist," he said slowly, "unless you are really looking for trouble."

"Then you aren't one?" I felt a wave of relief, although I still didn't understand him.

"No, I am not. Not that it is any of your business. My religious faith is a private matter between me and my God. What my inner beliefs are you will have to judge by my actions . . . for you are not invited to question me about them. I decline to explain them nor to justify them to you. Nor to anyone . . . not the Lodge Master . . . nor to the Grand Inquisitor, if it comes to that."

"But you do believe in God?"

"I told you so, didn't I? Not that you had any business asking me."

"Then you must believe in other things?"

"Of course I do! I believe that a man has an obligation to be merciful to the weak . . . patient with the stupid . . . generous with the poor. I think he is obliged to lay down his life for his brothers, should it be required of him. But I don't propose to prove any of those things; they are beyond proof. And I don't demand that you believe as I do."

I let out my breath. "I'm satisfied, Zeb."

Instead of looking pleased he answered, "That's mighty kind of you, brother, mighty kind! Sorry—I shouldn't be sarcastic. But I had no intention of asking for your approval. You goaded me—accidentally, I'm sure—into discussing matters that I never intend to discuss." He stopped to light up another of those stinking cigarettes and went on more quietly. "John, I suppose that I am, in my own cantankerous way, a very narrow man myself. I believe very strongly in freedom of religion —but I think that that freedom is best expressed as freedom to keep quiet. From my point of view, a great deal of openly expressed piety is insufferable conceit."

"Huh?"

"Not every case—I've known the good and the humble and the devout. But how about the man who claims to know what the Great Architect is thinking? The man who claims to be privy to His Inner Plans? It strikes me as sacrilegious conceit of the worst sort—this character probably has never been any closer to His Trestle Board than you or I. But it makes him feel good to claim to be on chummy terms with the Almighty, it builds his ego, and lets him lay down the law to you and me. Pfui! Along comes a knothead with a loud voice, an I.Q. around 90, hair in his ears, dirty underwear, and a lot of ambition. He's too lazy to be a farmer, too stupid to be an engineer, too unreliable to be a banker—but, brother, can he pray! After a while he has gathered around him other knotheads who don't have his vivid imagination and self-assurance but like the idea of having a direct line to Omnipotence. Then this character is no longer Nehemiah Scudder but the First Prophet."

I was going along with him, feeling shocked but rather pleasantly so, until he named the First Prophet. Perhaps my own spiritual state at that time could have been described as that of a "primitive" follower of the First Prophet—that is to say, I had decided that the Prophet Incarnate was the devil himself and that all of his works were bad, but that belief did not affect the basics of the faith I had learned from my mother. The thing to do was to purge and reform the Church, not to destroy it. I mention this because my own case paralleled a very serious military problem that was to develop later.

I found that Zeb was studying my face. "Did I get you on the raw again, old fellow? I didn't mean to."

"Not at all," I answered stiffly, and went on to explain that, in my opinion, the sinfulness of the present gang of devils that had taken over the Church in no way invalidated the true faith. "After all, no matter what you think nor how much you may like to show off your cynicism, the doctrines are a matter of logical necessity. The Prophet Incarnate and his cohorts can pervert them, but they can't destroy them—and it doesn't matter whether the real Prophet had dirty underwear or not."

Zeb sighed as if he were very tired. "Johnnie, I certainly did not intend to get into an argument about religion with you. I'm not the aggressive type—you know that. I had to be pushed into the Cabal." He paused. "You say the doctrines are a matter of logic?"

"You've explained the logic to me yourself. It's a perfect, consistent structure."

"So it is. Johnnie, the nice thing about citing God as an authority is that you can prove anything you set out to prove. It's just a matter of selecting the proper postulates, then insisting that your postulates are 'inspired.' Then no one can possibly prove that you are wrong."

"You are asserting that the First Prophet was *not* inspired?"

"I am asserting nothing. For all you know, *I* am the First Prophet, come back to kick out the defilers of my temple."

"Don't be—" I was all wound up to kick it around further when there came a knock at Zeb's door. I stopped and he called out, "Come in!"

It was Sister Magdalene.

She nodded at Zeb, smiled sweetly at my open-mouthed surprise and said, "Hello, John Lyle. Welcome." It was the first time I had even seen her other than in the robes of a holy deaconess. She seemed awfully pretty and much younger.

"Sister Magdalene!"

"No. Staff Sergeant Andrews. 'Maggie,' to my friends."

"But what happened? Why are you here?"

"Right at the moment I'm here because I heard at dinner that you had arrived. When I didn't find you in your own quarters I concluded that you would be with Zeb. As for the rest, I couldn't go back, any more than you or Zeb—and our hideout back in New Jerusalem was getting overcrowded, so they transferred me."

"Well, it's good to see you!"

"It's good to see you, John." She patted me on the cheek and smiled again. Then she climbed on Zeb's bed and squatted tailor-fashion, showing a rather immodest amount of limb in the process. Zeb lit another cigarette and handed it to her; she accepted it, drew smoke deep into her lungs, and let it go as if she had been smoking all her life.

I had never seen a woman smoke—never. I could see Zeb watching me, confound him!—and I most carefully ignored it. Instead I grinned and said, "This is a *wonderful* reunion! If only—"

"I know," agreed Maggie. "If only Judith were here. Have you heard from her yet, John?"

"Heard from her? How could I?"

"That's right, you couldn't—not yet. But you can write to her now."

"Huh? How?"

"I don't know the code number off hand, but you can drop it at my desk—I'm in G-2. Don't bother to seal it; all personal mail has to be censored and paraphrased. I wrote to her last week but I haven't had an answer yet."

I thought about excusing myself at once and writing a letter, but I didn't. It was wonderful to be with both of them and I didn't want to cut the evening short. I decided to write before I went to bed—while realizing, with surprise, that I had been so much on the go that, so far as I could remember, I hadn't even had time to think about Judith since . . . well, since Denver, at least.

But I did not get to write to her even later that night. It was past eleven o'clock and Maggie was saying something about reveille coming early when an orderly showed up: "The Commanding General's compliments and will Legate Lyle see him at once, sir."

I gave my hair a quick brush with Zeb's gear and hurried away, while wishing mightily that I had something fit to report in, rather than a civilian suit much the worse for wear.

The inner sanctum was deserted and dark except for a light that I could see in the far inner office—even Mr. Giles was not at his desk. I found my way in, knocked on the door frame, stepped inside, clicked my heels and saluted. "Legate Lyle reports to the Commanding General as ordered, sir."

An elderly man seated at a big desk with his back to me turned and looked up, and I got another surprise. "Ah, yes, John Lyle," he said gently. He got up and came toward me, with his hand out. "It's been a long time, hasn't it?"

It was Colonel Huxley, head of the Department of Applied Miracles when I was a cadet—and almost my only friend among the officers at that time. Many was the Sunday afternoon that I had relaxed in his quarters, my stock unhooked, free for the moment from the pressure of discipline.

I took his hand. "Colonel—I mean 'General,' sir. . . . I thought you were dead!"

"Dead colonel into live general, eh! No, Lyle, though I was listed as dead when I went underground. They usually do that when an officer disappears; it looks better. You're dead, too—did you know?"

"Uh, no, I didn't, sir. Not that it matters. This is wonderful, sir!"

"Good."

"But— I mean, how did you ever—well—" I shut up.

"How did I land here and in charge at that? I've been a Brother since I was your age, Lyle. But I didn't go underground until I had to—none of us do. In my case the pressure for me to join the priesthood became a bit too strong; the Superintendent was quite restless about having a lay officer know too much about the more abstruse branches of physics and chemistry. So I took a short leave and died. Very sad." He smiled. "But sit down. I've been meaning to send for you all day, but it's been a busy day. They all are. It wasn't until now that I've had time to listen to the record of your report."

We sat down and chatted, and I felt that my cup runneth over. Huxley I respected more than any officer I had ever served under. His very presence resolved any residual doubts I might have—if the Cabal was right for him, it was right for me, and never mind the subtleties of doctrine.

At last he said, "I didn't call you in at this late hour just to chat, Lyle. I've a job for you."

"Yes, sir?"

"No doubt you've already noticed what a raw militia we have here. This is between ourselves and I'm not criticizing our comrades--every one of them has pledged his life to our cause, a harder thing for them to do than for you and me, and they have all placed themselves under military discipline, a thing still harder. But I haven't enough trained soldiers to handle things properly. They mean well but I am tremendously handicapped in trying to turn the organization into an efficient fighting machine. I'm swamped with administrative details. Will you help me?"

I stood up. "I shall be honored to serve with the General to the best of my ability."

"Fine! We'll call you my personal aide for the time being. That's all for tonight, Captain. I'll see you in the morning."

I was halfway out the door before his parting designation sunk in—then I decided that it was a slip of the tongue.

But it was not. I found my own office the next morning by the fact that a sign had been placed on it reading: "CAPTAIN LYLE." From the standpoint of a professional military man there is one good thing about revolutions: the opportunities for swift promotion are excellent . . . even if the pay is inclined to be irregular.

My office adjoined General Huxley's and from then on I almost lived in it—eventually I had a cot installed back of my desk. The very first day I was still fighting my way down a stack of papers in my incoming basket at ten at night. I had promised myself that I would find the bottom, then write a long letter to Judith. But it turned out to be a very short note, as there was a memorandum addressed to me personally, rather than to the General, at the bottom.

It was addressed to "Legate J. Lyle," then someone had scratched out "Legate" and written "Captain." It went on:

MEMORANDUM FOR ALL PERSONNEL NEWLY REPORTED

SUBJECT: Personal Conversion Report

1. You are requested and directed to write out, as fully as possible, all of the events, thoughts, considerations, and incidents which led up to your decision to join our fight for freedom. This account should be as detailed as possible and as subjective as possible. A report written hastily, too briefly, or too superficially will be returned to be expanded and corrected and may be supplemented by hypno examination.

2. This report will be treated as confidential as a whole and any portion of it may be classified secret by the writer. You may substitute letters or numbers for proper names if this will help you to speak freely, but the report must be complete.

3. No time off from regular duties is allotted for this purpose, but this report must be treated as extra-duty of highest priority. A draft of your report will be expected by (*here someone had written in a date and hour less than forty-eight hours away; I used some profane expressions under my breath.*)

BY ORDER OF THE COMMANDING GENERAL

(s) M. NOVAK, Col., F.U.S.A.
Chief of Psychology

I was considerably annoyed by this demand and decided to

write to Judith first anyway. The note didn't go very well—how can one write a love letter when you know that one or more strangers will read it and that one of them will rephrase your tenderest words? Besides that, while writing to Judith, my thoughts kept coming back to that night on the rampart of the Palace when I had first met her. It seemed to me that my own personal conversion, as the nosy Colonel Novak called it, started then . . . although I had begun to have doubts before then. Finally I finished the note, decided not to go to bed at once but to tackle that blasted report.

After a while I noticed that it was one o'clock in the morning and I still hadn't carried my account up to the point where I was admitted to the Brotherhood. I stopped writing rather reluctantly (I found that I had grown interested) and locked it in my desk.

At breakfast the next morning I got Zebadiah aside, showed him the memorandum, and asked him about it. "What's the big idea?" I asked. "You work for this particular brass. Are they still suspicious of us, even after letting us in here?"

Zeb barely glanced at it. "Oh, that— Shucks, no. Although I might add that a spy, supposing one could get this far, would be bound to be caught when his personal story went through semantic analysis. Nobody can tell a lie that long and that complicated."

"But what's it for?"

"What do you care? Write it out—and be sure you do a thorough job. Then turn it in."

I felt myself grow warm. "I don't know as I will. I rather think I'll ask the General about it first."

"Do so, if you want to make a ruddy fool of yourself. But look, John, the psychomathematicians who will read that mess of bilge you will write, won't have the slightest interest in you as an individual. They don't even want to know who you are—a girl goes through your report and deletes all personal names, including your own, if you haven't done so yourself, and substitutes numbers . . . all this before an analyst sees it. You're just data, that's all; the Chief has some heap big project on the fire—I don't know what it is myself—and he is trying to gather together a large enough statistical universe to be significant."

I was mollified. "Well, why don't they say so, then? This memo is just a bald order—irritating."

Zeb shrugged. "That is because it was prepared by the semantics division. If the propaganda division had written it, you would have gotten up early and finished the job before breakfast." He added, "By the way, I hear you've been promoted. Congratulations."

"Thanks." I grinned at him slyly. "How does it feel to be junior to me, Zeb?"

"Huh? Did they bump you that far? I thought you were a captain."

"I am."

"Well, excuse me for breathing—but I'm a major."

"Oh. Congratulations."

"Think nothing of it. You have to be at least a colonel around here, or you make your own bed."

I was too busy to make my bed very often. More than half the time I slept on the couch in my office and once I went a week without bathing. It was evident at once that the Cabal was bigger and had more complicated ramifications to it than I had ever dreamed and furthermore that it was building to a crescendo. I was too close to the trees to see the woods, even though everything but the utter top-secret, burn-after-reading items passed across my desk.

I simply endeavored to keep General Huxley from being smothered in pieces of paper—and found myself smothered instead. The idea was to figure out what he would do, if he had time, and then do it for him. A person who has been trained in the principles of staff or doctrinal command can do this; the trick is to make your mind work like your boss's mind in all routine matters, and to be able to recognize what is routine and what he must pass on himself. I made my share of mistakes, but apparently not too many for he didn't fire me, and three months later I was a major with the fancy title of assistant chief of staff. Chalk most of it up to the West Point ring, of course—a professional has a great advantage.

I should add that Zeb was a short-tailed colonel by then and acting chief of propaganda, his section chief having been transferred to a regional headquarters I knew only by the code name JERICHO.

But I am getting ahead of my story. I heard from Judith about two weeks later—a pleasant-enough note but with the juice pressed out of it through rephrasing. I meant to answer her at once but actually delayed a week—it was so pesky hard to know what to say. I could not possibly tell her any news except that I was well and busy. If I had told her I loved her three times in one letter some idiot in cryptography would have examined it for "pattern" and rejected it completely when he failed to find one.

The mail went to Mexico through a long tunnel, partly artificial but mostly natural, which led right under the international border. A little electric railroad of the sort used in mines ran through this tunnel and carried not only my daily headaches in the way of official mail but also a great deal of freight to supply our fair-sized town. There were a dozen other entrances to GHQ on the Arizona side of the border, but I never knew where any of them were—it was not my pidgin. The whole area overlay a deep layer of paleozoic limestone and it may well be honeycombed from California to Texas. The area known as GHQ had been in use for more than twenty years as a hideout for refugee brethren. Nobody knew the extent of the caverns we were in; we simply lighted and used what we needed. It was a favorite sport of us troglodytes—permanent residents were "trogs"; transients were "bats" because they flew by night—we trogs liked to go on "spelling bees," picnics which included a little amateur speleology in the unexplored parts.

It was permitted by regulations, but just barely and subject to stringent safety precautions, for you could break a leg awfully easily in those holes. But the General permitted it because it was necessary; we had only such recreations as we could make ourselves and some of us had not seen daylight in years.

Zeb and Maggie and I went on a number of such outings when I could get away. Maggie always brought another woman along. I protested at first but she pointed out to me that it was necessary in order to avoid gossip . . . mutual chaperonage. She assured me that she was certain that Judith would not mind, under the circumstances. It was a different girl each time and it seemed to work out that Zeb always paid a lot of attention to the other girl while I talked with Maggie. I had thought once that Maggie and Zeb would marry, but now I began to wonder. They seemed to suit each other like ham and eggs, but Maggie did not seem jealous and I can only describe Zeb, in honesty, as shameless—that is, if he thought Maggie would care.

One Saturday morning Zeb stuck his head in my sweat box and said, "Spelling bee. Two o'clock. Bring a towel."

I looked up from a mound of papers. "I doubt if I can make it," I answered. "And why a towel?"

But he was gone. Maggie came through my office later to take the weekly consolidated intelligence report in to the Old Man, but I did not attempt to question her, as Maggie was all business during working hours—the perfect office sergeant. I had lunch at my desk, hoping to finish up, but knowing it was impossible. About a quarter of two I went in to get General Huxley's signature on an item that was to go out that night by hypnoed courier and therefore had to go at once to psycho in order that the courier might be operated. He glanced at it and signed it, then said, "Sergeant Andy tells me you have a date."

"Sergeant Andrews is mistaken," I said stiffly. "There are still the weekly reports from Jericho, Nod, and Egypt to be gone over."

"Place them on my desk and get out. That's an order. I can't have you going stale from overwork."

I did not tell him that he had not even been to lodge himself in more than a month; I got out.

I dropped the message with Colonel Novak and hurried to

where we always met near the women's mess. Maggie was there with the other girl—a blonde named Miriam Booth who was a clerk in Quartermaster's stores. I knew her by sight by had never spoken to her. They had our picnic lunch and Zeb arrived while I was being introduced. He was carrying, as usual, the portable flood we would use when we picked out a spot and a blanket to sit on and use as a table. "Where's your towel?" he demanded.

"Were you serious? I forgot it."

"Run get it. We'll start off along Appian Way. You can catch up. Come on, kids."

They started off, which left me with nothing but to do as I was told. After grabbng a towel from my room I dogtrotted until I had them in sight, then slowed to a walk, puffing. Desk work had ruined my wind. They heard me and waited.

We were all dressed alike, with the women in trousers and each with a safety line wrapped around the waist and torch clipped to the belt. I had gotten used to women in men's clothes, much as I disliked it—and, after all, it is impractical and quite immodest to climb around in caves wearing skirts.

We left the lighted area by taking a turn that appeared to lead into a blind wall; instead it led into a completely concealed but easily negotiated tunnel. Zeb tied our labyrinth string and started paying it out as soon as we left permanent and marked paths, as required by the standing order; Zeb was always careful about things that mattered.

For perhaps a thousand paces we could see blazes and other indications that others had been this way before, such as a place where someone had worked a narrow squeeze wider with a sledge. Then we left the obvious path and turned into a blind wall. Zeb put down the flood and turned it on. "Sling your torches. We climb this one."

"Where are we going?"

"A place Miriam knows about. Give me a leg up, Johnnie."

The climb wasn't much. I got Zeb up all right and the girls could have helped each other up, but we took them up roped, for safety's sake. We picked up our gear and Miriam led us away, each of us using his torch.

We went down the other side and there was another passage so well hidden that it could have been missed for ten thousand years. We stopped once while Zeb tied on another ball of string. Shortly Miriam said, "Slow up, everybody. I think we're there."

Zeb flashed his torch around, then set up the portable flood and switched it on. He whistled. "Whew! This is all right!"

Maggie said softly, "It's lovely." Miriam just grinned triumphantly.

I agreed with them all. It was a perfect small domed cavern, perhaps eighty feet wide and much longer. How long, I could not tell, as it curved gently away in a gloom-filled turn. But the feature of the place was a quiet, inky-black pool that filled most of the floor. In front of us was a tiny beach of real sand that might have been laid down a million years ago for all I know.

Our voices echoed pleasantly and a little bit spookily in the chamber, being broken up and distorted by stalactites and curtains hanging from the roof. Zeb walked down to the water's edge, squatted and tested it with his hand. "Not too cold," he announced. "Well, the last one in is a proctor's nark."

I recognized the old swimming hole call, even though the last time I had heard it, as a boy, it had been "last one in is a dirty pariah." But here I could not believe it.

Zeb was already unbuttoning his shirt. I stepped up to him quickly and said privately, "Zeb! Mixed bathing? You must be joking?"

"Not a bit of it." He searched my face. "Why not? What's the matter with you, boy? Afraid someone will make you do penance? They won't, you know. That's all over with."

"But——"

"But what?"

I could not answer. The only way I could make the words come out would have been in the terms we had been taught in the Church, and I knew that Zeb would laugh at me—in front of the women. Probably they would laugh, too, since they had known and I hadn't. "But Zeb," I insisted, "I *can't*. You didn't tell me. . . . and I don't even have a bathing outfit."

"Neither do I. Didn't you ever go in raw as a kid—and get paddled for it?" He turned away without waiting for me to answer this enormity and said, "Are you frail vessels waiting on something?"

"Just for you two to finish your debate," Maggie answered, coming closer. "Zeb, I think Mimi and I will use the other side of that boulder. All right?"

"Okay. But wait a second. No diving, you both understand. And a safety man on the bank at all times—John and I will take turns."

"Pooh!" said Miriam. "I dove the last time I was here."

"You weren't with me, that's sure. No diving—or I'll warm your pants where they are tightest."

She shrugged. "All right, Colonel Crosspatch. Come on, Mag." They went on past us and around a boulder half as big as a house. Miriam stopped, looked right at me, and waggled a finger. "No peeking, now!" I blushed to my ears.

They disappeared and we heard no more of them, except for giggles. I said hurriedly, "Look. You do as you please—and on your own head be it. But I'm not going in. I'll sit here on the bank and be safety man."

"Suit yourself. I was going to match you for first duty, but

95

nobody is twisting your arm. Pay out a line, though, and have it ready for heaving. Not that we'll need it; both the girls are strong swimmers."

I said desperately, "Zeb, I'm sure the General would forbid swimming in these underground pools."

"That's why we didn't mention it. 'Never worry the C.O. unnecessarily'—standing orders in Joshua's Army, circa 1400 B.C." He went right on peeling off his clothes.

I don't know why Miriam warned me not to peek—not that I would!—for when she was undressed she came straight out from behind that boulder, not toward us but toward the water. But the flood light was full on her and she even turned toward us for an instant, then shouted, "Come on, Maggie! Zeb is going to be last if you hurry."

I did not want to look and I could not take my eyes off her. I had never seen anything remotely resembling the sight she was in my life—and only once a picture, one in the possession of a boy in my parish school and on that occasion I had gotten only a glimpse and then had promptly reported him.

But I could not stop looking, burning with shame as I was.

Zeb beat Maggie into the water—I don't think she cared. He went into the water quickly, almost breaking his own injunction against diving. Sort of a surface dive I would call it, running into the water and then breaking into a racing start. His powerful crawl was soon overtaking Miriam, who had started to swim toward the far end.

Then Maggie came out from behind the boulder and went into the water. She did not make a major evolution of it, the way Miriam had, but simply walked quickly and with quiet grace into the water. When she was waist deep, she let herself sink forward and struck out in a strong breast stroke, then shifted to a crawl and followed the others, whom I could hear but hardly see in the distance.

Again I could not take my eyes away if my eternal soul had depended on it. What is it about the body of a human woman that makes it the most terribly beautiful sight on earth? Is it, as some claim, simply a necessary instinct to make sure that we comply with God's will and replenish the earth? Or is it some stranger, more wonderful thing?

I found myself quoting: "How fair and how pleasant art thou, O love, for delights!

"This thy stature is like to a palm tree, and thy breasts to clusters of grapes."

Then I broke off, ashamed, remembering that the Song of Songs which is Solomon's was a chaste and holy allegory having nothing to do with such things.

I sat down on the sand and tried to compose my soul. After a while I felt better and my heart stopped pounding so hard. When they all came swimming back with Zeb in the lead, racing Miriam, I even managed to throw them a smile. It no longer seemed quite so terrible and as long as they stayed in the water the women were not shockingly exposed. Perhaps evil was truly in the eye of the beholder—in which case the idea was to keep it out of mine.

Zeb called out, "Ready to be relieved?"

I answered firmly, "No. Go ahead and have your fun."

"Okay." He turned like a dolphin and started back the other way. Miriam followed him. Maggie came in to where it was shallow, rested her finger tips on the bottom, and held facing me, with just her head and her ivory shoulders out of the inky water, while her waist-length mane of hair floated around her.

"Poor John," she said softly. "I'll come out and spell you."

"Oh, no, really!"

"Are you sure?"

"Quite sure."

"All right." She turned, flipped herself over, and started after the others. For one ghostly, magic instant she was partly out of the water.

Maggie came back to my end of the cavern about ten minutes later. "I'm cold," she said briefly, climbed out and strode quickly to the protection of the boulder. Somehow she was not naked, but merely unclothed, like Mother Eve. There is a difference—Miriam had been naked.

With Maggie out of the water and neither one of us speaking I noticed for the first time that there was no other sound. Now there is nothing so quiet as a cave; anywhere else at all there is noise, but the complete zero decibel which obtains underground if one holds still and says nothing is very different.

The point is that I should have been able to hear Zeb and Miriam swimming. Swimming need not be noisy but it can't be as quiet as a cave. I sat up suddenly and started forward—then stopped with equal suddenness as I did not want to invade Maggie's dressing room, which another dozen steps would have accomplished.

But I was really worried and did not know what to do. Throw a line? Where? Peel down and search for them? If necessary. I called out softly, "Maggie!"

"What is it, John?"

"Maggie, I'm worried."

She came at once from behind the rock. She had already pulled on her trousers, but held her towel so that it covered her from the waist up; I had the impression she had been drying her hair. "Why, John?"

"Keep very quiet and listen."

She did so. "I don't hear anything."

"That's just it. We should. I could hear you all swimming even when you were down at the far end, out of my sight.

Now there isn't a sound, not a splash. Do you suppose they possibly could both have hit their heads on the bottom at the same time?"

"Oh. Stop worrying, John. They're all right."

"But I *am* worried."

"They're just resting, I'm sure. There is another little beach down there, about half as big as this. That's where they are. I climbed up on it with them, then I came back. I was cold."

I made up my mind, realizing that I had let my modesty hold me back from my plain duty. "Turn your back. No, go behind the boulder—I want to undress."

"What? I tell you it's not necessary." She did not budge.

I opened my mouth to shout. Before I got it out Maggie had a hand over my mouth, which caused her towel to be disarranged and flustered us both. "Oh, heavens!" she said sharply. "Keep your big mouth shut." She turned suddenly and flipped the towel; when she turned back she had it about her like a stole, covering her front well enough, I suppose, without the need to hold it.

"John Lyle, come here and sit down. Sit down by me." She sat on the sand and patted the place by her—and such was the firmness with which she spoke that I did as I was told.

"By me," she insisted. "Come closer. I don't want to shout." I inched gingerly closer until my sleeve brushed her bare arm. "That's better," she agreed, keeping her voice low so that it did not resound around the cavern. "Now listen to me. There are two people down there, of their own free will. They are entirely safe—I saw them. And they are both excellent swimmers. The thing for you to do, John Lyle, is to mind your own business and restrain that nasty itch to interfere."

"I'm afraid I don't understand you." Truthfully, I was afraid I did.

"Oh, goodness me! See here, does Miriam mean anything to you?"

"Why, no, not especially."

"I should think not, since you haven't addressed six words to her since we started out. Very well, then—since you have no cause to be jealous, if two people choose to be alone, why should you stick your nose in? Understand me now?"

"Uh, I guess so."

"Then just be quiet."

I was quiet. She didn't move. I was acutely aware of her nakedness—for now she was naked, though covered—and I hoped that she was not aware that I was aware. Besides that I was acutely aware of being almost a participant in—well, I don't know what. I told myself angrily that I had no right to assume the worst, like a morals proctor.

Presently I said, "Maggie . . ."

"Yes, John?"

"I don't understand you."

"Why not, John? Not that it is really needful."

"Uh, you don't seem to give a hoot that Zeb is down there, with Miriam—alone."

"Should I give a hoot?"

Confound the woman! She was deliberately misunderstanding me. "Well . . . look, somehow I had gotten the impression that you and Zeb—I mean . . . well, I suppose I sort of expected that you two meant to get married, when you could."

She laughed a low chuckle that had little mirth in it. "I suppose you could have gotten that impression. But, believe me, the matter is all settled and for the best."

"Huh?"

"Don't misunderstand me. I am very fond of Zebadiah and I know he is equally fond of me. But we are both dominant types psychologically—you should see my profile chart; it looks like the Rocky Mountains! Two such people should not marry. Such marriages are *not* made in Heaven, believe me! Fortunately we found it out in time."

"Oh."

"Oh, indeed."

Now I don't know just how the next thing happened. I was thinking that she seemed rather forlorn—and the next thing I knew I was kissing her. She lay back in my arms and returned the kiss with a fervor I would not have believed possible. As for me, my head was buzzing and my eyeballs were knocking together and I couldn't have told you whether I was a thousand feet underground or on dress parade.

Then it was over. She looked up for a bare moment into my eyes and whispered, "Dear John . . ." Then she got suddenly to her feet, leaned over me, careless of the towel, and patted my cheek. "Judith is a very lucky girl. I wonder if she knows it."

"Maggie!" I said.

She turned away and said, without looking back, "I really must finish dressing. I'm cold."

She had not felt cold to me.

She came out shortly, fully dressed and towelling her hair vigorously. I got my dry towel and helped her. I don't believe I suggested it; the idea just took care of itself. Her hair was thick and lovely and I enjoyed doing it. It sent goose pimples over me.

Zeb and Miriam came back while I was doing so, not racing but swimming slowly; we could hear them laughing long before they were in sight. Miriam climbed out of the water as shamelessly as any harlot of Gomorrah, but I hardly noticed her.

Zeb looked me in the eye and said aggressively, "Ready for your swim, chum?"

I started to say that I did not believe that I would bother and was going to make some excuse about my towel already being wet—when I noticed Maggie watching me . . . not saying anything but watching. I answered, "Why, surely! You two took long enough." I called out, "Miriam! Get out from behind that rock! I want to use it."

She squealed and giggled and came out, still arranging her clothes. I went behind it with quiet dignity.

I hope I still had quiet dignity when I came out. In any case I set my teeth, walked out and straight into the water. It was bitingly cold at first, but only for a moment. I was never varsity but I swam on my class team and I've even been in the Hudson on New Year's Day. I liked that black pool, once I was in.

I just had to swim down to the other end. Sure enough, there was a little shelf beach there. I did not go up on it.

On the way back I tried to swim down to the bottom. I could not find it, but it must have been over twenty feet down. I liked it down there—black and utterly still. Had I the breath for it, or gills, it seemed to me that it would have been a good place to stay, away from Prophets, away from Cabals, and paperwork, and worries, and problems too subtle for me.

I came up gasping, then struck out hard for our picnic beach. The girls already had the food laid out and Zeb shouted for me to hurry. Zeb and Maggie did not look up as I got out of the water, but I caught Miriam eyeing me. I don't think I blushed. I never did like blondes anyhow. I think Lilith must have been a blonde.

11

THE Supreme Council, consisting of heads of departments, General Huxley, and a few others, met weekly or oftener to advise the General, exchange views, and consider the field reports. About a month after our rather silly escapade in the underground pool they were in session and I was with them, not as a member but as recorder. My own girl was ill and I had borrowed Maggie from G-2 to operate the voicewriter, since she was cleared for top secret. We were always terribly shorthanded of competent personnel. My nominal boss, for example, was Wing General Penoyer, who carried the title of Chief of Staff. But I hardly ever saw him, as he was also Chief of Ordnance. Huxley was his own chief of staff and I was sort of a glorified aide—"midshipmite, and bosun tite, and crew of the captain's gig." I even tried to see to it that Huxley took his stomach medicine regularly.

This meeting was bigger than usual. The regional commanders of Gath, Canaan, Jericho, Babylon, and Egypt were present in person; Nod and Damascus were represented by deputies—every Cabal district of the United States except Eden and we were holding a sensitive hook-up to Louisville for that command, using idea code that the sensitives themselves would not understand. I could feel the pressure of something big coming up, although Huxley had not taken me into his confidence. The place was tyled so that a mouse couldn't have got in.

We droned through the usual routine reports. It was duly recorded that we now had eighty-seven hundred and nine accepted members, either lodge brethren or tested and bound members of the parallel military organization. There were listed as recruited and instructed more than ten times that number of fellow travelers who could be counted on to rise against the Prophet, but who had not been intrusted with knowledge of the actual conspiracy.

The figures themselves were not encouraging. We were always in the jaws of a dilemma; a hundred thousand men was a handful to conquer a continent-wide country whereas the less than nine thousand party to the conspiracy itself were 'way too many to keep a secret. We necessarily relied on the ancient cell system wherein no man knew more than he had to know and could not give away too much no matter what an inquisitor did to him—no, not even if he had been a spy. But we had our weekly losses even at this passive stage.

One entire lodge had been surprised in session and arrested in Seattle four days earlier; it was a serious loss but only three of the chairs had possessed critical knowledge and all three had suicided successfully. Prayers would be said for all of them at a grand session that night, but here it was a routine report. We had lost four hatchet men that week but twenty-three assassinations had been accomplished—one of them the Elder Inquisitor for the entire lower Mississippi Valley.

The Chief of Communications reported that the brethren were prepared to disable 91% (figured on population coverage) of the radio & TV stations in the country, and that with the aid of assault groups we could reasonably hope to account for the rest—with the exception of the Voice of God station at New Jerusalem, which was a special problem.

The Chief of Combat Engineering reported readiness to sabotage the power supply of the forty-six largest cities, again with the exception of New Jerusalem, the supply of which was self-contained with the pile located under the Temple. Even there major interruption could be accomplished at distribution stations if the operation warranted the expenditure of sufficient men. Major surface transportation and freight routes could be sabotaged sufficiently with present plans and personnel to reduce traffic to 12% of normal.

The reports went on and on—newspapers, student action groups, rocket field seizure or sabotage, miracles, rumor propagation, water supply, incident incitement, counter-espionage, long-range weather prediction, weapons distribution. War is a simple matter compared with revolution. War is an applied science, with well-defined principles tested in history; analogous solutions may be found from ballista to H-bomb. But every revolution is a freak, a mutant, a monstrosity, its conditions never to be repeated and its operations carried out by amateurs and individualists.

While Maggie recorded the data I was arranging it and transmitting it to the calculator room for analysis. I was much too busy even to attempt a horse-back evaluation in my head. There was a short wait while the analysts finished programming and let the "brain" have it—then the remote-printer in front of me chattered briefly and stopped. Huxley leaned across me and tore off the tape before I could reach it.

He glanced at it, then cleared his throat and waited for dead silence. "Brethren," he began, "comrades—we agreed long ago on our doctrine of procedure. When every predictable factor, calculated, discounted for probable error, weighted and correlated with all other significant factors, gave a calculated risk of two to one in our favor, we would strike. Today's solution of the probability equation, substituting this week's data for the variables, gives an answer of two point one three. I propose to set the hour of execution. How say you?"

It was a delayed shock; no one said anything. Hope delayed too long makes reality hard to believe—and all of these men had waited for years, some for most of a lifetime. Then they were on their feet, shouting, sobbing, cursing, pounding each others' backs.

Huxley sat still until they quieted, an odd little smile on his face. Then he stood up and said quietly, "I don't think we need poll the sentiment. I will set the hour after I have—"

"General! If you please! I do not agree." It was Zeb's boss, Sector General Novak, Chief of Psych. Huxley stopped speaking and the silence fairly ached. I was as stunned as the rest.

Then Huxley said quietly, "This council usually acts by unanimous consent. We have long since arrived at the method for setting the date. . . . but I know that you would not disagree without good reason. We will listen now to Brother Novak."

Novak came slowly forward and faced them. "Brethren," he began, running his eyes over bewildered and hostile faces,

102

"you know me, and you know I want this thing as much as you do. I have devoted the last seventeen years to it—it has cost me my family and my home. But I can't let you go ahead without warning you, when I am sure that the time is not yet. I think—no, I *know* with mathematical certainty that we are not ready for revolution." He had to wait and hold up both hands for silence; they did not want to hear him. "Hear me out! I concede that all military plans are ready. I admit that if we strike now we have a strong probability of being able to seize the country. Nevertheless we are not ready—"

"Why not?"

"—because a majority of the people still believe in the established religion, they believe in the Divine authority of the Prophet. We can seize power but we can't hold it."

"The Devil we won't!"

"*Listen* to me! No people was ever held in subjection long except through their own consent. For three generations the American people have been conditioned from cradle to grave by the cleverest and most thorough psycho-technicians in the world. They *believe!* If you turn them loose now, without adequate psychological preparation, they will go back to their chains . . . like a horse returning to a burning barn. We can win the revolution but it will be followed by a long and bloody civil war—which we will lose!"

He stopped, ran a trembling hand across his eyes, then said to Huxley, "That's all."

Several were on their feet at once. Huxley pounded for order, then recognized Wing General Penoyer.

Penoyer said, "I'd like to ask Brother Novak a few questions."

"Go ahead."

"Can his department tell us what percentage of the population is sincerely devout?"

Zebadiah, present to assist his chief, looked up; Novak nodded and he answered, "Sixty-two per cent, plus-or-minus three per cent."

"And the percentage who secretly oppose the government whether we have enlisted them or not?"

"Twenty-one per cent plus, proportional error. The balance can be classed as conformists, not devout but reasonably contented."

"By what means were the data obtained?"

"Surprise hypnosis of representative types."

"Can you state the trend?"

"Yes, sir. The government lost ground rapidly during the first years of the present depression, then the curve flattened out. The new tithing law and to some extent the vagrancy decrees were unpopular and the government again lost ground before the curve again flattened at a lower level. About that

103

time business picked up a little but we simultaneously started our present intensified propaganda campaign; the government has been losing ground slowly but steadily the past fifteen months."

"And what does the first derivative show?"

Zeb hesitated and Novak took over. "You have to figure the second derivative," he answered in a strained voice; "the rate is accelerating."

"Well?"

The Psych Chief answered firmly but reluctantly, "On extrapolation, it will be three years and eight months before we can risk striking."

Penoyer turned back to Huxley. "I have my answer, sir. With deep respect to General Novak and his careful scientific work, I say—win while we can! We may never have another chance."

He had the crowd with him. "Penoyer is right! If we wait, we'll be betrayed."—"You can't hold a thing like this together forever."—"I've been underground ten years; I don't want to be buried here."—"Win . . . and worry about making converts when we control communications."—"Strike now! Strike now!"

Huxley let them carry on, his own face expressionless, until they had it out of their systems. I kept quiet myself, since I was too junior to be entitled to a voice here, but I went along with Penoyer; I couldn't see waiting nearly four years.

I say Zeb talking earnestly with Novak. They seemed to be arguing about something and were paying no attention to the racket. But when Huxley at last held up a hand for silence Novak left his place and hurried up to Huxley's elbow. The General listened for a moment, seemed almost annoyed, then undecided. Novak crooked a finger at Zeb, who came running up. The three whispered together for several moments while the council waited.

Finally Huxley faced them again. "General Novak has proposed a scheme which may change the whole situation. The Council is recessed until tomorrow."

Novak's plan (or Zeb's, though he never admitted authorship) required a delay of nearly two months, to the date of the annual Miracle of the Incarnation. For what was contemplated was no less than tampering with the Miracle itself. In hindsight it was an obvious and probably essential stratagem; the psych boss was right. In essence, a dictator's strength depends not upon guns but on the faith his people place in him. This had been true of Caesar, of Napoleon, of Hitler, of Stalin. It was necessary to strike first at the foundation of the Prophet's power: the popular belief that he ruled by direct authority of God.

Future generations will undoubtedly find it impossible to

believe the importance, the extreme importance both to religious faith and political power, of the Miracle of Incarnation. To comprehend it even intellectually it is necessary to realize that the people literally believed that the First Prophet actually and physically returned from Heaven once each year to judge the stewardship of his Divinely appointed successor and to confirm him in his office. The people *believed* this—the minority of doubters dared not open their faces to dispute it for fear of being torn limb from limb . . . and I am speaking of a rending that leaves blood on the pavement, not some figure of speech. Spitting on the Flag would have been much safer.

I had believed it myself, all my life; it would never have occurred to me to doubt such a basic article of faith—and I was what is called an educated man, one who had been let into the secrets of and trained in the production of lesser miracles. I believed it.

The ensuing two months had all the endless time-stretching tension of the waiting period while coming into range and before "Commence firing!"—yet we were so busy that each day and each hour was too short. In addition to preparing the still-more-miraculous intervention in the Miracle we used the time to whet our usual weapons to greater fineness. Zeb and his boss, Sector General Novak, were detached almost at once. Novak's orders read "—proceed to BEULAHLAND and take charge of OPERATION BEDROCK." I cut the orders myself, not trusting them to a clerk, but no one told me where Beulahland might be found on a map.

Huxley himself left when they did and was gone for more than a week, leaving Penoyer as acting C.-in-C. He did not tell me why he was leaving, of course, nor where he was going, but I could fill in. Operation Bedrock was a psychological maneuver but the means must be physical—and my boss had once been head of the Department of Applied Miracles at the Point. He may have been the best physicist in the entire Cabal; in any case I could guess with certainty that he intended at the very least to see for himself that the means were adequate and the techniques foolproof. For all I know he may actually have used soldering iron and screwdriver and electronic micrometer himself that week—the General did not mind getting his hands dirty.

I missed Huxley personally. Penoyer was inclined to reverse my decisions on minor matters and waste my time and his on details a top C.O. can't and should not cope with. But he was gone part of the time, too. There was much coming and going and more than once I had to chase down the senior department head present, tell him that he was acting, and get him to sign where I had initialed. I took to scrawling "I. M. Dumbjohn, Wing General F.U.S.A., Acting" as indecipherably as possible on all routine internal papers—I don't think anybody ever noticed.

Before Zeb left another thing happened which really has nothing to do with the people of the United States and the struggle to regain their freedoms—but my own personal affairs are so tied into this account that I mention it. Perhaps the personal angle really is important; certainly the order under which this journal was started called for it to be "personal" and "subjective"—however I had retained a copy and added to it because I found it helped me to get my own confused thoughts straight while going through a metamorphosis as drastic as that from caterpillar into moth. I am typical, perhaps, of the vast majority, the sort of person who has to have his nose rubbed in a thing before he recognizes it, while Zeb and Maggie and General Huxley were of the elite minority of naturally free souls . . . the original thinkers, the leaders.

I was at my desk, trying to cope with the usual spate of papers, when I received a call to see Zeb's boss at my earliest convenience. Since he already had his orders, I left word with Huxley's orderly and hurried over.

He cut short the formalities. "Major, I have a letter for you which Communications sent over for analysis to determine whether it should be rephrased or simply destroyed. However, on the urgent recommendation of one of my division heads I am taking the responsibility of letting you read it without paraphrasing. You will have to read it here."

I said, "Yes, sir," feeling quite puzzled.

He handed it to me. It was fairly long and I suppose it could have held half a dozen coded messages, even idea codes that could come through paraphrasing. I don't remember much of it—just the impact it had on me. It was from Judith.

"My dear John. . . . I shall always think of you fondly and I shall never forget what you have done for me. . . . never meant for each other . . . Mr. Mendoza has been most considerate . . . I know you will forgive me. . . . he needs me; it must have been fate that brought us together. . . . if you ever visit Mexico City, you must think of our home as yours. . . . I will always think of you as my strong and wise older brother and I will always be a sister—" There was more, lots more, all of the same sort—I think the process is known as "breaking it gently."

Novak reached out and took the letter from me. "I didn't intend for you to have time to memorize it," he said dryly, then dropped it at once into his desk incinerator. He glanced back at me. "Maybe you had better sit down, Major. Do you smoke?"

I did not sit down, but I was spinning so fast that I accepted the cigarette and let him light it for me. Then I choked on tobacco smoke and the sheer physical discomfort helped to bring me back to reality. I thanked him and got out—went straight to my room, called my office and left word where I could be found if the General really wanted me. But I told my secretary that I was suddenly quite ill and not to disturb me if it could possibly be helped.

I may have been there about an hour—I wouldn't know—lying face down and doing nothing, not even thinking. There came a gentle tap at the door, then it was pushed open; it was Zeb. "How do you feel?" he said.

"Numb," I answered. It did not occur to me to wonder how he knew and at the time I had forgotten the "division head" who had prevailed upon Novak to let me see it in the clear.

He came on in, sprawled in a chair, and looked at me. I rolled over and sat on the edge of the bed. "Don't let it throw you, Johnnie," he said quietly. " 'Men have died and worms have eaten them—but not for love.' "

"You don't know!"

"No, I don't," he agreed. "Each man is his own prisoner, in solitary confinement for life. Nevertheless on this particular point the statistics are fairly reliable. Try something for me. Visualize Judith in your mind. See her features. Listen to her voice."

"Huh?"

"Do it."

I tried, I really tried—and, do you know, I couldn't. I had never had a picture of her; her face now eluded me.

Zeb was watching me. "You'll get well," he said firmly. "Now look here, Johnnie. . . . I could have told you. Judith is a very female sort of woman, all gonads and no brain. And she's quite attractive. Turned loose, she was bound to find a man, as sure as nascent oxygen will recombine. But there is no use in talking to a man in love."

He stood up. "Johnnie, I've got to go. I hate like the mischief to walk out and leave you in the shape you are in, but I've already checked out and Grandfather Novak is ready to leave. He'll eat me out as it is, for holding him up this long. But one more word of advice before I go—"

I waited. "I suggest," he continued, "that you see a lot of Maggie while I'm away. She's good medicine."

He started to leave; I said sharply, "Zeb—what happened to you and Maggie? Something like this?"

He looked back at me sharply. "Huh? No. Not at all the same thing. It wasn't . . . well, it wasn't similar."

"I don't understand you—I guess I just don't understand people. You're urging me to see a lot of Maggie—and I thought she was your girl. Uh, wouldn't you be jealous?"

He stared at me, laughed, and clapped me on the shoulder. "She's a free citizen, Johnnie, believe me. If you ever did anything to hurt Maggie, I'd tear off your head and beat you to death with it. Not that you ever would. But jealous of her? No. It doesn't enter the picture. I think she's the greatest gal that ever trod shoe leather—but I would rather marry a mountain lioness."

He left on that, leaving me again with my mouth open. But I took his advice, or Maggie took it for me. Maggie knew all about it—Judith, I mean—and I assumed that Zeb had told her. He hadn't; it seemed that Judith had written to her first. In any case I didn't have to look her up; she looked me up right after dinner that night. I talked with her a while and felt much better, so much so that I went back to my office and made up for time lost that afternoon.

Maggie and I made a habit thereafter of taking a walk together after dinner. We went on no more spelling bees; not only was there no time for such during those last days but also neither one of us felt like trying to work up another foursome with Zeb away. Sometimes I could spare only twenty minutes or even less before I would have to be back at my desk—but it was the high point of the day; I looked forward to it.

Even without leaving the floodlighted main cavern, without leaving the marked paths, there were plenty of wonderfully beautiful walks to take. If I could afford to be away as much as an hour, there was one place in particular we liked to go— north in the big room, a good half mile from the buildings. The path meandered among frozen limestone mushrooms, great columns, domes, and fantastic shapes that have no names and looked equally like souls in torment or great exotic flowers, depending on the mood one was in. At a spot nearly a hundred feet higher than the main floor we had found a place only a few feet off the authorized path where nature had contrived a natural stone bench. We could sit there and stare down at the toy village, talk, and Maggie would smoke. I had taken to lighting her cigarettes for her, as I had seen Zeb do. It was a little attention she liked and I had learned to avoid getting smoke caught in my throat.

About six weeks after Zeb had left and only days before M-Hour we were doing this and were talking about what it would be like after the revolution and what we would do with ourselves. I said that I supposed I would stay in the regular army, assuming that there was such and that I was eligible for it. "What will you do, Maggie?"

She exhaled smoke slowly. "I haven't thought that far, John. I haven't any profession—that is to say, we are trying our best to make the one I did have obsolete." She smiled wryly. "I'm not educated in anything useful. I can cook and I can sew and I can keep house; I suppose I should try to find a job as a housekeeper—competent servants are always scarce, they say."

The idea of the courageous and resourceful Sister Magdalene, so quick with a vibroblade when the need arose, tramping from one employment bureau to another in search of menial work to keep her body fed was an idea at once distasteful to me—"General Housework & Cooking, live in, Thur. eve. & alternate Sundays off; references required." Maggie? Maggie who had saved my own probably worthless life at least twice and never hesitated nor counted the cost. Not Maggie!

I blurted out, "Look, you don't have to do *that*."

"It's what I know."

"Yes, but—well, why don't you cook and keep house for *me*? I'll be drawing enough to support both of us, even if I have to go back to my permanent rank. Maybe it isn't much but—shucks! you're welcome to it."

She looked up. "Why, John, how very generous!" She crushed out the cigarette and threw it aside. "I do appreciate it—but it wouldn't work. I imagine there will be just as many gossips after we have won as before. Your colonel would not like it."

I blushed red and almost shouted, "That wasn't what I meant at all!"

"What? Then what did you mean?"

I had not really known until the words came out. Now I knew but not how to express it. "I meant— Look, Maggie, you seem to like me well enough . . . and we get along well together. That is, why don't we—" I halted, hung up.

She stood up and faced me. "John, are you proposing marriage—to *me*?"

I said gruffly, "Uh, that was the general idea." It bothered me to have her standing in front of me, so I stood up, too.

She looked at me gravely, searching my face, then said humbly, "I'm honored . . . and grateful . . . and I am deeply touched. But—*oh, no, John!*" The tears started out of her eyes and she started to bawl. She stopped as quickly, wiping her face with her sleeve, and said brokenly, "Now you've made me cry. I haven't cried in years."

I started to put my arms around her; she pushed me back. "No, John! Listen to me first. I'll accept that job as your housekeeper, but I won't marry you."

"Why not?"

" 'Why not?' Oh, my dear, my very dear— Because I am an old, tired woman, that's why."

"Old? You can't be more than a year or two older than I am—three, at the outside. It doesn't matter."

"I'm a thousand years older than you are. Think who I am—where I've been—what I've known. First I was 'bride,' if you care to call it that, to the Prophet."

"Not your fault!"

"Perhaps. Then I was mistress to your friend Zebadiah. You knew that?"

"Well . . . I was pretty sure of it."

"That isn't all. There were other men. Some because it was needful and a woman has few bribes to offer. Some from loneliness, or even boredom. After the Prophet has tired of her, a woman doesn't seem very valuable, even to herself."

"I don't care. I don't care! It doesn't matter!"

"You say that now. Later it would matter to you, dreadfully. I think I know you, my dear."

"Then you don't know me. We'll start fresh."

She sighed deeply. "You think that you love me, John?"

"Uh? Yes, I guess that's it."

"You loved Judith. Now you are hurt—so you think you love me."

"But— Oh, I don't know what love is! I know I want you to marry me and live with me."

"Neither do I know," she said so softly that I almost missed it. Then she moved into my arms as easily and naturally as if she had always lived there.

When we had finished kissing each other I said, "You will marry me, then?"

She threw her head back and stared as if she were frightened. "Oh, no!"

"Huh? But I thought—"

"No, dear, no! I'll keep your house and cook your food and make your bed—and sleep in it, if you want me to. But you don't need to marry me."

"But—Sheol! Maggie, I won't have it that way."

"You won't? We'll see." She was out of my arms although I had not let go. "I'll see you tonight. About one—after everyone is asleep. Leave your door unlatched."

"Maggie!" I shouted.

She was headed down the path, running as if she were flying. I tried to catch up, tripped on a stalagmite and fell. When I picked myself up she was out of sight.

Here is an odd thing—I had always thought of Maggie as quite tall, stately, almost as tall as I was. But when I held her in my arms, she was short. I had to lean way over to kiss her.

O N the night of the Miracle all that were left of us gathered in the main communications room—my boss and myself, the chief of communications and his technical crew, a few staff officers. A handful of men and a few dozen women, too many to crowd into the comm shack, were in the main mess-hall where a relay screen had been rigged for them. Our underground city was a ghost town now, with only a skeleton crew to maintain communications for the commanding general; all the rest had gone to battle stations. We few who were left had no combat stations in this phase. Strategy had been settled; the hour of execution was set for us by the Miracle. Tactical decisions for a continent could not be made from headquarters and Huxley was too good a general to try. His troops had been disposed and his subordinate commanders were now on their own; all he could do was wait and pray.

All that we could do, too—I didn't have any fingernails left to bite.

The main screen in front of us showed, in brilliant color and perfect perspective, the interior of the Temple. The services had been going on all day—processional, hymns, prayers and more prayers, sacrifice, genuflexion, chanting, endless monotony of colorful ritual. My old regiment was drawn up in two frozen ranks, helmets shining, spears aligned like the teeth of a comb. I made out Peter van Eyck, Master of my home lodge, his belly corseted up, motionless before his platoon.

I knew, from having handled the despatch, that Master Peter had stolen a print of the film we had to have. His presence in the ceremonies was reassuring; had his theft even been suspected our plans could not possibly succeed. But there he was.

Around the other three walls of the comm room were a dozen smaller screens, scenes from as many major cities—crowds in Rittenhouse Square, the Hollywood Bowl jam-packed, throngs in local temples. In each case the eyes of all were riveted on a giant television screen showing the same scene in the Great Temple that we were watching. Throughout all America it would be the same—every mortal soul who could possibly manage it was watching some television screen somewhere—waiting, waiting, waiting for the Miracle of the Incarnation.

Behind us a psychoperator bent over a sensitive who worked

under hypnosis. The sensitive, a girl about nineteen, stirred and muttered; the operator bent closer.

Then he turned to Huxley and the communications chief. "The Voice of God Station has been secured, sir."

Huxley merely nodded; I felt like turning handsprings, if my knees had not been so weak. This was the key tactic and one that could not possibly be executed until minutes before the Miracle. Since television moves only on line-of-sight or in its own special cable the only possible way to tamper with this nationwide broadcast was at the station of origin. I felt a wild burst of exaltation at their success—followed by an equally sudden burst of sorrow, knowing that not one of them could hope to live out the night.

Never mind—if they could hold out for a few more minutes their lives would have counted. I commended their souls to the Great Architect. We had men for such jobs where needed, mostly brethren whose wives had faced an inquisitor.

The comm chief touched Huxley's sleeve. "It's coming, sir." The scene panned slowly up to the far end of the Temple, passed over the altar, and settled in close-up on an ivory archway above and behind the altar—the entrance to the Sanctum Sanctorum. It was closed with heavy cloth-of-gold drapes.

The pick-up camera held steady with the curtained entranceway exactly filling the screen. "They can take over any time now, sir."

Huxley turned his head to the psychoperator. "Is that ours yet? See if you can get a report from the Voice of God."

"Nothing, sir. I'll let you know."

I could not take my eyes off the screen. After an interminable wait, the curtains stirred and slowly parted, drawn up and out on each side—and there, standing before us almost life size and so real that I felt he could step out of the screen, was the Prophet Incarnate!

He turned his head, letting his gaze rove from side to side, then looked right at me, his eyes staring right into mine. I wanted to hide. I gasped and said involuntarily, "You mean we can duplicate *that?*"

The comm chief nodded. "To the millimeter, or I'll eat the difference. Our best impersonator, prepared by our best plastic surgeons. That may be our film already."

"But it's real."

Huxley glanced at me. "A little less talk, please, Lyle." It was the nearest he had ever come to bawling me out; I shut up and studied the screen. That powerful, totally unscrupulous face, that burning gaze—an actor? No! I knew that face; I had seen it too many times in too many ceremonies. Something had gone wrong and this was the Prophet Incarnate himself. I began to sweat that stinking sweat of fear. I very much believe that had he called me by name out of that screen I would have confessed my treasons and thrown myself on his mercy.

Huxley said crossly, "Can't you raise New Jerusalem?"

The psychoperator answered, "No, sir. I'm sorry, sir."

The Prophet started his invocation.

His compelling, organlike voice rolled through magnificent periods. Then he asked the blessings of Eternal God for the people this coming year. He paused, looked at me again, then rolled his eyes up to Heaven, lifted his hands and commenced his petition to the First Prophet, asking him to confer on his people the priceless bounty of seeing and hearing him in the flesh, and offering for that purpose the flesh of the present prophet as an instrument. He waited.

The transformation started—and my hackles stood up. I knew now that we had lost; something had gone wrong . . . and God alone knew how many men had died through the error.

The features of the Prophet began to change; he stretched an inch or two in height; his rich robes darkened—and there standing in his place, dressed in a frock coat of a bygone era, was the Reverend Nehemiah Scudder, First Prophet and founder of the New Crusade. I felt my stomach tighten with fear and dread and I was a little boy again, watching it for the first time in my parish church.

He spoke to us first with his usual yearly greeting of love and concern for his people. Gradually he worked himself up, his face sweating and his hands clutching in the style that had called down the Spirit in a thousand Mississippi Valley camp meetings; my heart began to beat faster. He was preaching against sin in all its forms—the harlot whose mouth is like honey, the sins of the flesh, the sins of the spirit, the money changers.

At the height of his passion he led into a new subject in a fashion that caught me by surprise: "But I did not return to you this day to speak to you of the little sins of little people. No! I come to tell you of a truly hellish thing and to bid you to gird on your armor and fight. Armageddon is upon you! Rise up, mine hosts, and fight you the Battle of the Lord! For Satan is upon you! He is here! Here among you! Here tonight in the flesh! With the guile of the serpent he has come among you, taking on the form of the Vicar of the Lord! Yea! He has disguised himself falsely, taken on the shape of the *Prophet Incarnate!*

"Smite him! Smite his hirelings! In the Name of God destroy them all!"

13

BRUEHLER from Voice of God," the psychoperator said quietly. "The station is now off the air and demolition will take place in approximately thirty seconds. An attempt will be made to beat a retreat before the building goes up. Good luck. Message ends."

Huxley muttered something and left the now-dark big screen. The smaller screens, monitoring scenes around the country, were confusing but heartening. There was fighting and rioting everywhere. I watched it, still stunned, and tried to figure out which was friend and which was foe. In the Hollywood Bowl the crowd boiled up over the stage and by sheer numbers overran and trampled the officials and clergy seated there. There were plenty of guards stationed around the edges of the bowl and it should not have happened that way. But instead of the murderous enfilading fire one would have expected, there was one short blast from a tripod mounted on the hillside northeast of the stage, then the guard was shot—apparently by another of the guards.

Apparently the chancy tour de force against the Prophet himself was succeeding beyond all expectations. If government forces were everywhere as disorganized as they were at the Hollywood Bowl, the job would not be one of fighting but of consolidating an accomplished fact.

The monitor from Hollywood went dead and I shifted to another screen, Portland, Oregon. More fighting. I could see men with white armbands, the only uniform we had allowed ourselves for M-Hour—but not all the violence came from our brethren in the armbands. I saw an armed proctor go down before bare fists and not get up.

Testing messages and early reports were beginning to come in, now that it was feasible to use our own radio—now that we had at long, long last shown our hand. I stopped looking and went back to help my boss keep track of them. I was still dazed and could still see in my mind the incredible face of the Prophet—both Prophets. If I had been emotionally battered by it, what did the people think? The devout, the believers?

The first clear-cut report other than contact messages was from Lucas in New Orleans:

HAVE TAKEN CONTROL OF CITY CENTER, POWER AND COMM STATIONS. MOP-UP SQUADS SEIZING WARD POLICE STATIONS. FEDERAL GUARDS HERE DEMORALIZED BY STEREOCAST. SPORADIC FIGHT-

ING BROKE OUT AMONG GUARDS THEMSELVES. LITTLE ORGANIZED RESISTANCE. ESTABLISHING ORDER UNDER MARTIAL LAW. SO MOTE IT BE!— LUCAS.

Then reports started pouring in: Kansas City, Detroit, Philadelphia, Denver, Boston, Minneapolis—all the major cities. They varied but told the same story; our synthetic Prophet's call to arms, followed at once by a cutting of all regular methods of communication, had made of the government forces a body without a head, flopping around and fighting itself. The power of the Prophet was founded on superstition and fraud; we had turned superstition back on him to destroy him.

Lodge that night was the grandest I have ever attended. We tyled the communications room itself, with the comm chief sitting as secretary and passing incoming messages to General Huxley, sitting as Master in the east, as fast as they came in. I was called on to take a chair myself, Junior Warden, an honor I had never had before. The General had to borrow a hat and it was ridiculously too small for him, but it didn't matter—I have never seen ritual so grand, before or since. We all spake the ancient words from our hearts, as if we were saying them for the first time. If the stately progress was interrupted to hear that Louisville was ours, what better interruption? We were building anew; after an endless time of building in speculation we were at last building operatively.

14

TEMPORARY capital was set up at St. Louis, for its central location. I piloted Huxley there myself. We took over the Prophet's proctor base there, restoring to it its old name of Jefferson Barracks. We took over the buildings of the University, too, and handed back to it the name of Washington. If the people no longer recalled the true significance of those names, they soon would and here was a good place to start. (I learned for the first time that Washington had been one of us.)

However, one of Huxley's first acts as military governor— he would not let himself be called even "Provisional President"—was to divorce all official connection between the Lodge and the Free United States Army. The Brotherhood had served its purpose, had kept alive the hopes of free men; now it was time to go back to its ancient ways and let public affairs be handled publicly. The order was not made public, since the public had no real knowledge of us, always a secret society and for three generations a completely clandestine one. But it was read and recorded in all lodges and, so far as I know, honored.

There was one necessary exception: my home lodge at New Jerusalem and the cooperating sister order there of which Maggie had been a member. For we did not yet hold New Jerusalem although the country as a whole was ours.

This was more serious than it sounds. While we had the country under military control, with all communication centers in our hands, with the Federal Forces demoralized, routed, and largely dispersed or disarmed and captured, we did not hold the country's heart in our hands. More than half of the population were not with us; they were simply stunned, confused, and unorganized. As long as the Prophet was still alive, as long as the Temple was still a rallying point, it was still conceivably possible for him to snatch back the victory from us.

A fraud, such as we had used, has only a temporary effect; people revert to their old thinking habits. The Prophet and his cohorts were not fools; they included some of the shrewdest applied psychologists this tired planet has ever seen. Our own counterespionage became disturbingly aware that they were rapidly perfecting their own underground, using the still devout and that numerous minority, devout or not, who had waxed fat under the old regime and saw themselves growing leaner under the new. We could not stop this counterrevolution—Sheol! the Prophet had not been able to stop *us* and we had worked under much greater handicaps. The Prophet's spies could work almost openly in the smaller towns and the country; we had barely enough men to guard the television stations —we could not possibly put a snooper under every table.

Soon it was an open secret that we had faked the call to Armageddon. One would think that this fact in itself would show to anyone who knew it that *all* of the Miracles of Incarnation had been frauds—trick television and nothing more. I mentioned this to Zebadiah and got laughed at for being naive. People believe what they want to believe and logic has no bearing on it, he assured me. In this case they wanted to believe in their old time religion as they learned it at their mothers' knees; it restored security to their hearts. I could sympathize with that, I understood it.

In any case, New Jerusalem must fall—and time was against us.

While we were worrying over this, a provisional constitutional convention was being held in the great auditorium of the university. Huxley opened it, refused again the title, offered by acclamation, of president—then told them bluntly that all laws since the inauguration of President Nehemiah Scudder were of no force, void, and that the old constitution

116

and bill of rights were effective as of now, subject to the exigencies of temporary military control. Their single purpose, he said, was to work out orderly methods of restoring the old free democratic processes; any permanent changes in the constitution, if needed, would have to wait until after free elections.

Then he turned the gavel over to Novak and left.

I did not have time for politics, but I hid out from work and caught most of one afternoon session because Zebadiah had tipped me off that significant fireworks were coming up. I slipped into a back seat and listened. One of Novak's bright young men was presenting a film. I saw the tail end of it only, but it seemed to be more or less a standard instruction film, reviewing the history of the United States, discussing civil liberty, explaining the duties of a citizen in a free democracy —not the sort of thing ever seen in the Prophet's schools but making use of the same techniques which had long been used in every school in the country. The film ended and the bright young man—I could never remember his name, perhaps because I disliked him. Stokes? Call him Stokes, anyway. Stokes began to speak.

"This reorientation film," he began, "is of course utterly useless in recanalizing an adult. His habits of thought are much too set to be affected by anything as simple as this."

"Then why waste our time with it?" someone called out.

"Please! Nevertheless this film was prepared for adults— provided the adult has been placed in a receptive frame of mind. Here is the prologue—" the screen lighted up again. It was a simple and beautiful pastoral scene with very restful music. I could not figure what he was getting at, but it was soothing; I remembered that I had not had much sleep the past four nights—come to think about it, I couldn't remember when I had had a good night's sleep. I slouched back and relaxed.

I didn't notice the change from scenery to abstract patterns. I think the music continued but it was joined by a voice, warm, soothing, monotonous. The patterns were going round and around and I was beginning to bore . . . right . . . into . . . the . . . screen. . . .

Then Novak had left his chair and switched off the projector with a curse. I jerked awake with that horrid shocked feeling that makes one almost ready to cry. Novak was speaking sharply but quietly to Stokes—then Novak faced the rest of us. "Up on your feet!" he ordered. "Seventh inning stretch. Take a deep breath. Shake hands with the man next to you. Slap him on the back, hard!"

We did so and I felt foolish. Also irritated. I had felt so good just a moment before and now I was reminded of the mountain of work I must move if I were to have ten minutes

117

with Maggie that evening. I thought about leaving but the b. y. m. had started talking again.

"As Dr. Novak has pointed out," he went on, not sounding quite so sure of himself, "it is not necessary to use the prologue on this audience, since you don't need reorientation. But this film, used with the preparatory technique and possibly in some cases with a light dose of one of the hypnotic drugs, can be depended on to produce an optimum political temperament in 83% of the populace. This has been demonstrated on a satisfactory test group. The film itself represents several years of work analyzing the personal conversion reports of almost everyone—surely everyone in this audience!—who joined our organization while it was still underground. The irrelevant has been eliminated; the essential has been abstracted. What remains will convert a devout follower of the Prophet to free manhood—provided he is in a state receptive to suggestion when he is exposed to it."

So *that* was why we had each been required to bare our souls. It seemed logical to me. God knew that we were sitting on a time bomb, and we couldn't wait for every lunk to fall in love with a holy deaconess and thereby be shocked out of his groove; there wasn't time. But an elderly man whom I did not know was on his feet on the other side of the hall—he looked like the pictures of Mark Twain, an angry Mark Twain. "Mr. Chairman!"

"Yes, comrade? State your name and district."

"You know what my name is, Novak—Winters, from Vermont. Did you okay this scheme?"

"No." It was a simple declarative.

"He's one of your boys."

"He's a free citizen. I supervised the preparation of the film itself and the research which preceded it. The use of null-vol suggestion techniques came from the research group he headed. I disapproved the proposal, but agreed to schedule time to present it. I repeat, he is a free citizen, free to speak, just as you are."

"May I speak now?"

"You have the floor."

The old man drew himself up and seemed to swell up. "I shall! Gentlemen . . . ladies . . . comrades! I have been in this for more than forty years—more years than that young pup has been alive. I have a brother, as good a man as I am, but we haven't spoken in many years—because he is honestly devout in the established faith and he suspects me of heresy. Now this cub, with his bulging forehead and his whirling lights, would 'condition' my brother to make him 'politically reliable.' "

He stopped to gasp asthmatically and went on. "Free men aren't 'conditioned!' Free men are free because they are ornery

118

and cussed and prefer to arrive at their own prejudices in their own way—not have them spoonfed by a self-appointed mind tinkerer! We haven't fought, our brethren haven't bled and died, just to change bosses, no matter how sweet their motives. I tell you, we got into the mess we are in through the efforts of those same mind tinkerers. They've studied for years how to saddle a man and ride him. They started with advertising and propaganda and things like that, and they perfected it to the point where what used to be simple, honest swindling such as any salesman might use became a mathematical science that left the ordinary man helpless." He pointed his finger at Stokes. "I tell you that the American citizen needs no protection from anything—except the likes of him."

"This is ridiculous," Stokes snapped, his voice rather high. "You wouldn't turn high explosives over to children. That is what the franchise would be now."

"The American people are not children."

"They might as well be!—most of them."

Winters turned his eyes around the hall. "You see what I mean, friends? He's as ready to play God as the Prophet was. I say give 'em their freedom, give 'em their clear rights as men and free men and children under God. If they mess it up again, that's their doing—but we have no right to operate on their minds." He stopped and labored again to catch his breath; Stokes looked contemptuous. "We *can't* make the world safe for children, nor for men either—and God didn't appoint us to do it."

Novak said gently, "Are you through, Mr. Winters?"

"I'm through."

"And you've had *your* say, too, Stokes. Sit down."

Then I had to leave, so I slipped out—and missed what must have been a really dramatic event if you care for that sort of thing; I don't. Old Mr. Winters dropped dead about the time I must have been reaching the outer steps.

Novak did not let them recess on that account. They passed two resolutions; that no citizen should be subjected to hypnosis or other psychomanipulative technique without his written consent, and that no religious or political test should be used for franchise in the first elections.

I don't know who was right. It certainly would have made life easier in the next few weeks if we had known that the people were solidly behind us. Temporarily rulers we might be, but we hardly dared go down a street in uniform at night in groups of less than six.

Oh yes, we had uniforms now—almost enough for one for each of us, of the cheapest materials possible and in the standard army sizes, either too large or too small. Mine was too tight. They had been stockpiled across the Canadian border and we got our own people into uniform as quickly as possible. A handkerchief tied around the arm is not enough.

Besides our own simple powder-blue dungarees there were several other uniforms around, volunteer brigades from outside the country and some native American outfits. The Mormon Battalions had their own togs and they were all growing beards as well—they went into action singing the long-forbidden "Come, Come, Ye Saints!" Utah was one state we didn't have to worry about, now that the Saints had their beloved temple back. The Catholic Legion had its distinctive uniform, which was just as well since hardly any of them spoke English. The Onward Christian Soldiers dressed differently from us because they were a rival underground and rather resented our coup d'état—we should have waited. Joshua's Army from the pariah reservations in the northwest (plus volunteers from all over the world) had a get-up that can only be described as outlandish.

Huxley was in tactical command of them all. But it wasn't an army; it was a rabble.

The only thing that was hopeful about it was that the Prophet's army had not been large, less than two hundred thousand, more of an internal police than an army, and of that number only a few had managed to make their way back to New Jerusalem to augment the Palace garrison. Besides that, since the United States had not had an external war for more than a century, the Prophet could not recruit veteran soldiers from the remaining devout.

Neither could we. Most of our effectives were fit only to guard communication stations and other key installations around the country and we were hard put to find enough of them to do that. Mounting an assault on New Jerusalem called for scraping the bottom of the barrel.

Which we did, while smothering under a load of paperwork that made the days in the old GHQ seem quiet and untroubled. I had thirty clerks under me now and I don't know what half of them did. I spent a lot of my time just keeping Very Important Citizens who Wanted to Help from getting in to see Huxley.

I recall one incident which, while not important, was not exactly routine and was important to me. My chief secretary came in with a very odd look on her face. "Colonel," she said, "your twin brother is out there."

"Eh? I have no brothers."

"A Sergeant Reeves," she amplified.

He came in, we shook hands, and exchanged inanities. I really was glad to see him and told him about all the orders I had sold and then lost for him. I apologized, pled exigency of war and added, "I landed one new account in K.C.—Emery, Bird, Thayer. You might pick it up some day."

"I will. Thanks."

"I didn't know you were a soldier."

"I'm not, really. But I've been practicing at it ever since my travel permit, uh—got itself lost."

"I'm sorry about that."

"Don't be. I've learned to handle a blaster and I'm pretty good with a grenade now. I've been okayed for Operation Strikeout."

"Eh? That code word is supposed to be confo."

"It is? Better tell the boys; they don't seem to realize it. Anyhow, I'm in. Are you? Or shouldn't I ask that?"

I changed the subject. "How do you like soldiering? Planning to make a career of it?"

"Oh, it's all right—but not *that* all right. But what I came in to ask you, Colonel, are *you?*"

"Eh?"

"Are you staying in the army afterwards? I suppose you can make a good thing out of it, with your background—whereas they wouldn't let me shine brightwork, once the fun is over. But if by any chance you aren't, what do you think of the textile business?"

I was startled but I answered, "Well, to tell the truth I rather enjoyed it—the selling end, at least."

"Good. I'm out of a job where I was, of course—and I've been seriously considering going in on my own, a jobbing business and manufacturers' representative. I'll need a partner. Eh?"

I thought it over. "I don't know," I said slowly. "I haven't thought ahead any farther than Operation Strikeout. I might stay in the army—though soldiering does not have the appeal for me it once had . . . too many copies to make out and certify. But I don't know. I think what I really want is simply to sit under my own vine and my own fig tree."

" '—and none shall make you afraid,' " he finished. "A good thought. But there is no reason why you shouldn't unroll a few bolts of cloth while you are sitting there. The fig crop might fail. Think it over."

"I will. I surely will."

15

MAGGIE and I were married the day before the assault on New Jerusalem. We had a twenty-minute honeymoon, holding hands on the fire escape outside my office, then I flew Huxley to the jump-off area. I was in the flagship during the attack. I had asked permission to pilot a rocket-jet as my combat assignment but he had turned me down.

"What for, John?" he had asked. "This isn't going to be won in the air; it will be settled on the ground."

He was right, as usual. We had few ships and still fewer pilots who could be trusted. Some of the Prophet's air force had been sabotaged on the ground; a goodly number had escaped to Canada and elsewhere and been interned. With what planes we had we had been bombing the Palace and Temple regularly, just to make them keep their heads down.

But we could not hurt them seriously that way and both sides knew it. The Palace, ornate as it was above ground, was probably the strongest bombproof ever built. It had been designed to stand direct impact of a fission bomb without damage to personnel in its deepest tunnels—and that was where the Prophet was spending his days, one could be sure. Even the part above ground was relatively immune to ordinary HE bombs such as we were using.

We weren't using atomic bombs for three reasons: we didn't have any; the United States was not known to have had any since the Johannesburg Treaty after World War III. We could not get any. We might have negotiated a couple of bombs from the Federation had we been conceded to be the legal government of the United States, but, while Canada had recognized us, Great Britain had not and neither had the North African Confederacy. Brazil was teetering; she had sent a chargé d'affaires to St. Louis. But even if we had actually been admitted to the Federation, it is most unlikely that a mass weapon would have been granted for an internal disorder.

Lastly, we would not have used one if it had been laid in our laps. No, we weren't chicken hearted. But an atom bomb, laid directly on the Palace, would certainly have killed around a hundred thousand or more of our fellow citizens in the surrounding city—and almost as certainly would not have killed the Prophet.

It was going to be necessary to go in and dig him out, like a holed-up badger.

Rendezvous was made on the east shore of the Delaware River. At one minute after midnight we moved east, thirty-four land cruisers, thirteen of them modern battlewagons, the rest light cruisers and obsolescent craft—all that remained of the Prophet's mighty East Mississippi fleet; the rest had been blown up by their former commanders. The heavy ships would be used to breach the walls; the light craft were escort to ten armored transports carrying the shock troops—five thousand fighting men hand-picked from the whole country. Some of them had had some military training in addition to what we had been able to give them in the past few weeks; all of them had taken part in the street fighting.

We could hear the bombing at New Jerusalem as we started out, the dull *Crrump!*, the gooseflesh shiver of the concussion wave, the bass rumble of the ground sonic. The bombing had been continuous the last thirty-six hours; we hoped that no one in the Palace had had any sleep lately, whereas our troops had just finished twelve hours impressed sleep.

None of the battlewagons had been designed as a flagship, so we had improvised a flag plot just abaft the conning tower, tearing out the long-range televisor to make room for the battle tracker and concentration plot. I was sweating over my jury-rigged tracker, hoping to Heaven that the makeshift shock absorbers would be good enough when we opened up. Crowded in behind me was a psychoperator and his crew of sensitives, eight women and a neurotic fourteen-year-old boy. In a pinch, each would have to handle four circuits. I wondered if they could do it. One thin blonde girl had a dry, chronic cough and a big thyroid patch on her throat.

We lumbered along in approach zigzag. Huxley wandered from comm to plot and back again, calm as a snail, looking over my shoulder, reading despatches casually, watching the progress of the approach on the screens.

The pile of despatches at my elbow grew. The *Cherub* had fouled her starboard tread; she had dropped out of formation but would rejoin in thirty minutes. Penoyer reported his columns extended and ready to deploy. Because of the acute shortage of command talent, we were using broad-command organization; Penoyer commanded the left wing and his own battlewagon; Huxley was force commander, right wing commander, and skipper of his own flagship.

At 12:32 the televisors went out. The enemy had analyzed our frequency variation pattern, matched us and blown every tube in the circuits. It is theoretically impossible; they did it. At 12:37 radio went out.

Huxley seemed unperturbed. "Shift to light-phone circuits," was all he said.

The communications officer had anticipated him; our audio circuits were now on infra-red beams, ship to ship. Huxley hung over my shoulder most of the next hour, watching the position plot lines grow. Presently he said, "I think we will deploy now, John. Some of those pilots aren't any too steady; I think we will give them time to settle down in their positions before anything more happens."

I passed the order and cut my tracker out of circuit for fifteen minutes; it wasn't built for so many variables at such high speeds and there was no sense in overloading it. Nineteen minutes later the last transport had checked in by phone, I made a preliminary set up, threw the starting switch and let the correction data feed in. For a couple of minutes I was very busy balancing data, my hands moving among knobs and keys; then the machine was satisfied with its own predictions and I reported, "Tracking, sir."

Huxley leaned over my shoulder. The line was a little ragged but I was proud of them—some of those pilots had been freighter jacks not four weeks earlier.

At three A.M. we made the precautionary signal, "Coming on the range," and our own turret rumbled as they loaded it.

At 3:31 Huxley gave the command, "Concentration Plan III, open fire."

Our own big fellow let go. The first shot shook loose a lot of dust and made my eyes water. The craft rolled back on her treads to the recoil and I nearly fell out of my saddle. I had never ridden one of the big booster guns before and I hadn't expected the long recoil. Our big rifle had secondary firing chambers up the barrel, electronically synchronized with the progress of the shell; it maintained max pressure all the way up and gave a much higher muzzle velocity and striking power. It also gave a bone-shaking recoil. But the second time I was ready for it.

Huxley was at the periscope between shots, trying to observe the effects of our fire. New Jerusalem had answered our fire but did not yet have us ranged. We had the advantage of firing at a stationary target whose range we knew to the meter; on the other hand even a heavy land cruiser could not show the weight of armor that underlay the Palace's gingerbread.

Huxley turned from the scope and remarked, "Smoke, John."

I turned to the communications officer. "Stand by, sensitives; all craft!"

The order never got through. Even as I gave it the comm officer reported loss of contact. But the psychoperator was already busy and I knew the same thing was happening in all the ships; it was normal casualty routine.

Of our nine sensitives, three—the boy and two women—were wide-awakes; the other six were hypnos. The technician hooked the boy first to one in Penoyer's craft. The kid established rapport almost at once and Penoyer got through a report:

"BLANKETED BY SMOKE. HAVE SHIFTED LEFT WING TO PSYCHO. WHAT HOOK-UP?—PENOYER."

I answered, "Pass down the line." Doctrine permitted two types of telepathic hook-up: relay, in which a message would be passed along until it reached its destination; and command mesh, in which there was direct hook-up from flag to each ship under that flag, plus ship-to-ship for adjacent units. In the first case each sensitive carries just one circuit, that is, is in rapport with just one other telepath; in the second they might

124

have to handle as many as four circuits. I wanted to hold off overloading them as long as possible.

The technician tied the other two wide-awakes into our flanking craft in the battle line, then turned his attention to the hypnos. Four of them required hypodermics; the other two went under in response to suggestion. Shortly we were hooked up with the transports and second-line craft, as well as with the bombers and the rocket-jet spotting the fall of shot. The jet reported visibility zero and complained that he wasn't getting anything intelligible by radar. I told him to stand by; the morning breeze might clear the smoke away presently.

We weren't dependent on him anyway; we knew our positions almost to the inch. We had taken departure from a benchmark and our deadreckoning was checked for the whole battle line every time any skipper identified a map-shown landmark. In addition, the deadreckoners of a tread-driven cruiser are surprisingly accurate; the treads literally measure every yard of ground as they pass over it and a little differential gadget compares the treads and keeps just as careful track of direction. The smoke did not really bother us and we could keep on firing accurately even if radar failed. On the other hand, if the Palace commander kept us in smoke he himself was entirely dependent on radar.

His radar was apparently working; shot was falling all around us. We hadn't been hit yet but we could feel the concussions when shells struck near us and some of the reports were not cheerful. Penoyer reported the *Martyr* hit; the shell had ruptured her starboard engine room. The skipper had tried to cross connect and proceed at half speed, but the gear train was jammed; she was definitely out of action. The *Archangel* had overheated her gun. She was in formation but would be harmless until the turret captain got her straightened out.

Huxley ordered them to shift to Formation E, a plan which used changing speeds and apparently random courses—carefully planned to avoid collision between ships, however. It was intended to confuse the fire control of the enemy.

At 4:11 Huxley sent the bombers back to base. We were inside the city now and the walls of the Palace lay just beyond —too close to target for comfort; we didn't want to lose ships to our own bombs.

At 4:17 we were struck. The port upper tread casing was split, the barbette was damaged so that the gun would no longer train, and the conning tower was cracked along its after surface. The pilot was killed at his controls.

I helped the psychoperator get gas helmets over the heads of the hypnos. Huxley picked himself up off the floor plates, put on his own helmet, and studied the set-up on my battle tracker, frozen at the instant the shell hit us.

"The *Benison* should pass by this point in three minutes, John. Tell them to proceed dead slow, come along starboard side, and pick us up. Tell Penoyer I am shifting my flag."

We made the transfer without mishap, Huxley, myself, the psychoperator, and his sensitives. One sensitive was dead, killed by a flying splinter. One went into a deep trance and we could not rouse her. We left her in the disabled battlewagon; she was as safe there as she could be.

I had torn the current plot from my tracker and brought it along. It had the time-predicted plots for Formation E. We would have to struggle along with those, as the tracker could not be moved and was probably beyond casual repair in any case. Huxley studied the chart.

"Shift to full communication mesh, John. I plan to assault shortly."

I helped the psychoperator get his circuits straightened out. By dropping the *Martyr* out entirely and by using "Pass down the line" on Penoyer's auxiliaries, we made up for the loss of two sensitives. All carried four circuits now, except the boy who had five, and the girl with the cough, who was managing six. The psychoperator was worried but there was nothing to do about it.

I turned back to General Huxley. He had seated himself and at first I thought he was in deep thought; then I saw that he was unconscious. It was not until I tried to rouse him and failed that I saw the blood seeping down the support column of his chair and wetting the floor plates. I moved him gently and found, sticking out from between his ribs near his spine, a steel splinter.

I felt a touch at my elbow, it was the psychoperator. "Penoyer reports that he will be within assault radius in four minutes. Requests permission to change formation and asks time of execution."

Huxley was out. Dead or wounded, he would fight no more this battle. By all rules, command devolved on Penoyer, and I should tell him so at once. But time was pressing hard, it would involve a drastic change of set-up, and we had been forced to send Penoyer into battle with only three sensitives. It was a physical impossibility.

What should I do? Turn the flag over to the skipper of the *Benison?* I knew the man, stolid, unimaginative, a gunner by disposition. He was not even in his conning tower but had been fighting his ship from the fire control station in the turret. If I called him down here, he would take many minutes to comprehend the situation—and then give the wrong orders.

With Huxley out I had not an ounce of real authority. I was a brevet short-tailed colonel, only days up from major and a legate by rights; I was what I was as Huxley's flunky. Should I turn command over to Penoyer—and lose the battle with proper military protocol? *What would Huxley have me do, if he could make the decision?*

It seemed to me that I worried that problem for an hour. The chronograph showed thirteen seconds between reception of Penoyer's despatch and my answer:

"Change formation at will. Stand by for execution signal in six minutes." The order given, I sent word to the forward dressing station to attend to the General.

I shifted the right wing to assault echelon, then called the transport *Sweet Chariot:* "Sub-plan D; leave formation and proceed on duty assigned." The psychoperator eyed me but transmitted my orders. Sub-plan D called for five hundred light infantry to enter the Palace through the basement of the department store that was connected with the lodge room. From the lodge room they would split into squads and proceed on assigned tasks. All of our shock troops had all the plans of the Palace graven into their brains; these five hundred had had additional drill as to just where they were to go, what they were to do.

Most of them would be killed, but they should be able to create confusion during the assault. Zeb had trained them and now commanded them.

We were ready. "All units, stand by to assault. Right wing, outer flank of right bastion; left wing, outer flank of left bastion. Zigzag emergency full speed until within assault distance. Deploy for full concentration fire, one salvo, and assault. Stand by to execute. Acknowledge."

The acknowledgments were coming in and I was watching my chronometer preparatory to giving the command of execution when the boy sensitive broke off in the middle of a report and shook himself. The technician grabbed the kid's wrist and felt for his pulse; the boy shook him off.

"Somebody new," he said. "I don't quite get it." Then he commenced in a sing-song, "To commanding general from Lodge Master Peter van Eyck: assault center bastion with full force. I will create a diversion."

"Why the center?" I asked.

"It is much more damaged."

If this were authentic, it was crucially important. But I was suspicious. If Master Peter had been detected, it was a trap. And I didn't see how he, in his position, had been able to set up a sensitive circuit in the midst of battle.

"Give me the word," I said.

"Nay, you give me."

"Nay, I will not."

"I will spell it, or halve it."

"Spell it, then."

We did so. I was satisfied. "Cancel last signal. Heavy cruisers assault center bastion, left wing to left flank, right wing to right flank. Odd numbered auxiliaries make diversion assaults on right and left bastions. Even numbers remain with transports. Acknowledge."

Nineteen seconds later I gave the command to execute, then we were off. It was like riding a rocket plane with a dirty, over-heated firing chamber. We crashed through walls of masonry, lurched sickeningly on turns, almost overturned when we crashed into the basement of some large demolished building and lumbered out again. It was out of my hands now, up to each skipper.

As we slewed into firing position, I saw the psychoperator peeling back the boy's eyelids. "I'm afraid he's gone," he said tonelessly. "I had to overload him too much on that last hook-up." Two more of the women had collapsed.

Our big gun cut loose for the final salvo; we waited for an interminable period—all of ten seconds. Then we were moving, gathering speed as we rolled. The *Benison* hit the Palace wall with a blow that I thought would wreck her, but she did not mount. But the pilot had his forward hydraulic jacks down as soon as we hit; her bow reared slowly up. We reached an angle so steep that it seemed she must turn turtle, then the treads took hold, we ground forward and slid through the breach in the wall.

Our gun spoke again, at point-blank range, right into the inner Palace. A thought flashed through my head—this was the exact spot where I had first laid eyes on Judith. I had come full circle.

The *Benison* was rampaging around, destroying by her very weight. I waited until the last cruiser had had time to enter, then gave the order, "Transports, assault." That done, I called Penoyer, informed him that Huxley was wounded and that he was now in command.

I was all through. I did not even have a job, a battle station. The battle surged around me, but I was not part of it—I, who two minutes ago had been in usurped full command.

I stopped to light a cigarette and wondered what to do with myself. I put it out after one soul-satisfying drag and scrambled up into the fire control tower of the turret and peered out the after slits. A breeze had come up and the smoke was clearing; the transport *Jacob's Ladder* I could see just pulling out of the breach. Her sides fell away and ranks of infantry sprang out, blasters ready. A sporadic fire met them; some fell but most returned the fire and charged the inner Palace. The *Jacob's Ladder* cleared the breach and the *Ark* took her place.

The troops commander in the *Ark* had orders to take the Prophet alive. I hurried down ladders from the turret, ran down the passageway between the engine rooms, and located the escape hatch in the floor plates, clear at the stern of the

Benison. Somehow I got it unclamped, swung up the hatch cover, and stuck my head down. I could see men running, out beyond the treads. I drew my blaster, dropped to the ground, and tried to catch up with them, running out the stern between the big treads.

They were men from the *Ark,* right enough. I attached myself to a platoon and trotted along with them. We swarmed into the inner Palace.

But the battle was over; we encountered no organized resistance. We went on down and down and down and found the Prophet's bombproof. The door was open and he was there.

But we did not arrest him. The Virgins had gotten to him first; he no longer looked imperious. They had left him barely something to identify at an inquest.

Coventry

"HAVE you anything to say before sentence is pronounced on you?" The mild eyes of the Senior Judge studied the face of the accused. His question was answered by a sullen silence.

"Very well—the jury has determined that you have violated a basic custom agreed to under the Covenant, and that through this act did damage another free citizen. It is the opinion of the jury and of the court that you did so knowingly, and aware of the probability of damage to a free citizen. Therefore, you are sentenced to choose between the Two Alternatives."

A trained observer might have detected a trace of dismay breaking through the mask of indifference with which the young man had faced his trial. Dismay was unreasonable; in view of his offence, the sentence was inevitable—but reasonable men do not receive the sentence.

After waiting a decent interval, the judge turned to the bailiff. "Take him away."

The prisoner stood up suddenly, knocking over his chair. He glared wildly around at the company assembled and burst into speech.

"Hold on!" he yelled. "I've got something to say first!" In spite of his rough manner there was about him the noble dignity of a wild animal at bay. He stared at those around him, breathing heavily, as if they were dogs waiting to drag him down.

"Well?" he demanded, "Well? Do I get to talk, or don't I? It 'ud be the best joke of this whole comedy, if a condemned man couldn't speak his mind at the last!"

"You may speak," the Senior Judge told him, in the same unhurried tones with which he had pronounced sentence; "David MacKinnon, as long as you like, and in any manner that you like. There is no limit to that freedom, even for those who have broken the Covenant. Please speak into the recorder."

MacKinnon glanced with distaste at the microphone near his face. The knowledge that any word he spoke would be recorded and analyzed inhibited him. "I don't ask for records," he snapped.

"But we must have them," the judge replied patiently, "in order that others may determine whether, or not, we have dealt with you fairly, and according to the Covenant. Oblige us, please."

"Oh—very well!" He ungraciously conceded the requirement and directed his voice toward the instrument. "There's no sense in me talking at all—but, just the same, I'm going to talk and you're going to listen. . . . You talk about your precious 'Covenant' as if it were something holy. I don't agree to it and I don't accept it. You act as if it had been sent down from Heaven in a burst of light. My grandfathers fought in the Second Revolution—but they fought to abolish superstition . . . not to let sheep-minded fools set up new ones.

"There were men in those days!" He looked contemptuously around him. "What is there left today? Cautious, compromising 'safe' weaklings with water in their veins. You've planned your whole world so carefully that you've planned the fun and zest right out of it. Nobody is ever hungry, nobody ever gets hurt. Your ships can't crack up and your crops can't fail. You even have the weather tamed so it rains politely—after midnight. Why wait till midnight, I don't know . . . you all go to bed at nine o'clock!

"If one of you safe little people *should* have an unpleasant emotion—perish the thought!—you'd trot right over to the nearest psychodynamics clinic and get your soft little minds readjusted. Thank God I never succumbed to that dope habit. I'll keep my own feelings, thanks, no matter how bad they taste.

"You won't even make love without consulting a psychotechnician— Is her mind as flat and insipid as mine? Is there any emotional instability in her family? It's enough to make a man gag. As for fighting over a woman—if any one had the guts to do that, he'd find a proctor at his elbow in two minutes, looking for the most convenient place to paralyze him, and inquiring with sickening humility, 'May I do you a service, sir?' "

The bailiff edged closer to MacKinnon. He turned on him. "Stand back, you. I'm not through yet." He turned and added, "You've told me to choose between the Two Alternatives. Well, it's no hard choice for me. Before I'd submit to treatment, before I'd enter one of your neat little, safe little, pleasant little reorientation homes and let my mind be pried into by a lot of soft-fingered doctors—before I did anything like that, I'd choose a nice, clean death. Oh, no—there is just one choice for me, not two. I take the choice of going to Coventry—and glad of it, too . . . I hope I never hear of the United States again!

"But there is just one thing I want to ask you before I go— Why do you bother to live anyhow? I would think that anyone of you would welcome an end to your silly, futile lives just from sheer boredom. That's all." He turned back to the bailiff. "Come on, you."

"One moment, David MacKinnon." The Senior Judge held up a restraining hand. "We have listened to you. Although custom does not compel it, I am minded to answer some of your statements. Will you listen?"

Unwilling, but less willing to appear loutish in the face of a request so obviously reasonable, the younger man consented.

The judge commenced to speak in gentle, scholarly words appropriate to a lecture room. "David MacKinnon, you have spoken in a fashion that doubtless seems wise to you. Nevertheless, your words were wild, and spoken in haste. I am moved to correct your obvious misstatements of fact. The Covenant is not a superstition, but a simple temporal contract entered into by those same revolutionists for pragmatic reasons. They wished to insure the maximum possible liberty for every person.

"You yourself have enjoyed that liberty. No possible act, nor mode of conduct, was forbidden to you, as long as your action did not damage another. Even an act specifically prohibited by law could not be held against you, unless the state was able to prove that your particular act damaged, or caused evident danger of damage, to a particular individual.

"Even if one should willfully and knowingly damage another —as you have done—the state does not attempt to sit in moral judgment, nor to punish. We have not the wisdom to do that, and the chain of injustices that have always followed such moralistic coercion endanger the liberty of all. Instead, the convicted is given the choice of submitting to psychological readjustment to correct his tendency to wish to damage others, or of having the state withdraw itself from him—of sending him to Coventry.

"You complain that our way of living is dull and unromantic, and imply that we have deprived you of excitement to which you feel entitled. You are free to hold and express your esthetic opinion of our way of living, but you must not expect us to live to suit your tastes. You are free to seek danger and adventure if you wish—there is danger still in experimental laboratories; there is hardship in the mountains of the Moon,

131

and death in the jungles of Venus—but you are not free to expose us to the violence of your nature."

"Why make so much of it?" MacKinnon protested contemptuously. "You talk as if I had committed a murder—I simply punched a man in the nose for offending me outrageously!"

"I agree with your esthetic judgment of that individual," the judge continued calmly, "and am personally rather gratified that you took a punch at him—but your psychometrical tests show that you believe yourself capable of judging morally your fellow citizens and feel justified in personally correcting and punishing their lapses. You are a dangerous individual, David MacKinnon, a danger to all of us, for we can not predict what damage you may do next. From a social standpoint, your delusion makes you as mad as the March Hare.

"You refuse treatment—therefore we withdraw our society from you, we cast you out, we divorce you. To Coventry with you." He turned to the bailiff. "Take him away."

MacKinnon peered out of a forward port of the big transport helicopter with repressed excitement in his heart. There! That must be it—that black band in the distance. The helicopter drew closer, and he became certain that he was seeing the Barrier—the mysterious, impenetrable wall that divided the United States from the reservation known as Coventry.

His guard looked up from the magazine he was reading and followed his gaze. "Nearly there, I see," he said pleasantly. "Well, it won't be long now."

"It can't be any too soon for me!"

The guard looked at him quizzically, but with tolerance. "Pretty anxious to get on with it, eh?"

MacKinnon held his head high. "You've never brought a man to the Gateway who was more anxious to pass through!"

"Mmm—maybe. They all say that, you know. Nobody goes through the Gate against his own will."

"I mean it!"

"They all do. Some of them come back, just the same."

"Say—maybe you can give me some dope as to conditions inside?"

"Sorry," the guard said, shaking his head, "but that is no concern of the United States, nor of any of its employees. You'll know soon enough."

MacKinnon frowned a little. "It seems strange—I tried inquiring, but found no one who would admit that they had any notion about the inside. And yet you say that some come out. Surely some of them must talk. . . ."

"That's simple," smiled the guard, "part of their reorientation is a subconscious compulsion not to discuss their experiences."

132

"That's a pretty scabby trick. Why should the government deliberately conspire to prevent me, and people like me, from knowing what we are going up against?"

"Listen, buddy," the guard answered, with mild exasperation, "you've told the rest of us to go to the devil. You've told us that you could get along without us. You are being given plenty of living room in some of the best land on this continent, and you are being allowed to take with you everything that you own, or your credit could buy. What the deuce else do you expect?"

MacKinnon's face settled in obstinate lines. "What assurance have I that there will be any land left for me?"

"That's your problem. The government sees to it that there is plenty of land for the population. The divvy-up is something you rugged individualists have to settle among yourselves. You've turned down our type of social cooperation; why should you expect the safeguards of our organization?" The guard turned back to his reading and ignored him.

They landed on a small field which lay close under the blank black wall. No gate was apparent, but a guardhouse was located at the side of the field. MacKinnon was the only passenger. While his escort went over to the guardhouse, he descended from the passenger compartment and went around to the freight hold. Two members of the crew were letting down a ramp from the cargo port. When he appeared, one of them eyed him, and said, "Okay, there's your stuff. Help yourself."

He sized up the job, and said, "It's quite a lot, isn't it? I'll need some help. Will you give me a hand with it?"

The crew member addressed paused to light a cigarette before replying, "It's your stuff. If you want it, get it out. We take off in ten minutes." The two walked around him and re-entered the ship.

"Why, you—" MacKinnon shut up and kept the rest of his anger to himself. The surly louts! Gone was the faintest trace of regret at leaving civilization. He'd show them! He could get along without them.

But it was twenty minutes and more before he stood beside his heaped up belongings and watched the ship rise. Fortunately the skipper had not been adamant about the time limit. He turned and commenced loading his steel tortoise. Under the romantic influence of the classic literature of a bygone day he had considered using a string of burros, but had been unable to find a zoo that would sell them to him. It was just as well— he was completely ignorant of the limits, foibles, habits, vices, illnesses, and care of those useful little beasts, and unaware of his own ignorance. Master and servant would have vied in making each other unhappy.

The vehicle he had chosen was not an unreasonable substitute for burros. It was extremely rugged, easy to operate, and almost fool-proof. It drew its power from six square yards of sunpower screens on its low curved roof. These drove a constant-load motor, or, when halted, replenished the storage battery against cloudy weather, or night travel. The bearings were "ever-lasting," and every moving part, other than the caterpillar treads and the controls, were sealed up, secure from inexpert tinkering.

It could maintain a steady six miles per hour on smooth, level pavement. When confronted by hills, or rough terrain, it did not stop, but simply slowed until the task demanded equalled its steady power output.

The steel tortoise gave MacKinnon a feeling of Crusoe-like independence. It did not occur to him his chattel was the end product of the cumulative effort and intelligent co-operation of hundreds of thousands of men, living and dead. He had been used all his life to the unfailing service of much more intricate machinery, and honestly regarded the tortoise as a piece of equipment of the same primitive level as a woodsman's axe, or a hunting knife. His talents had been devoted in the past to literary criticism rather than engineering, but that did not prevent him from believing that his native intelligence and the aid of a few reference books would be all that he would really need to duplicate the tortoise, if necessary.

Metal ores were necessary, he knew, but saw no obstacle in that, his knowledge of the difficulties of prospecting, mining, and metallurgy being as sketchy as his knowledge of burros.

His goods filled every compartment of the compact little freighter. He checked the last item from his inventory and ran a satisfied eye down the list. Any explorer or adventurer of the past might well be pleased with such equipment, he thought. He could imagine showing Jack London his knock-down cabin. See, Jack, he would say, it's proof against any kind of weather —perfectly insulated walls and floor—and can't rust. It's so light that you can set it up in five minutes by yourself, yet it's so strong that you can sleep sound with the biggest grizzly in the world snuffling right outside your door.

And London would scratch his head, and say, Dave, you're a wonder. If I'd had that in the Yukon, it would have been a cinch!

He checked over the list again. Enough concentrated and desiccated food and vitamin concentrates to last six months. That would give him time enough to build hothouses for hydroponics, and get his seeds started. Medical supplies—he did not expect to need those, but foresight was always best. Reference books of all sorts. A light sporting rifle—vintage: last century. His face clouded a little at this. The War Department had positively refused to sell him a portable blaster. When he had claimed the right of common social heritage, they had grudgingly provided him with the plans and specifications, and told him to build his own. Well, he would, the first spare time he got.

Everything else was in order. MacKinnon climbed into the cockpit, grasped the two hand controls, and swung the nose of the tortoise toward the guardhouse. He had been ignored since the ship had landed; he wanted to have the gate opened and to leave.

Several soldiers were gathered around the guardhouse. He picked out a legate by the silver stripe down the side of his kilt and spoke to him. "I'm ready to leave. Will you kindly open the Gate?"

"Okay," the officer answered him, and turned to a soldier who wore the plain grey kilt of a private's field uniform. "Jenkins, tell the power house to dilate—about a number three opening, tell them," he added, sizing up the dimensions of the tortoise.

He turned to MacKinnon. "It is my duty to tell you that you may return to civilization, even now, by agreeing to be hospitalized for your neurosis."

"I have no neurosis!"

"Very well. If you change your mind at any future time, return to the place where you entered. There is an alarm there with which you may signal to the guard that you wish the gate opened."

"I can't imagine needing to know that."

The legate shrugged. "Perhaps not—but we send refugees to quarantine all the time. If I were making the rules, it might be harder to get out again." He was cut off by the ringing of an alarm. The soldiers near them moved smartly away, drawing their blasters from their belts as they ran. The ugly snout of a fixed blaster poked out over the top of the guardhouse and pointed toward the Barrier.

The legate answered the question on MacKinnon's face. "The power house is ready to open up." He waved smartly toward that building, then turned back. "Drive straight through the center of the opening. It takes a lot of power to suspend the stasis; if you touch the edge, we'll have to pick up the pieces."

A tiny, bright dot appeared in the foot of the barrier opposite where they waited. It spread into a half circle across the lampblack nothingness. Now it was large enough for MacKinnon to see the countryside beyond through the arch it had formed. He peered eagerly.

The opening grew until it was twenty feet wide, then stopped. It framed a scene of rugged, barren hills. He took this in, and turned angrily on the legate. "I've been tricked!" he exclaimed. "That's not fit land to support a man."

"Don't be hasty," he told MacKinnon. "There's good land

beyond. Besides—you don't have to enter. But if you are going, go!"

MacKinnon flushed, and pulled back on both hand controls. The treads bit in and the tortoise lumbered away, straight for the Gateway to Coventry.

When he was several yards beyond the Gate, he glanced back. The Barrier loomed behind him, with nothing to show where the opening had been. There was a little sheetmetal shed adjacent to the point where he had passed through. He supposed that it contained the alarm the legate had mentioned, but he was not interested and turned his eyes back to his driving.

Stretching before him, twisting between rocky hills, was a road of sorts. It was not paved and the surface had not been repaired recently, but the grade averaged downhill and the tortoise was able to maintain a respectable speed. He continued down it, not because he fancied it, but because it was the only road which led out of surroundings obviously unsuited to his needs.

The road was untravelled. This suited him; he had no wish to encounter other human beings until he had located desirable land to settle on, and had staked out his claim. But the hills were not devoid of life; several times he caught glimpses of little dark shapes scurrying among the rocks, and occasionally bright, beady eyes stared back into his.

It did not occur to him at first that these timid little animals, streaking for cover at his coming, could replenish his larder—he was simply amused and warmed by their presence. When he did happen to consider that they might be used as food, the thought was at first repugnant to him—the custom of killing for "sport" had ceased to be customary long before his time; and inasmuch as the development of cheap synthetic proteins in the latter half of the preceding century had spelled the economic ruin of the business of breeding animals for slaughter, it is doubtful if he had ever tasted animal tissue in his life.

But once considered, it was logical to act. He expected to live off the country; although he had plenty of food on hand for the immediate future, it would be wise to conserve it by using what the country offered. He suppressed his esthetic distaste and ethical misgivings, and determined to shoot one of the little animals at the first opportunity.

Accordingly, he dug out the rifle, loaded it, and placed it handy. With the usual perversity of the world-as-it-is, no game was evident for the next half hour. He was passing a little shoulder of rocky outcropping when he saw his prey. It peeked at him from behind a small boulder, its sober eyes wary but unperturbed. He stopped the tortoise and took careful aim, resting and steadying the rifle on the side of the cockpit. His quarry accommodated him by hopping out into full view.

136

He pulled the trigger, involuntarily tensing his muscles and squinting his eyes as he did so. Naturally, the shot went high and to the right.

But he was much too busy just then to be aware of it. It seemed that the whole world had exploded. His right shoulder was numb, his mouth stung as if he had been kicked there, and his ears rang in a strange and unpleasant fashion. He was surprised to find the gun still intact in his hands and apparently none the worse for the incident.

He put it down, clambered out of the car, and rushed up to where the small creature had been. There was no sign of it anywhere. He searched the immediate neighborhood, but did not find it. Mystified, he returned to his conveyance, having decided that the rifle was in some way defective, and that he should inspect it carefully before attempting to fire it again.

His recent target watched his actions cautiously from a vantage point yards away, to which it had stampeded at the sound of the shot. It was equally mystified by the startling events, being no more used to firearms than was MacKinnon.

Before he started the tortoise again, MacKinnon had to see to his upper lip, which was swollen and tender and bleeding from a deep scratch. This increased his conviction that the gun was defective. Nowhere in the romantic literature of the nineteenth and twentieth centuries, to which he was addicted, had there been a warning that, when firing a gun heavy enough to drop a man in his tracks, it is well not to hold the right hand in such a manner that the recoil will cause the right thumb and thumb nail to strike the mouth.

He applied an antiseptic and a dressing of sorts, and went on his way, somewhat subdued. The arroyo by which he had entered the hills had widened out, and the hills were greener. He passed around one sharp turn in the road, and found a broad fertile valley spread out before him. It stretched away until it was lost in the warm day's haze.

Much of the valley was cultivated, and he could make out human habitations. He continued toward it with mixed feelings. People meant fewer hardships, but it did not look as if staking out a claim would be as simple as he had hoped. However—Coventry was a big place.

He had reached the point where the road gave onto the floor of the valley, when two men stepped out into his path. They were carrying weapons of some sort at the ready. One of them called out to him:

"Halt!"

MacKinnon did so, and answered him as they came abreast. "What do you want?"

"Customs inspection. Pull over there by the office." He indicated a small building set back a few feet from the road, which MacKinnon had not previously noticed. He looked from it back to the spokesman, and felt a slow, unreasoning heat spread up from his viscera. It rendered his none too stable judgment still more unsound.

"What the deuce are you talking about?" he snapped. "Stand aside and let me pass."

The one who had remained silent raised his weapon and aimed it at MacKinnon's chest. The other grabbed his arm and pulled the weapon out of line. "Don't shoot the dumb fool, Joe," he said testily. "You're always too anxious." Then to MacKinnon, "You're resisting the law. Come on—be quick about it!"

"The law?" MacKinnon gave a bitter laugh and snatched his rifle up from the seat. It never reached his shoulder— the man who had done all the talking fired casually, without apparently taking time to aim. MacKinnon's rifle was smacked from his grasp and flew into the air, landing in the roadside ditch behind the tortoise.

The man who had remained silent followed the flight of the gun with detached interest, and remarked, "Nice shot, Blackie. Never touched him."

"Oh, just luck," the other demurred, but grinned his pleasure at the compliment. "Glad I didn't nick him, though—saves writing out a report." He reassumed an official manner, spoke again to MacKinnon, who had been sitting dumbfounded, rubbing his smarting hands. "Well, tough guy? Do you behave, or do we come up there and get you?"

MacKinnon gave in. He drove the tortoise to the designated spot, and waited sullenly for orders. "Get out and start unloading," he was told.

He obeyed, under compulsion. As he piled his precious possessions on the ground, the one addressed as Blackie separated the things into two piles, while Joe listed them on a printed form. He noticed presently that Joe listed only the items that went into the first pile. He understood this when Blackie told him to reload the tortoise with the items from that pile, and commenced himself to carry goods from the other pile into the building. He started to protest—

Joe punched him in the mouth, coolly and without rancor. MacKinnon went down, but got up again, fighting. He was in such a blind rage that he would have tackled a charging rhino. Joe timed his rush, and clipped him again. This time he could not get up at once.

Blackie stepped over to a washstand in one corner of the office. He came back with a wet towel and chucked it at MacKinnon. "Wipe your face on that, bud, and get back in the buggy. We got to get going."

MacKinnon had time to do a lot of serious thinking as he drove Blackie into town. Beyond a terse answer of "Prize court" to MacKinnon's inquiry as to their destination, Blackie did not converse, nor did MacKinnon press him, anxious as he was to have information. His mouth pained him from repeated punishment, his head ached, and he was no longer tempted to precipitate action by hasty speech.

Evidently Coventry was not quite the frontier anarchy he had expected it to be. There was a government of sorts, apparently, but it resembled nothing that he had ever been used to. He had visualized a land of noble, independent spirits who gave each other wide berth and practised mutual respect. There would be villains, of course, but they would be treated to summary, and probably lethal, justice as quickly as they demonstrated their ugly natures. He had a strong, though subconscious, assumption that virtue is necessarily triumphant.

But having found government, he expected it to follow the general pattern that he had been used to all his life—honest, conscientious, reasonably efficient, and invariably careful of a citizen's rights and liberties. He was aware that government had not always been like that, but he had never experienced it—the idea was as remote and implausible as cannibalism, or chattel slavery.

Had he stopped to think about it, he might have realized that public servants in Coventry would never have been examined psychologically to determine their temperamental fitness for their duties, and, since every inhabitant of Coventry was there—as he was—for violating a basic custom and refusing treatment thereafter, it was a foregone conclusion that most of them would be erratic and arbitrary.

He pinned his hope on the knowledge that they were going to court. All he asked was a chance to tell his story to the judge.

His dependence on judicial procedure may appear inconsistent in view of how recently he had renounced all reliance on organized government, but while he could renounce government verbally, he could not do away with a lifetime of environmental conditioning. He could curse the court that had humiliated him by condemning him to the Two Alternatives, but he expected courts to dispense justice. He could assert his own rugged independence, but he expected persons he encountered to behave as if they were bound by the Covenant —he had met no other sort. He was no more able to discard his past history than he would have been to discard his accustomed body.

But he did not know it yet.

MacKinnon failed to stand up when the judge entered the court room. Court attendants quickly set him right, but not before he had provoked a glare from the bench. The judge's appearance and manner were not reassuring. He was a well-fed man, of ruddy complexion, whose sadistic temper was evident in face and mien. They waited while he dealt drastically with several petty offenders. It seemed to MacKinnon, as he listened, that almost everything was against the law.

Nevertheless, he was relieved when his name was called. He stepped up and undertook at once to tell his story. The judge's gavel cut him short.

"What is this case?" the judge demanded, his face set in grim lines. "Drunk and disorderly, apparently. I shall put a stop to this slackness among the young if it takes the last ounce of strength in my body!" He turned to the clerk. "Any previous offences?"

The clerk whispered in his ear. The judge threw MacKinnon a look of mixed annoyance and suspicion, then told the customs' guard to come forward. Blackie told a clear, straight-forward tale with the ease of a man used to giving testimony. MacKinnon's condition was attributed to resisting an officer in the execution of his duty. He submitted the inventory his colleague had prepared, but failed to mention the large quantity of goods which had been abstracted before the inventory was made.

The judge turned to MacKinnon. "Do you have anything to say for yourself?"

"I certainly have, Doctor," he began eagerly. "There isn't a word of—"

Bang! The gavel cut him short. A court attendant hurried to MacKinnon's side and attempted to explain to him the proper form to use in addressing the court. The explanation confused him. In his experience, "judge" naturally implied a medical man—a psychiatrist skilled in social problems. Nor had he heard of any special speech forms appropriate to a courtroom. But he amended his language as instructed.

"May it please the Honorable Court, this man is lying. He and his companion assaulted and robbed me. I was simply—"

"Smugglers generally think they are being robbed when customs officials catch them," the judge sneered. "Do you deny that you attempted to resist inspection?"

"No, Your Honor, but—"

"That will do. Penalty of fifty per cent is added to the established scale of duty. Pay the clerk."

"But, Your Honor, I can't—"

"Can't you pay it?"

"I haven't any money. I have only my possessions."

"So?" He turned to the clerk. "Condemnation proceedings. Impound his goods. Ten days for vagrancy. The community can't have these immigrant paupers roaming at large, and preying on law-abiding citizens. Next case!"

They hustled him away. It took the sound of a key grating

in a barred door behind him to make him realize his predicament.

"Hi, pal, how's the weather outside?" The detention cell had a prior inmate, a small, well-knit man who looked up from a game of solitaire to address MacKinnon. He sat astraddle a bench on which he had spread his cards, and studied the newcomer with unworried, bright, beady eyes.

"Clear enough outside—but stormy in the courtroom," MacKinnon answered, trying to adopt the same bantering tone and not succeeding very well. His mouth hurt him and spoiled his grin.

The other swung a leg over the bench and approached him with a light, silent step. "Say, pal, you must 'a' caught that in a gear box," he commented, inspecting MacKinnon's mouth. "Does it hurt?"

"Like the devil," MacKinnon admitted.

"We'll have to do something about that." He went to the cell door and rattled it. "Hey! Lefty! The house is on fire! Come arunnin'!"

The guard sauntered down and stood opposite their cell door. "Wha' d'yuh want, Fader?" he said noncommittally.

"My old school chum has been slapped in the face with a wrench, and the pain is inordinate. Here's a chance for you to get right with Heaven by oozing down to the dispensary, snagging a dressing and about five grains of neoanodyne."

The guard's expression was not encouraging. The prisoner looked grieved. "Why, Lefty," he said, "I thought you would jump at a chance to do a little pure charity like that." He waited for a moment, then added, "Tell you what—you do it, and I'll show you how to work that puzzle about 'How old is Ann?' Is it a go?"

"Show me first."

"It would take too long. I'll write it out and give it to you."

When the guard returned, MacKinnon's cellmate dressed his wounds with gentle deftness, talking the while. "They call me Fader Magee. What's your name, pal?"

"David MacKinnon. I'm sorry, but I didn't quite catch your first name."

"Fader. It isn't," he explained with a grin, "the name my mother gave me. It's more a professional tribute to my shy and unobtrusive nature."

MacKinnon looked puzzled. "Professional tribute? What is your profession?"

Magee looked pained. "Why, Dave," he said, "I didn't ask *you* that. However," he went on, "it's probably the same as yours—self-preservation."

Magee was a sympathetic listener, and MacKinnon welcomed the chance to tell someone about his troubles. He related the story of how he had decided to enter Coventry

141

rather than submit to the sentence of the court, and how he had hardly arrived when he was hijacked and hauled into court. Magee nodded. "I'm not surprised," he observed. "A man has to have larceny in his heart, or he wouldn't be a customs guard."

"But what happens to my belongings?"

"They auction them off to pay the duty."

"I wonder how much there will be left for me?"

Magee stared at him. "Left over? There won't be anything left over. You'll probably have to pay a deficiency judgment."

"Huh? What's that?"

"It's a device whereby the condemned pays for the execution," Magee explained succinctly, if somewhat obscurely. "What it means to you is that when your ten days is up, you'll still be in debt to the court. Then it's the chain gang for you, my lad—you'll work it off at a dollar a day."

"Fader—you're kidding me."

"Wait and see. You've got a lot to learn, Dave."

Coventry was an even more complex place than MacKinnon had gathered up to this time. Magee explained to him that there were actually three sovereign, independent jurisdictions. The jail where they were prisoners lay in the so-called New America. It had the forms of democratic government, but the treatment he had already received was a fair sample of the fashion in which it was administered.

"This place is heaven itself compared with the Free State," Magee maintained. "I've been there—" The Free State was an absolute dictatorship; the head man of the ruling clique was designated the "Liberator." Their watchwords were Duty and Obedience; an arbitrary discipline was enforced with a severity that left no room for any freedom of opinion. Governmental theory was vaguely derived from the old functionalist doctrines. The state was thought of as a single organism with a single head, a single brain, and a single purpose. Anything not compulsory was forbidden. "Honest so help me," claimed Magee, "you can't go to bed in that place without finding one of their damned secret police between the sheets."

"But at that," he continued, "it's an easier place to live than with the Angels."

"The Angels?"

"Sure. We still got 'em. Must have been two or three thousand die-hards that chose to go to Coventry after the Revolution—you know that. There's still a colony up in the hills to the north, complete with Prophet Incarnate and the works. They aren't bad hombres, but they'll pray you into heaven even if it kills you."

All three states had one curious characteristic in common —each one claimed to be the only legal government of the entire United States, and each looked forward to some future

142

day when they would reclaim the "unredeemed" portion; i. e., outside Coventry. To the Angels, this was an event which would occur when the First Prophet returned to earth to lead them again. In New America it was hardly more than a convenient campaign plank, to be forgotten after each election. But in the Free State it was a fixed policy.

Pursuant to this purpose there had been a whole series of wars between the Free State and New America. The Liberator held, quite logically, that New America was an unredeemed section, and that it was necessary to bring it under the rule of the Free State before the advantages of their culture could be extended to the outside.

Magee's words demolished MacKinnon's dream of finding an anarchistic utopia within the barrier, but he could not let his fond illusion die without a protest. "But see here, Fader," he persisted, "isn't there some place where a man can live quietly by himself without all this insufferable interference?"

"No—" considered Fader, "no . . . not unless you took to the hills and hid. Then you 'ud be all right, as long as you steered clear of the Angels. But it would be pretty slim pickin's, living off the country. Ever tried it?"

"No . . . not exactly—but I've read all the classics: Zane Grey, and Emerson Hough, and so forth."

"Well . . . maybe you could do it. But if you really want to go off and be a hermit, you 'ud do better to try it on the Outside, where there aren't so many objections to it."

"No"—MacKinnon's backbone stiffened at once—"no, I'll never do that. I'll never submit to psychological reorientation just to have a chance to be let alone. If I could go back to where I was before a couple of months ago, before I was arrested, it might be all right to go off to the Rockies, or look up an abandoned farm somewhere . . . But with that diagnosis staring me in the face . . . after being told I wasn't fit for human society until I had had my emotions re-tailored to fit a cautious little pattern, I couldn't face it. Not if it meant going to a sanatarium—"

"I see," agreed Fader, nodding, "you want to go to Coventry, but you don't want the Barrier to shut you off from the rest of the world."

"No, that's not quite fair . . . Well, maybe, in a way. Say, you don't think I'm not fit to associate with, do you?"

"You look all right to me," Magee reassured him, with a grin, "but I'm in Coventry too, remember. Maybe I'm no judge."

"You don't talk as if you liked it much. Why are you here?"

Magee held up a gently admonishing finger. "Tut! Tut! That is the one question you must never ask a man here.

143

You must assume that he came here because he knew how swell everything is here."

"Still . . . you don't seem to like it."

"I didn't say I didn't like it. I do like it; it has flavor. Its little incongruities are a source of innocent merriment. And anytime they turn on the heat I can always go back through the Gate and rest up for a while in a nice quiet hospital, until things quiet down."

MacKinnon was puzzled again. "Turn on the heat? Do they supply too hot weather here?"

"Huh? Oh, I didn't mean weather control—there isn't any of that here, except what leaks over from outside. I was just using an old figure of speech."

"What does it mean?"

Magee smiled to himself. "You'll find out."

After supper—bread, stew in a metal dish, a small apple —Magee introduced MacKinnon to the mysteries of cribbage. Fortunately, MacKinnon had no cash to lose. Presently Magee put the cards down without shuffling them. "Dave," he said, "are you enjoying the hospitality offered by this institution?"

"Hardly— Why?"

"I suggest that we check out."

"A good idea, but how?"

"That's what I've been thinking about. Do you suppose you could take another poke on that battered phiz of yours, in a good cause?"

MacKinnon cautiously fingered his face. "I suppose so— if necessary. It can't do me much more harm, anyhow."

"That's mother's little man! Now listen—this guard, Lefty, in addition to being kind o' unbright, is sensitive about his appearance. When they turn out the lights, you—"

"Let me out of here! Let me out of here!" MacKinnon beat on the bars and screamed. No answer came. He renewed the racket, his voice an hysterical falsetto. Lefty arrived to investigate, grumbling.

"What the hell's eating on you?" he demanded, peering through the bars.

MacKinnon changed to tearful petition. "Oh, Lefty, please let me out of here. Please! I can't stand the dark. It's dark in here—please don't leave me alone." He flung himself, sobbing, on the bars.

The guard cursed to himself. "Another slugnutty. Listen, you—shut up, and go to sleep, or I'll come in there, and give you something to yelp for!" He started to leave.

MacKinnon changed instantly to the vindictive, unpredictable anger of the irresponsible. "You big ugly baboon! You rat-faced idiot! Where'd you get that nose?"

Lefty turned back, fury in his face. He started to speak.

MacKinnon cut him short. "Yah! Yah! Yah!" he gloated, like a nasty little boy, "Lefty's mother was scared by a wart-hog—"

The guard swung at the spot where MacKinnon's face was pressed between the bars of the door. MacKinnon ducked and grabbed simultaneously. Off balance at meeting no resistance, the guard rocked forward, thrusting his forearm between the bars. MacKinnon's fingers slid along his arm, and got a firm purchase on Lefty's wrist.

He threw himself backwards, dragging the guard with him, until Lefty was jammed up against the outside of the barred door, with one arm inside, to the wrist of which MacKinnon clung as if welded.

The yell which formed in Lefty's throat miscarried; Magee had already acted. Out of the darkness, silent as death, his slim hands had snaked between the bars and imbedded themselves in the guard's fleshy neck. Lefty heaved, and almost broke free, but MacKinnon threw his weight to the right and twisted the arm he gripped in an agonizing, bone-breaking leverage.

It seemed to MacKinnon that they remained thus, like some grotesque game of statues, for an endless period. His pulse pounded in his ears until he feared that it must be heard by others, and bring rescue to Lefty. Magee spoke at last:

"That's enough," he whispered. "Go through his pockets."

He made an awkward job of it, for his hands were numb and trembling from the strain, and it was anything but convenient to work between the bars. But the keys were there, in the last pocket he tried. He passed them to Magee, who let the guard slip to the floor, and accepted them.

Magee made a quick job of it. The door swung open with a distressing creak. Dave stepped over Lefty's body, but Magee kneeled down, unhooked a truncheon from the guard's belt, and cracked him behind the ear with it. MacKinnon paused.

"Did you kill him?" he asked.

"Cripes, no," Magee answered softly, "Lefty is a friend of mine. Let's go."

They hurried down the dimly lighted passageway between cells toward the door leading to the administrative offices—their only outlet. Lefty had carelessly left it ajar, and light shone through the crack, but as they silently approached it, they heard ponderous footsteps from the far side. Dave looked hurriedly for cover, but the best he could manage was to slink back into the corner formed by the cell block and the wall. He glanced around for Magee, but he had disappeared.

The door swung open; a man stepped through, paused, and looked around. MacKinnon saw that he was carrying a black-light, and wearing its complement—rectifying spectacles. He

145

realized then that the darkness gave him no cover. The black-light swung his way; he tensed to spring—

He heard a dull *"clunk!"* The guard sighed, swayed gently, then collapsed into a loose pile. Magee stood over him, poised on the balls of his feet, and surveyed his work, while caressing the business end of the truncheon with the cupped fingers of his left hand.

"That will do," he decided. "Shall we go, Dave?"

He eased through the door without waiting for an answer; MacKinnon was close behind him. The lighted corridor led away to the right and ended in a large double door to the street. On the left wall, near the street door, a smaller office door stood open.

Magee drew MacKinnon to him. "It's a cinch," he whispered. "There'll be nobody in there now but the desk sergeant. We get past him, then out that door, and into the ozone—" He motioned Dave to keep behind him, and crept silently up to the office door. After drawing a small mirror from a pocket in his belt, he lay down on the floor, placed his head near the door frame, and cautiously extended the tiny mirror an inch or two past the edge.

Apparently he was satisfied with the reconnaissance the improvised periscope afforded, for he drew himself back onto his knees and turned his head so that MacKinnon could see the words shaped by his silent lips. "It's all right," he breathed, "there is only—"

Two hundred pounds of uniformed nemesis landed on his shoulders. A clanging alarm sounded through the corridor. Magee went down fighting, but he was outclassed and caught off guard. He jerked his head free and shouted, "Run for it, kid!"

MacKinnon could hear running feet somewhere, but could see nothing but the struggling figures before him. He shook his head and shoulders like a dazed animal, then kicked the larger of the two contestants in the face. The man screamed and let go his hold. MacKinnon grasped his small companion by the scruff of the neck and hauled him roughly to his feet.

Magee's eyes were still merry. "Well played, my lad," he commended in clipped syllables, as they burst out the street door, "—if hardly cricket! Where did you learn *La Savate?*"

MacKinnon had not time to answer, being fully occupied in keeping up with Magee's weaving, deceptively rapid progress. They ducked across the street, down an alley, and between two buildings.

The succeeding minutes, or hours, were confusion to MacKinnon. He remembered afterwards crawling along a roof top and letting himself down to crouch in the blackness of an interior court, but he could not remember how they had gotten on the roof. He also recalled spending an interminable period alone, compressed inside a most unsavory refuse bin, and his terror when footsteps approached the bin and a light flashed through a crack.

A crash and the sound of footsteps in flight immediately thereafter led him to guess that Fader had drawn the pursuit away from him. But when Fader did return, and open the top of the bin, MacKinnon almost throttled him before identification was established.

When the active pursuit had been shaken off, Magee guided him across town, showing a sophisticated knowledge of back ways and shortcuts, and a genius for taking full advantage of cover. They reached the outskirts of the town in a dilapidated quarter, far from the civic center. Magee stopped. "I guess this is the end of the line, kid," he told Dave. "If you follow this street, you'll come to open country shortly. That's what you wanted, wasn't it?"

"I suppose so," MacKinnon replied uneasily, and peered down the street. Then he turned back to speak again to Magee.

But Magee was gone. He had faded away into the shadows. There was neither sight nor sound of him.

MacKinnon started in the suggested direction with a heavy heart. There was no possible reason to expect Magee to stay with him; the service Dave had done him with a lucky kick had been repaid with interest—yet he had lost the only friendly companionship he had found in a strange place. He felt lonely and depressed.

He continued along, keeping to the shadows, and watching carefully for shapes that might be patrolmen. He had gone a few hundred yards, and was beginning to worry about how far it might be to open countryside, when he was startled into gooseflesh by a hiss from a dark doorway.

He did his best to repress the panic that beset him, and was telling himself that policemen never hiss, when a shadow detached itself from the blackness and touched him on the arm.

"Dave," it said softly.

MacKinnon felt a childlike sense of relief and wellbeing. "Fader!"

"I changed my mind, Dave. The gendarmes would have you in tow before morning. You don't know the ropes. . . . so I came back."

Dave was both pleased and crestfallen. "Hell's bells, Fader," he protested, "you shouldn't worry about me. I'll get along."

Magee shook him roughly by the arm. "Don't be a chump. Green as you are, you'd start to holler about your civil rights, or something, and get clipped in the mouth again.

"Now see here," he went on, "I'm going to take you to some friends of mine who will hide you until you're smartened up to the tricks around here. But they're on the wrong

147

side of the law, see? You'll have to be all three of the three sacred monkeys—see no evil, hear no evil, tell no evil. Think you can do it?"

"Yes, but—"

"No 'buts' about it. Come along!"

The entrance was in the rear of an old warehouse. Steps led down into a little sunken pit. From this open areaway— foul with accumulated refuse—a door let into the back wall of the building. Magee tapped lightly but systematically, waited and listened. Presently he whispered, "Pssst! It's the Fader."

The door opened quickly, and Magee was encircled by two great, fat arms. He was lifted off his feet, while the owner of those arms planted a resounding buss on his cheek. "Fader!" she exclaimed, "are you all right, lad? We've missed you."

"Now that's a proper welcome, Mother," he answered, when he was back on his own feet, "but I want you to meet a friend of mine. Mother Johnston, this is David MacKinnon."

"May I do you a service?" David acknowledged, with automatic formality, but Mother Johnston's eyes tightened with instant suspicion.

"Is he stooled?" she snapped.

"No, Mother, he's a new immigrant—but I vouch for him. He's on the dodge, and I've brought him here to cool."

She softened a little under his sweetly persuasive tones. "Well—"

Magee pinched her cheek. "That's a good girl! When are you going to marry me?"

She slapped his hand away. "Even if I were forty years younger, I'd not marry such a scamp as you! Come along then," she continued to MacKinnon, "as long as you're a friend of the Fader—though it's no credit to you!" She waddled quickly ahead of them, down a flight of stairs, while calling out for someone to open the door at its foot.

The room was poorly lighted and was furnished principally with a long table and some chairs, at which an odd dozen people were seated, drinking and talking. It reminded MacKinnon of prints he had seen of old English pubs in the days before the Collapse.

Magee was greeted with a babble of boisterous welcome. "Fader!"—"It's the kid himself!"—"How d'ja do it this time, Fader? Crawl down the drains?"—"Set 'em up, Mother—the Fader's back!"

He accepted the ovation with a wave of his hand and a shout of inclusive greeting, then turned to MacKinnon. "Folks," he said, his voice cutting through the confusion, "I want you to know Dave—the best pal that ever kicked a jailer at the right moment. If it hadn't been for Dave, I wouldn't be here."

Dave found himself seated between two others at the table and a stein of beer thrust into his hand by a not uncomely

148

young woman. He started to thank her, but she had hurried off to help Mother Johnston take care of the sudden influx of orders. Seated opposite him was a rather surly young man who had taken little part in the greeting to Magee. He looked Mac-Kinnon over with a face expressionless except for a recurrent tic which caused his right eye to wink spasmodically every few seconds.

"What's your line?" he demanded.

"Leave him alone, Alec," Magee cut in swiftly, but in a friendly tone. "He's just arrived inside; I told you that. But he's all right," he continued, raising his voice to include the others present, "he's been here less than twenty-four hours, but he's broken jail, beat up two customs busies, and sassed old Judge Fleishacker right to his face. How's that for a busy day?"

Dave was the center of approving interest, but the party with the tic persisted. "That's all very well, but I asked him a fair question: What's his line? If it's the same as mine, I won't stand for it—it's too crowded now."

"That cheap racket you're in is always crowded, but he's not in it. Forget about his line."

"Why don't he answer for himself," Alec countered suspiciously. He half stood up. "I don't believe he's stooled—"

It appeared that Magee was cleaning his nails with the point of a slender knife. "Put your nose back in your glass, Alec," he remarked in a conversational tone, without looking up, "—or must I cut it off and put it there?"

The other fingered something nervously in his hand. Magee seemed not to notice it, but nevertheless told him, "If you think you can use a vibrator on me faster than I use steel, go ahead—it will be an interesting experiment."

The man facing him stood uncertainly for a moment longer, his tic working incessantly. Mother Johnston came up behind him and pushed him down by the shoulders, saying, "Boys! Boys! Is that any way to behave?—and in front of a guest, too! Fader, put that toadsticker away—I'm ashamed of you."

The knife was gone from his hands. "You're right as always, Mother," he grinned. "Ask Molly to fill up my glass again."

An old chap sitting on MacKinnon's right had followed these events with alcoholic uncertainty, but he seemed to have gathered something of the gist of it, for now he fixed Dave with serum-filled eye, and enquired, "Boy, are you stooled to the rogue?" His sweetly sour breath reached MacKinnon as the old man leaned toward him and emphasized his question with a trembling, joint-swollen finger.

Dave looked to Magee for advice and enlightenment. Magee answered for him. "No, he's not—Mother Johnston knew that when she let him in. He's here for sanctuary—as our customs provide!"

An uneasy stir ran around the room. Molly paused in her serving and listened openly. But the old man seemed satisfied. "True . . . true enough," he agreed, and took another pull at his drink, "sanctuary may be given when needed, if—" His words were lost in a mumble.

The nervous tension slackened. Most of those present were subconsciously glad to follow the lead of the old man, and excuse the intrusion on the score of necessity. Magee turned back to Dave. "I thought that what you didn't know couldn't hurt you—or us—but the matter has been opened."

"But what did he mean?"

"Gramps asked you if you had been stooled to the rogue— whether or not you were a member of the ancient and honorable fraternity of thieves, cutthroats, and pickpockets!"

Magee stared into Dave's face with a look of sardonic amusement. Dave looked uncertainly from Magee to the others, saw them exchange glances, and wondered what answer was expected of him. Alec broke the pause. "Well," he sneered, "what are you waiting for? Go ahead and put the question to him—or are the great Fader's friends free to use this club without so much as a by-your-leave?"

"I thought I told you to quiet down, Alec," the Fader replied evenly. "Besides—you're skipping a requirement. All the comrades present must first decide whether or not to put the question at all."

A quiet little man with a chronic worried look in his eyes answered him. "I don't think that quite applies, Fader. If he had come himself, or fallen into our hands—in that case, yes. But you brought him here. I think I speak for all when I say he should answer the question. Unless someone objects, I will ask him myself." He allowed an interval to pass. No one spoke up. "Very well then . . . Dave, you have seen too much and heard too much. Will you leave us now—or will you stay and take the oath of our guild? I must warn you that once stooled you are stooled for life—and there is but one punishment for betraying the rogue."

He drew his thumb across his throat in an age-old deadly gesture. Gramps made an appropriate sound effect by sucking air wetly through his teeth, and chuckled.

Dave looked around. Magee's face gave him no help. "What is it that I have to swear to?" he temporized.

The parley was brought to an abrupt ending by the sound of pounding outside. There was a shout, muffled by two closed doors and a stairway, of "Open up down there!" Magee got lightly to his feet and beckoned to Dave.

"That's for us, kid," he said. "Come along."

He stepped over to a ponderous, old-fashioned radio-phonograph which stood against the wall, reached under it, fiddled for a moment, then swung out one side panel of it. Dave saw that the mechanism had been cunningly rearranged in such a fashion that a man could squeeze inside it. Magee urged him into it, slammed the panel closed, and left him.

His face was pressed up close to the slotted grill which was intended to cover the sound box. Molly had cleared off the two extra glasses from the table, and was dumping one drink so that it spread along the table top and erased the rings their glasses had made.

MacKinnon saw the Fader slide under the table, and reach up. Then he was gone. Apparently he had, in some fashion, attached himself to the underside of the table.

Mother Johnston made a great-to-do of opening up. The lower door she opened at once, with much noise. Then she clumped slowly up the steps, pausing, wheezing, and complaining aloud. He heard her unlock the outer door.

"A fine time to be waking honest people up!" she protested. "It's hard enough to get the work done and make both ends meet, without dropping what I'm doing every five minutes, and—"

"Enough of that, old girl," a man's voice answered, "just get along downstairs. We have business with you."

"What sort of business?" she demanded.

"It might be selling liquor without a license, but it's not —this time."

"I don't—this is a private club. The members own the liquor; I simply serve it to them."

"That's as may be. It's those members I want to talk to. Get out of the way now, and be spry about it."

They come pushing into the room with Mother Johnston, still voluble, carried along in by the van. The speaker was a sergeant of police; he was accompanied by a patrolman. Following them were two other uniformed men, but they were soldiers. MacKinnon judged by the markings on their kilts that they were corporal and private—provided the insignia in New America were similar to those used by the United States Army.

The sergeant paid no attention to Mother Johnston. "All right, you men," he called out, "line up!"

They did so, ungraciously but promptly. Molly and Mother Johnston watched them, and moved closer to each other. The police sergeant called out, "All right, corporal—take charge!"

The boy who washed up in the kitchen had been staring round-eyed. He dropped a glass. It bounced around on the hard floor, giving out bell-like sounds in the silence.

The man who had questioned Dave spoke up. "What's all this?"

The sergeant answered with a pleased grin. "Conscription—that's what it is. You are all enlisted in the army for the duration."

151

"Press gang!" It was an involuntary gasp that came from no particular source.

The corporal stepped briskly forward. "Form a column of twos," he directed. But the little man with the worried eyes was not done.

"I don't understand this," he objected. "We signed an armistice with the Free State three weeks ago."

"That's not your worry," countered the sergeant, "nor mine. We are picking up every able-bodied man not in essential industry. Come along."

"Then you can't take me."

"Why not?"

He held up the stump of a missing hand. The sergeant glanced from it to the corporal, who nodded grudgingly, and said, "Okay—but report to the office in the morning, and register."

He started to march them out when Alec broke ranks and backed up to the wall, screaming, "You can't do this to me! I won't go!" His deadly little vibrator was exposed in his hand, and the right side of his face was drawn up in a spastic wink that left his teeth bare.

"Get him, Steeves," ordered the corporal. The private stepped forward, but stopped when Alec brandished the vibrator at him. He had no desire to have a vibroblade between his ribs, and there was no doubt as to the uncontrolled dangerousness of his hysterical opponent.

The corporal, looking phlegmatic, almost bored, levelled a small tube at a spot on the wall over Alec's head. Dave heard a soft *pop!*, and a thin tinkle. Alec stood motionless for a few seconds, his face even more strained, as if he were exerting the limit of his will against some unseen force, then slid quietly to the floor. The tonic spasm in his face relaxed, and his features smoothed into those of a tired and petulant, and very bewildered, little boy.

"Two of you birds carry him," directed the corporal. "Let's get going."

The sergeant was the last to leave. He turned at the door and spoke to Mother Johnston. "Have you seen the Fader lately?"

"The Fader?" She seemed puzzled. "Why, he's in jail."

"Ah, yes . . . so he is." He went out.

Magee refused the drink that Mother Johnston offered him. Dave was surprised to see that he appeared worried for the first time. "I don't understand it," Magee muttered, half to himself, then addressed the one-handed man. "Ed—bring me up to date."

"Not much news since they tagged you, Fader. The armistice

152

was before that. I thought from the papers that things were going to be straightened out for once."

"So did I. But the government must expect war if they are going in for general conscription." He stood up. "I've got to have more data. Al!" The kitchen boy stuck his head into the room.

"What 'cha want, Fader?"

"Go out and make palaver with five or six of the beggars. Look up their 'king.' You know where he makes his pitch?"

"Sure—over by the auditorium."

"Find out what's stirring, but don't let them know I sent you."

"Right, Fader. It's in the bag." The boy swaggered out.

"Molly."

"Yes, Fader?"

"Will you go out, and do the same thing with some of the business girls? I want to know what they hear from their customers." She nodded agreement. He went on, "Better look up that little redhead that has her beat up on Union Square. She can get secrets out of a dead man. Here—" He pulled a wad of bills out of his pocket and handed her several. "You better take this grease . . . You might have to pay off a cop to get back out of the district."

Magee was not disposed to talk, and insisted that Dave get some sleep. He was easily persuaded, not having slept since he entered Coventry. That seemed like a lifetime past; he was exhausted. Mother Johnston fixed him a shakedown in a dark, stuffy room on the same underground level. It had none of the hygienic comforts to which he was accustomed—air-conditioning, restful music, hydraulic mattress, nor soundproofing—and he missed his usual relaxing soak and auto-massage, but he was too tired to care. He slept in clothing and under covers for the first time in his life.

He woke up with a headache, a taste in his mouth like tired sin, and a sense of impending disaster. At first he could not remember where he was—he thought he was still in detention Outside. His surroundings were inexplicably sordid; he was about to ring for the attendant and complain, when his memory pieced in the events of the day before. Then he got up and discovered that his bones and muscles were painfully sore, and—which was worse—that he was, by his standards, filthy dirty. He itched.

He entered the common room, and found Magee sitting at the table. He greeted Dave. "Hi, kid. I was about to wake you. You've slept almost all day. We've got a lot to talk about."

"Okay—shortly. Where's the 'fresher?"

"Over there."

It was not Dave's idea of a refreshing chamber, but he managed to take a sketchy shower in spite of the slimy floor.

153

Then he discovered that there was no air blast installed, and he was forced to dry himself unsatisfactorily with his handkerchief. He had no choice in clothes. He must put back on the ones he had taken off, or go naked. He recalled that he had seen no nudity anywhere in Coventry, even at sports—a difference in customs, no doubt.

He put his clothes back on, though his skin crawled at the touch of the once-used linen.

But Mother Johnston had thrown together an appetizing breakfast for him. He let coffee restore his courage as Magee talked. It was, according to Fader, a serious situation. New America and the Free State had compromised their differences and had formed an alliance. They quite seriously proposed to break out of Coventry and attack the United States.

MacKinnon looked up at this. "That's ridiculous, isn't it? They would be outnumbered enormously. Besides, how about the Barrier?"

"I don't know—yet. But they have some reason to think that they can break through the Barrier. . . . and there are rumors that whatever it is can be used as a weapon, too, so that a small army might be able to whip the whole United States."

MacKinnon looked puzzled. "Well," he observed, "I haven't any opinion of a weapon I know nothing about, but as to the Barrier. . . . I'm not a mathematical physicist, but I was always told that it was theoretically impossible to break the Barrier—that it was just a nothingness that there was no way to touch. Of course, you can fly over it, but even that is supposed to be deadly to life."

"Suppose they had found some way to shield from the effects of the Barrier's field?" suggested Magee. "Anyhow, that's not the point, for us. The point is: they've made this combine; the Free State supplies the techniques and most of the officers; and New America, with its bigger population, supplies most of the men. And that means to us that we don't dare show our faces any place, or we are in the army before you can blink.

"Which brings me to what I was going to suggest. I'm going to duck out of here as soon as it gets dark, and light out for the Gateway, before they send somebody after me who is bright enough to look under a table. I thought maybe you might want to come along."

"Back to the psychologists?" MacKinnon was honestly aghast.

"Sure—why not? What have you got to lose? This whole damn place is going to be just like the Free State in a couple of days—and a Joe of your temperament would be in hot water all the time. What's so bad about a nice, quiet hospital room as a place to hide out until things quiet down? You don't have to pay any attention to the psych boys—just make animal noises at 'em every time one sticks his nose into your room, until they get discouraged."

Dave shook his head. "No," he said slowly, "I can't do that."

"Then what will you do?"

"I don't know yet. Take to the hills I guess. Go live with the Angels if it comes to a showdown. I wouldn't mind them praying for my soul as long as they left my mind alone."

They were each silent for a while. Magee was mildly annoyed at MacKinnon's bullheaded stubbornness in the face of what seemed to him a reasonable offer. Dave continued busily to stow away grilled ham, while considering his position. He cut off another bite. "My, but this is good," he remarked, to break the awkward silence, "I don't know when I've had anything taste so good—Say!"

"What?" inquired Magee, looking up, and seeing the concern written on MacKinnon's face.

"This ham—is it synthetic, or is it *real meat?*"

"Why, it's real. What about it?"

Dave did not answer. He managed to reach the refreshing room before that which he had eaten departed from him.

Before he left, Magee gave Dave some money with which he could have purchased for him things that he would need in order to take to the hills. MacKinnon protested, but the Fader cut him short. "Quit being a damn fool, Dave. I can't use New American money on the Outside, and you can't stay alive in the hills without proper equipment. You lie doggo here for a few days while Al, or Molly, picks up what you need, and you'll stand a chance—unless you'll change your mind and come with me?"

Dave shook his head at this, and accepted the money.

It was lonely after Magee left. Mother Johnston and Dave were alone in the club, and the empty chairs reminded him depressingly of the men who had been impressed. He wished that Gramps or the one-handed man would show up. Even Alec, with his nasty temper, would have been company—he wondered if Alec had been punished for resisting the draft.

Mother Johnston inveigled him into playing checkers in an attempt to relieve his evident low spirits. He felt obligated to agree to her gentle conspiracy, but his mind wandered. It was all very well for the Senior Judge to tell him to seek adventure in interplanetary exploration, but only engineers and technicians were eligible for such billets. Perhaps he should have gone in for science, or engineering, instead of literature; then he might now be on Venus, contending against the forces of nature in high adventure, instead of hiding from uniformed bullies. It wasn't fair. No—he must not kid himself; there was no room for an expert in literary history in the raw frontier of the planets; that was not human injustice, that was a hard fact of nature, and he might as well face it.

He thought bitterly of the man whose nose he had broken, and thereby landed himself in Coventry. Maybe he was an "upholstered parasite" after all—but the recollection of the phrase brought back the same unreasoning anger that had gotten him into trouble. He was *glad* that he had socked that so-and-so! What right had he to go around sneering and calling people things like that?

He found himself thinking in the same vindictive spirit of his father, although he would have been at loss to explain the connection. The connection was not superficially evident, for his father would never have stooped to name-calling. Instead, he would have offered the sweetest of smiles, and quoted something nauseating in the way of sweetness-and-light. Dave's father was one of the nastiest little tyrants that ever dominated a household under the guise of loving-kindness. He was of the more-in-sorrow-than-in-anger, this-hurts-me-more-than-it-does-you school, and all his life had invariably been able to find an altruistic rationalization for always having his own way. Convinced of his own infallible righteousness, he had never valued his son's point of view on anything, but had dominated him in everything—always from the highest moralistic motives.

He had had two main bad effects on his son: the boy's natural independence, crushed at home, rebelled blindly at every sort of discipline, authority, or criticism which he encountered elsewhere and subconsciously identified with the not-to-be-criticized paternal authority. Secondly, through years of association Dave imitated his father's most dangerous social vice—that of passing unself-critical moral judgments on the actions of others.

When Dave was arrested for breaking a basic custom; to wit, atavistic violence; his father washed his hands of him with the statement that he had tried his best to "make a man of him," and could not be blamed for his son's failure to profit by his instruction.

A faint knock caused them to put away the checker board in a hurry. Mother Johnston paused before answering. "That's not our knock," she considered, "but it's not loud enough to be the nosies. Be ready to hide."

MacKinnon waited by the fox hole where he had hidden the night before, while Mother Johnston went to investigate. He heard her unbar and unlock the upper door, then she called out to him in a low but urgent voice, "Dave! Come here, Dave—hurry!"

It was Fader, unconscious, with his own bloody trail behind him.

Mother Johnston was attempting to pick up the limp form. MacKinnon crowded in, and between the two of them they

156

managed to get him downstairs and to lay him on the long table. He came to for a moment as they straightened his limbs. "Hi, Dave," he whispered, managing to achieve the ghost of his debonair grin. "Somebody trumped my ace."

"You keep quiet!" Mother Johnston snapped at him, then in a lower voice to Dave, "Oh, the poor darling—Dave, we must get him to the Doctor."

"Can't . . . do . . . that," muttered the Fader. "Got . . . to get to the . . . Gate—" His voice trailed off. Mother Johnston's fingers had been busy all the while, as if activated by some separate intelligence. A small pair of scissors, drawn from some hiding place about her large person, clipped away at his clothing, exposing the superficial extent of the damage. She examined the trauma critically.

"This is no job for me," she decided, "and he must sleep while we move him. Dave, get that hypodermic kit out of the medicine chest in the 'fresher."

"No, Mother!" It was Magee, his voice strong and vibrant. "Get me a pepper pill," he went on. "There's—"

"But Fader—"

He cut her short. "I've got to get to the Doctor all right, but how the devil will I get there if I don't walk?"

"We would carry you."

"Thanks, Mother," he told her, his voice softened, "I know you would—but the police would be curious. Get me that pill."

Dave followed her into the 'fresher, and questioned her while she rummaged through the medicine chest. "Why don't we just send for a doctor?"

"There is only one doctor we can trust, and that's *the* Doctor. Besides, none of the others are worth the powder to blast them."

Magee was out again when they came back into the room. Mother Johnston slapped his face until he came around, blinking and cursing. Then she fed him the pill.

The powerful stimulant, improbable offspring of common coal tar, took hold almost at once. To all surface appearance Magee was a well man. He sat up and tried his own pulse, searching it out in his left wrist with steady, sensitive fingers. "Regular as a metronome," he announced, "the old ticker can stand that dosage all right."

He waited while Mother Johnston applied sterile packs to his wounds, then said goodbye. MacKinnon looked at Mother Johnston. She nodded.

"I'm going with you," he told the Fader.

"What for? It will just double the risk."

"You're in no fit shape to travel alone—stimulant, or no stimulant."

"Nuts. *I'd* have to look after *you*."

"I'm going with you."

Magee shrugged his shoulders and capitulated.

Mother Johnston wiped her perspiring face, kissed both of them.

Until they were well out of town their progress reminded MacKinnon of their nightmare flight of the previous evening. Thereafter they continued to the north-northwest by a highway which ran toward the foothills, and they left the highway only when necessary to avoid the sparse traffic. Once they were almost surprised by a police patrol car, equipped with black-light and almost invisible, but the Fader sensed it in time and they crouched behind a low wall which separated the adjacent field from the road.

Dave inquired how he had known the patrol was near. Magee chuckled. "Damned if I know," he said, "but I believe I could smell a cop staked out in a herd of goats."

The Fader talked less and less as the night progressed. His usually untroubled countenance became lined and old as the effect of the drug wore off. It seemed to Dave as if this unaccustomed expression gave him a clearer insight into the man's character—that the mask of pain was his true face rather than the unworried features Magee habitually showed the world. He wondered for the ninth time what the Fader had done to cause a court to adjudge him socially insane.

This question was uppermost in his mind with respect to every person he met in Coventry. The answer was obvious in most cases; their types of instability were gross and showed up at once. Mother Johnston had been an enigma until she had explained it herself. She had followed her husband into Coventry. Now that she was a widow, she preferred to remain with the friends she knew and the customs and conditions she was adjusted to, rather than change for another and possibly less pleasing environment.

Magee sat down beside the road. "It's no use, kid," he admitted, "I can't make it."

"The hell we can't. I'll carry you."

Magee grinned faintly. "No, I mean it." Dave persisted. "How much farther is it?"

"Matter of two or three miles, maybe."

"Climb aboard." He took Magee pickaback and started on. The first few hundred yards were not too difficult; Magee was forty pounds lighter than Dave. After that the strain of the additional load began to tell. His arms cramped from supporting Magee's knees; his arches complained at the weight and the unnatural load distribution; and his breathing was made difficult by the clasp of Magee's arms around his neck.

Two miles to go—maybe more. Let your weight fall forward, and your foot must follow it, else you fall to the ground. It's automatic—as automatic as pulling teeth. How long is a mile? Nothing in a rocket ship, thirty seconds in a pleasure car, a ten minute crawl in a steel snail, fifteen minutes to trained troops in good condition. How far is it with a man on your back, on a rough road, when you are tired to start with?

Five thousand, two hundred, and eighty feet—a meaningless figure. But every step takes twenty-four inches off the total. The remainder is still incomprehensible—an infinity. Count them. Count them till you go crazy—till the figures speak themselves outside your head, and the jar! . . . jar! . . . jar! . . . of your enormous, benumbed feet beats in your brain. Count them backwards, subtracting two each time—no, that's worse; each remainder is still an unattainable, inconceivable figure.

His world closed in, lost its history and held no future. There was nothing, nothing at all, but the torturing necessity of picking up his foot again and placing it forward. No feeling but the heartbreaking expenditure of will necessary to achieve that meaningless act.

He was brought suddenly to awareness when Magee's arms relaxed from around his neck. He leaned forward, and dropped to one knee to keep from spilling his burden, then eased it slowly to the ground. He thought for a moment that the Fader was dead—he could not locate his pulse, and the slack face and limp body were sufficiently corpse-like, but he pressed an ear to Magee's chest, and heard with relief the steady *flub-dub* of his heart.

He tied Magee's wrists together with his handkerchief, and forced his own head through the encircled arms. But he was unable, in his exhausted condition, to wrestle the slack weight into position on his back. Fader regained consciousness while MacKinnon was struggling. His first words were, "Take it easy, Dave. What's the trouble?"

Dave explained. "Better untie my wrists," advised the Fader, "I think I can walk for a while."

And walk he did, for nearly three hundred yards, before he was forced to give up again. "Look, Dave," he said, after he had partially recovered, "did you bring along any more of those pepper pills?"

"Yes—but you can't take any more dosage. It would kill you."

"Yeah, I know—so they say. But that isn't the idea—yet. I was going to suggest that you might take one."

"Why, of course! Good grief, Fader, but I'm dumb."

Magee seemed no heavier than a light coat, the morning star shone brighter, and his strength seemed inexhaustible. Even when they left the highway and started up the cart trail that led to the Doctor's home in the foothills, the going was tolerable and the burden not too great. MacKinnon knew that the drugs burned the working tissue of his body long after his proper reserves were gone, and that it would take him days to recover from the reckless expenditure, but he did not mind.

No price was too high to pay for the moment when he at last arrived at the gate of the Doctor's home—on his own two feet, his charge alive and conscious.

MacKinnon was not allowed to see Magee for four days. In the meantime, he was encouraged to keep the routine of a semi-invalid himself in order to recover the twenty-five pounds he had lost in two days and two nights, and to make up for the heavy strain on his heart during the last night. A high-caloric diet, sun baths, rest, and peaceful surroundings plus his natural good health caused him to regain weight and strength rapidly, but he "enjoyed ill health" exceedingly because of the companionship of the Doctor himself—and Persephone.

Persephone's calendar age was fifteen. Dave never knew whether to think of her as much older, or much younger. She had been born in Coventry, and had lived her short life in the house of the Doctor, her mother having died in childbirth in that same house. She was completely childlike in many respects, being without experience in the civilized world Outside, and having had very little contact with the inhabitants of Coventry, except when she saw them as patients of the Doctor. But she had been allowed to read unchecked from the library of a sophisticated and protean-minded man of science. MacKinnon was continually being surprised at the extent of her academic and scientific knowledge—much greater than his own. She made him feel as if he were conversing with some aged and omniscient matriarch, then she would come out with some naive concept of the outer world, and he would be brought up sharply with the realization that she was, in fact, an inexperienced child.

He was mildly romantic about her. Not seriously, of course, in view of her barely nubile age, but she was pleasant to see, and he was hungry for feminine companionship. He was quite young enough himself to feel continual interest in the delightful differences, mental and physical, between male and female.

Consequently, it was a blow to his pride as sharp as had been the sentence to Coventry to discover that she classed him with the other inhabitants of Coventry as a poor unfortunate who needed help and sympathy because he was not quite right in his head.

He was furious and for one whole day he sulked alone, but the human necessity for self-justification and approval forced him to seek her out and attempt to reason with her. He explained carefully and with emotional candor the circumstances leading up to his trial and conviction, and embellished the account with his own philosophy and evaluations, then confidently awaited her approval.

It was not forthcoming. "I don't understand your view-

160

point," she said. "You broke his nose, yet he had done you no harm of any sort. You expect me to approve that?"

"But Persephone," he protested, "you ignore the fact that he called me a most insulting name."

"I don't see the connection," she said. "He made a noise with his mouth—a verbal label. If the label does not fit you, the noise is meaningless. If the label is true in your case—if you *are* the thing that the noise refers to, you are neither more, nor less, that thing by reason of some one uttering the verbal label. In short, he did not damage you.

"But what you did to him was another matter entirely. You broke his nose. That is damage. In self-protection the rest of society must seek you out, and determine whether or not you are so unstable as to be likely to damage some one else in the future. If you are, you must be quarantined for treatment, or leave society—whichever you prefer."

"You think I'm crazy, don't you?" he accused.

"Crazy? Not the way you mean it. You haven't paresis, or a brain tumor, or any other lesion that the Doctor could find. But from the viewpoint of your semantic reactions you are as socially *unsane* as any fanatic witch-burner."

"Come now—that's not just!"

"What is justice?" She picked up the kitten she had been playing with. "I'm going in—it's getting chilly." Off she went into the house, her bare feet noiseless in the grass.

Had the science of semantics developed as rapidly as psycho-dynamics and its implementing arts of propaganda and mob psychology, the United States might never have fallen into dictatorship, then been forced to undergo the Second Revolution. All of the scientific principles embodied in the Covenant which marked the end of the revolution were formulated as far back as the first quarter of the twentieth century.

But the work of the pioneer semanticists, C. K. Ogden, Alfred Korzybski, and others, were known to but a handful of students, whereas psycho-dynamics, under the impetus of repeated wars and the frenzy of high-pressure merchandising, progressed by leaps and bounds.

Semantics, "the meaning of meaning," gave a method for the first time of applying the scientific method to every act of everyday life. Because semantics dealt with spoken and written words as a determining aspect of human behavior it was at first mistakenly thought by many to be concerned *only* with words and of interest only to professional word manipulators, such as advertising copy writers and professors of etymology. A handful of unorthodox psychiatrists attempted to apply it to personal human problems, but their work was swept away by the epidemic mass psychoses that destroyed Europe and returned the United States to the Dark Ages.

The Covenant was the first scientific social document ever drawn up by man, and due credit must be given to its principal author, Dr. Micah Novak, the same Novak who served as staff psychologist in the revolution. The revolutionists wished to establish maximum personal liberty. How could they accomplish that to a degree of high mathematical probability?

First they junked the concept of "justice." Examined semantically "justice" has no referent—there is no observable phenomenon in the space-time-matter continuum to which one can point, and say, "This is justice." Science can deal only with that which can be observed and measured. Justice is not such a matter; therefore it can never have the same meaning to one as to another; any "noises" said about it will only add to confusion.

But damage, physical or economic, can be pointed to and measured. Citizens were forbidden by the Covenant to damage another. Any act not leading to damage, physical or economic, to some particular person, they declared to be lawful.

Since they had abandoned the concept of "justice," there could be no rational standards of punishment. Penology took its place with lycanthropy and other forgotten witchcrafts. Yet, since it was not practical to permit a source of danger to remain in the community, social offenders were examined and potential repeaters were given their choice of psychological readjustment, or of having society withdraw itself from them—Coventry.

Early drafts of the Covenant contained the assumption that the socially unsane would naturally be hospitalized and readjusted, particularly since current psychiatry was quite competent to cure all non-lesional psychoses and cure or alleviate lesional psychoses, but Novak set his face against this.

"No!" he protested. "The government must never again be permitted to tamper with the mind of any citizen without his consent, or else we set up a greater tyranny than we had before. Every man must be free to accept, or reject, the Covenant, even though we think him insane!"

The next time David MacKinnon looked up Persephone he found her in a state of extreme agitation. His own wounded pride was forgotten at once. "Why, my dear," he said, "whatever in the world is the matter?"

Gradually he gathered that she had been present at a conversation between Magee and the Doctor, and had heard, for the first time, of the impending military operation against the United States. He patted her hand. "So that's all it is," he observed in a relieved voice. "I thought something was wrong with you yourself."

" 'That's all—' David MacKinnon, do you mean to stand

there and tell me that you knew about this, and don't consider it worth worrying about?"

"Me? Why should I? And for that matter, what could *I* do?"

"What could you do? You could go outside and warn them —that's what you could do . . . As to why you should— Dave, you're impossible!" She burst into tears and ran from the room.

He stared after her, mouth open, then borrowed from his remotest ancestor by observing to himself that women are hard to figure out.

Persephone did not appear at lunch. MacKinnon asked the Doctor where she was.

"Had her lunch," the Doctor told him, between mouthfuls. "Started for the Gateway."

"What! Why did you let her do that?"

"Free agent. Wouldn't have obeyed me anyway. She'll be all right."

Dave did not hear the last, being already out of the room and running out of the house. He found her just backing her little monocycle runabout out of its shed. "Persephone!"

"What do you want?" she asked with frozen dignity beyond her years.

"You mustn't do this! That's where the Fader got hurt!"

"I am going. Please stand aside."

"Then I'm going with you."

"Why should you?"

"To take care of you."

She sniffed. "As if anyone would dare to touch me."

There was a measure of truth in what she said. The Doctor, and every member of his household, enjoyed a personal immunity unlike that of anyone else in Coventry. As a natural consequence of the set-up, Coventry had almost no competent medical men. The number of physicians who committed social damage was small. The proportion of such who declined psychiatric treatment was negligible, and this negligible remainder were almost sure to be unreliable bunglers in their profession. The Doctor was a natural healer, in voluntary exile in order that he might enjoy the opportunity to practice his art in the richest available field. He cared nothing for dry research; what he wanted was patients, the sicker the better, that he might make them well again.

He was above custom and above law. In the Free State the Liberator depended on him for insulin to hold his own death from diabetes at arm's length. In New America his beneficiaries were equally powerful. Even among the Angels of the Lord the Prophet himself accepted the dicta of the Doctor without question.

But MacKinnon was not satisfied. Some ignorant fool, he was afraid, might do the child some harm without realizing

163

her protected status. He got no further chance to protest; she started the little runabout suddenly, and forced him to jump out of its path. When he had recovered his balance, she was far down the lane. He could not catch her.

She was back in less than four hours. He had expected that; if a person as elusive as Fader had not been able to reach the Gate at night, it was not likely that a young girl could do so in daylight.

His first feeling was one of simple relief, then he eagerly awaited an opportunity to speak to her. During her absence he had been turning over the situation in his mind. It was a foregone conclusion that she would fail; he wished to rehabilitate himself in her eyes; therefore, he would help her in the project nearest her heart—he himself would carry the warning to the Outside!

Perhaps she would ask for such help. In fact, it seemed likely. By the time she returned he had convinced himself that she was certain to ask his help. He would agree—with simple dignity—and off he would go, perhaps to be wounded, or killed, but an heroic figure, even if he failed.

He pictured himself subconsciously as a blend of Sidney Carton, the White Knight, the man who carried the message to Garcia—and just a dash of d'Artagnan.

But she did not ask him—she would not even give him a chance to talk with her.

She did not appear at dinner. After dinner she was closeted with the Doctor in his study. When she reappeared she went directly to her room. He finally concluded that he might as well go to bed himself.

To bed, and then to sleep, and take it up again in the morning— But it's not as simple as that. The unfriendly walls stared back at him, and the other, critical half of his mind decided to make a night of it. Fool! She doesn't want your help. Why should she? What have you got that Fader hasn't got?—and better. To her, you are just one of the screwloose multitude you've seen all around you in this place.

But *I*'m not crazy!—just because I choose not to submit to the dictation of others doesn't make me *crazy*. Doesn't it, though? All the rest of them in here are lamebrains, what's so fancy about you? Not all of them—how about the Doctor, and— Don't kid yourself, chump, the Doctor and Mother Johnston are here for their own reasons; they weren't sentenced. And Persephone was born here.

How about Magee?—He was certainly rational—or seemed so. He found himself resenting, with illogical bitterness, Magee's apparent stability. Why should he be any different from the rest of us?

The rest of us? He had classed himself with the other inhabitants of Coventry. All right, all right, admit it, you fool—

164

you're just like the rest of them; turned out because the decent people won't have you—and too damned stubborn to admit that you need treatment.

But the thought of treatment turned him cold, and made him think of his father again. Why should that be? He recalled something the Doctor had said to him a couple of days before: "What you need, son, is to stand up to your father and tell him off. Pity more children don't tell their parents to go to hell!"

He turned on the light and tried to read. But it was no use. Why should Persephone care what happened to the people Outside?—She didn't know them; she had no friends there. If *he* had no obligations to them, how could *she* possibly care? No obligations? You had a soft, easy life for many years—all they asked was that you behave yourself. For that matter, where would you be now, if the Doctor had stopped to ask whether or not he owed you anything?

He was still wearily chewing the bitter cud of self-examination when the first cold and colorless light of morning filtered in. He got up, threw a robe around him, and tiptoed down the hall to Magee's room. The door was ajar. He stuck his head in, and whispered, "Fader— Are you awake?"

"Come in, kid," Magee answered quietly. "What's the trouble? No can sleep?"

"No—"

"Neither can I. Sit down, and we'll carry the banner together."

"Fader, I'm going to make a break for it. I'm going Outside."

"Huh? When?"

"Right away."

"Risky business, kid. Wait a few days, and I'll try it with you."

"No, I can't wait for you to get well. I'm going out to warn the United States!"

Magee's eyes widened a little, but his voice was unchanged. "You haven't let that spindly kid sell you a bill of goods, Dave?"

"No. Not exactly. I'm doing this for myself—it's something I need to do. See here, Fader, what about this weapon? Have they really got something that could threaten the United States?"

"I'm afraid so," Magee admitted. "I don't know much about it, but it makes blasters look sick. More range— I don't know what they expect to do about the Barrier, but I saw 'em stringing heavy power lines before I got winged. Say, if you do get outside, here's a chap you might look up; in fact, be sure to. He's got influence." Magee scrawled something on a

165

scrap of paper, folded the scrap, and handed it to MacKinnon, who pocketed it absent-mindedly and went on:

"How closely is the Gate guarded, Fader?"

"You can't get out the Gate; that's out of the question. Here's what you will have to do—" He tore off another piece of paper and commenced sketching and explaining.

Dave shook hands with Magee before he left. "You'll say goodbye for me, won't you? And thank the Doctor? I'd rather just slide out before anyone is up."

"Of course, kid," the Fader assured him.

MacKinnon crouched behind bushes and peered cautiously at the little band of Angels filing into the bleak, ugly church. He shivered, both from fear and from the icy morning air. But his need was greater than his fear. Those zealots had food —and he must have it.

The first two days after he left the house of the Doctor had been easy enough. True, he had caught cold from sleeping on the ground; it had settled in his lungs and slowed him down. But he did not mind that now if only he could refrain from sneezing or coughing until the little band of faithful were safe inside the temple. He watched them pass—dour-looking men, women in skirts that dragged the ground and whose work-lined faces were framed in shawls—sallow drudges with too many children. The light had gone out of their faces. Even the children were sober.

The last of them filed inside, leaving only the sexton in the churchyard, busy with some obscure duty. After an interminable time, during which MacKinnon pressed a finger against his upper lip in a frantic attempt to forestall a sneeze, the sexton entered the grim building and closed the doors.

MacKinnon crept out of his hiding place and hurried to the house he had previously selected, on the edge of the clearing, farthest from the church.

The dog was suspicious, but he quieted him. The house was locked, but the rear door could be forced. He was a little giddy at the sight of food when he found it—hard bread, and strong, unsalted butter made from goats' milk. A misstep two days before had landed him in a mountain stream. The mishap had not seemed important until he discovered that his food tablets were a pulpy mess. He had eaten them the rest of the day, then mold had taken them, and he had thrown the remainder away.

The bread lasted him through three more sleeps, but the butter melted and he was unable to carry it. He soaked as much of it as he could into the bread, then licked up the rest, after which he was very thirsty.

Some hours after the last of the bread was gone, he reached his first objective—the main river to which all other streams in Coventry were tributary. Some place, down stream, it dived under the black curtain of the Barrier, and continued seaward. With the gateway closed and guarded, its outlet constituted the only possible egress to a man unassisted.

In the meantime it was water, and thirst was upon him again, and his cold was worse. But he would have to wait until dark to drink; there were figures down there by the bank—some in uniform, he thought. One of them made fast a little skiff to a landing. He marked it for his own and watched it with jealous eyes. It was still there when the sun went down.

The early morning sun struck his nose and he sneezed. He came wide awake, raised his head, and looked around. The little skiff he had appropriated floated in midstream. There were no oars. He could not remember whether or not there had been any oars. The current was fairly strong; it seemed as if he should have drifted clear to the Barrier in the night. Perhaps he had passed under it—no, that was ridiculous.

Then he saw it, less than a mile away, black and ominous—but the most welcome sight he had seen in days. He was too weak and feverish to enjoy it, but it renewed the determination that kept him going.

The little boat scraped against bottom. He saw that the current at a bend had brought him to the bank. He hopped awkwardly out, his congealed joints complaining, and drew the bow of the skiff up onto the sand. Then he thought better of it, pushed it out once more, shoved as hard as he was able and watched it disappear around the meander. No need to advertise where he had landed.

He slept most of that day, rousing himself once to move out of the sun when it grew too hot. But the sun had cooked much of the cold out of his bones, and he felt much better by nightfall.

Although the Barrier was only a mile or so away, it took most of the night to reach it by following the river bank. He knew when he had reached it by the clouds of steam that rose from the water. When the sun came up, he considered the situation. The Barrier stretched across the water, but the juncture between it and the surface of the stream was hidden by billowing clouds. Someplace, down under the surface of the water—how far down he did not know—somewhere down there, the Barrier ceased, and its raw edge turned the water it touched to steam.

Slowly, reluctantly and most unheroically, he commenced to strip off his clothes. The time had come and he did not relish it. He came across the scrap of paper that Magee had handed him, and attempted to examine it. But it had been pulped by his involuntary dip in the mountain stream and was quite illegible. He chucked it away. It did not seem to matter.

He shivered as he stood hesitating on the bank, although

167

the sun was warm. Then his mind was made up for him; he spied a patrol on the far bank.

Perhaps they had seen him, perhaps not. He dived.

Down, down, as far as his strength would take him. Down and try to touch bottom, to be sure of avoiding that searing, deadly base. He felt mud with his hands. Now to swim under it. Perhaps it was death to pass under it, as well as over it; he would soon know. But which way was it? There was no direction down here.

He stayed down until his congested lungs refused. Then he rose part way, and felt scalding water on his face. For a timeless interval of unutterable sorrow and loneliness he realized that he was trapped between heat and water—trapped under the Barrier.

Two private soldiers gossiped idly on a small dock which lay under the face of the Barrier. The river which poured out from beneath it held no interest for them, they had watched it for many dull tours of guard duty. An alarm clanged behind them and brought them to alertness. "What sector, Jack?"

"This bank. There he is now—see!"

They fished him out and had him spread out on the dock by the time the sergeant of the guard arrived. "Alive, or dead?" he enquired.

"Dead, I think," answered the one who was not busy giving artificial resuscitation.

The sergeant clucked in a manner incongruous to his battered face, and said, "Too bad. I've ordered the ambulance; send him up to the infirmary anyhow."

The nurse tried to keep him quiet, but MacKinnon made such an uproar that she was forced to get the ward surgeon. "Here! Here! What's all this nonsense?" the medico rebuked him, while reaching for his pulse. Dave managed to convince him that he would not quiet down, not accept a soporific until he had told his story. They struck a working agreement that MacKinnon was to be allowed to talk—"But keep it short, mind you!"—and the doctor would pass the word along to his next superior, and in return Dave would submit to a hypodermic.

The next morning two other men, unidentified, were brought to MacKinnon by the surgeon. They listened to his full story and questioned him in detail. He was transferred to corps area headquarters that afternoon by ambulance. There he was questioned again. He was regaining his strength rapidly, but he was growing quite tired of the whole rigamarole, and wanted assurance that his warning was being taken seriously. The latest of his interrogators reassured him. "Compose yourself," he told Dave, "you are to see the commanding officer this afternoon."

The corps area commander, a nice little chap with a quick, birdlike manner and a most unmilitary appearance, listened gravely while MacKinnon recited his story for what seemed to him the fiftieth time. He nodded agreement when David finished. "Rest assured, David MacKinnon, that all necessary steps are being taken."

"But how about their weapon?"

"That is taken care of—and as for the Barrier, it may not be as easy to break as our neighbors think. But your efforts are appreciated. May I do you some service?"

"Well, no—not for myself, but there are two of my friends in there—" He asked that something be done to rescue Magee, and that Persephone be enabled to come out, if she wished.

"I know of that girl," the general remarked. "We will get in touch with her. If at any time she wishes to become a citizen, it can be arranged. As for Magee, that is another matter—" He touched the stud of his desk visiphone. "Send Captain Randall in."

A neat, trim figure in the uniform of a captain of the United States Army entered with a light step. MacKinnon glanced at him with casual, polite interest, then his expression went to pieces. "Fader!" he yelled.

Their mutual greeting was hardly sufficiently decorous for the private office of a commanding general, but the general did not seem to mind. When they had calmed down, MacKinnon had to ask the question uppermost in his mind. "But see here, Fader, all this doesn't make sense—" He paused, staring, then pointed a finger accusingly, "I know! You're in the secret service!"

The Fader grinned cheerfully. "Did you think," he observed, "that the United States Army would leave a plague spot like that unwatched?"

The general cleared his throat. "What do you plan to do now, David MacKinnon?"

"Eh? Me? Why, I don't have any plans—" He thought for a moment, then turned to his friend. "Do you know, Fader, I believe I'll turn in for psychological treatment after all. You're on the Outside—"

"I don't believe that will be necessary," interrupted the general gently.

"No? Why not, sir?"

"You have cured yourself. You may not be aware of it, but four psycho-technicians have interviewed you. Their reports agree. I am authorized to tell you that your status as a free citizen has been restored, if you wish it."

The general and Captain "the Fader" Randall managed tactfully between them to terminate the interview. Randall walked back to the infirmary with his friend. Dave wanted a thousand questions answered at once. "But Fader," he demanded, "you must have gotten out before I did."

"A day or two."

"Then my job was unnecessary!"

"I wouldn't say that," Randall contradicted. "I might not have gotten through. As a matter of fact, they had all the details even before I reported. There are others—Anyhow," he continued, to change the subject, "now that you are here, what will you do?"

"Me? It's too soon to say . . . It won't be classical literature, that's a cinch. If I wasn't such a dumbie in math, I might still try for interplanetary."

"Well, we can talk about it tonight," suggested Fader, glancing at his chrono. "I've got to run along, but I'll stop by later, and we'll go over to the mess for dinner."

He was out the door with speed reminiscent of the thieves' kitchen. Dave watched him, then said suddenly, "Hey! Fader! Why couldn't I get into the secret ser—"

But the Fader was gone—he must ask himself.

Misfit

> ". . . for the purpose of conserving and improving our interplanetary resources, and providing useful, healthful occupations for the youth of this planet."
>
> Excerpt from the enabling act, H.R. 7118, setting up the Cosmic Construction Corps.

ATTENTION to muster!" The parade ground voice of a First Sergeant of Space Marines cut through the fog and drizzle of a nasty New Jersey morning. "As your names are called, answer 'Here', step forward with your baggage, and embark. Atkins!"

"Here!"

"Austin!"

"Hyar!"

"Ayres!"

"Here!"

One by one they fell out of ranks, shouldered the hundred and thirty pounds of personal possessions allowed them, and trudged up the gangway. They were young—none more than twenty-two—in some cases luggage outweighed the owner.

"Kaplan!"

"Here!"

"Keith!"

"Heah!"

"Libby!"

"Here!" A thin gangling blonde had detached himself from the line, hastily wiped his nose, and grabbed his belongings. He slung a fat canvas bag over his shoulder, steadied it, and lifted a suitcase with his free hand. He started for the companionway in an unsteady dog trot. As he stepped on the gangway his suitcase swung against his knees. He staggered against a short wiry form dressed in the powder-blue of the Space Navy. Strong fingers grasped his arm and checked his fall.

"Steady, son. Easy does it." Another hand readjusted the canvas bag.

"Oh, excuse me, uh"—the embarrassed youngster automatically counted the four bands of silver braid below the shooting star—"Captain. I didn't—"

"Bear a hand and get aboard, son."

"Yes, sir."

The passage into the bowels of the transport was gloomy. When the lad's eyes adjusted he saw a gunner's mate wearing the brassard of a Master-at-Arms, who hooked a thumb towards an open air-tight door.

"In there. Find your locker and wait by it." Libby hurried to obey. Inside he found a jumble of baggage and men in a wide low-ceilinged compartment. A line of glow-tubes ran around the junction of bulkhead and ceiling and trisected the overhead; the soft roar of blowers made a background to the voices of his shipmates. He picked his way through heaped luggage and located his locker, seven-ten, on the far wall outboard. He broke the seal on the combination lock, glanced at the combination, and opened it. The locker was very small, the middle of a tier of three. He considered what he should keep in it. A loudspeaker drowned out the surrounding voices and demanded his attention:

"Attention! Man all space details; first section. Raise ship in twelve minutes. Close air-tight doors. Stop blowers at minus two minutes. Special orders for passengers; place all gear on deck, and lie down on red signal light. Remain down until release is sounded. Masters-at-Arms check compliance."

The gunner's mate popped in, glanced around and immediately commenced supervising rearrangement of the baggage. Heavy items were lashed down. Locker doors were closed. By the time each boy had found a place on the deck and the Master-at-Arms had okayed the pad under his head, the glow-tubes turned red and the loudspeaker brayed out.

"All hands—Up Ship! Stand by for acceleration." The

Master-at-Arms hastily reclined against two cruise bags, and watched the room. The blowers sighed to a stop. There followed two minutes of dead silence. Libby felt his heart commence to pound. The two minutes stretched interminably. Then the deck quivered and a roar like escaping high-pressure steam beat at his ear drums. He was suddenly very heavy and a weight lay across his chest and heart. An indefinite time later the glow-tubes flashed white, and the announcer bellowed:

"Secure all getting underway details; regular watch, first section." The blowers droned into life. The Master-at-Arms stood up, rubbed his buttocks and pounded his arms, then said:

"Okay, boys." He stepped over and undogged the airtight door to the passageway. Libby got up and blundered into a bulkhead, nearly falling. His legs and arms had gone to sleep, besides which he felt alarmingly light, as if he had sloughed off at least half of his inconsiderable mass.

For the next two hours he was too busy to think, or to be homesick. Suitcases, boxes, and bags had to be passed down into the lower hold and lashed against angular acceleration. He located and learned how to use a waterless water closet. He found his assigned bunk and learned that it was his only eight hours in twenty-four; two other boys had the use of it too. The three sections ate in three shifts, nine shifts in all— twenty-four youths and a master-at-arms at one long table which jam-filled a narrow compartment off the galley.

After lunch Libby restowed his locker. He was standing before it, gazing at a photograph which he intended to mount on the inside of the locker door, when a command filled the compartment:

"Attention!"

Standing inside the door was the Captain flanked by the Master-at-Arms. The Captain commenced to speak. "At rest, men. Sit down. McCoy, tell control to shift this compartment to smoke filter." The gunner's mate hurried to the communicator on the bulkhead and spoke into it in a low tone. Almost at once the hum of the blowers climbed a half-octave and stayed there. "Now light up if you like. I'm going to talk to you.

"You boys are headed out on the biggest thing so far in your lives. From now on you're men, with one of the hardest jobs ahead of you that men have ever tackled. What we have to do is part of a bigger scheme. You, and hundreds of thousands of others like you, are going out as pioneers to fix up the solar system so that human beings can make better use of it.

"Equally important, you are being given a chance to build yourselves into useful and happy citizens of the Federation. For one reason or another you weren't happily adjusted back on Earth. Some of you saw the jobs you were trained for abolished by new inventions. Some of you got into trouble

172

from not knowing what to do with the modern leisure. In any case you were misfits. Maybe you were called bad boys and had a lot of black marks chalked up against you.

"But everyone of you starts even today. The only record you have in this ship is your name at the top of a blank sheet of paper. It's up to you what goes on that page.

"Now about our job—We didn't get one of the easy repair-and-recondition jobs on the Moon, with week-ends at Luna City, and all the comforts of home. Nor did we draw a high-gravity planet where a man can eat a full meal and expect to keep it down. Instead we've got to go out to Asteroid HS-5388 and turn it into Space Station E-M3. She has no atmosphere at all, and only about two per cent Earth-surface gravity. We've got to play human fly on her for at least six months, no girls to date, no television, no recreation that you don't devise yourselves, and hard work every day. You'll get space sick, and so homesick you can taste it, and agoraphobia. If you aren't careful you'll get ray-burnt. Your stomach will act up, and you'll wish to God you'd never enrolled.

"But if you behave yourself, and listen to the advice of the old spacemen, you'll come out of it strong and healthy, with a little credit stored up in the bank, and a lot of knowledge and experience that you wouldn't get in forty years on Earth. You'll be men, and you'll know it.

"One last word. It will be pretty uncomfortable to those that aren't used to it. Just give the other fellow a little consideration, and you'll get along all right. If you have any complaint and can't get satisfaction any other way, come see me. Otherwise, that's all. Any questions?"

One of the boys put up his hand. "Captain?" he enquired timidly.

"Speak up, lad, and give your name."

"Rogers, sir. Will we be able to get letters from home?"

"Yes, but not very often. Maybe every month or so. The chaplain will carry mail, and any inspection and supply ships."

The ship's loudspeaker blatted out, "All hands! Free flight in ten minutes. Stand by to lose weight." The Master-at-Arms supervised the rigging of grab-lines. All loose gear was made fast, and little cellulose bags were issued to each man. Hardly was this done when Libby felt himself get light on his feet—a sensation exactly like that experienced when an express elevator makes a quick stop on an upward trip, except that the sensation continued and became more intense. At first it was a pleasant novelty, then it rapidly became distressing. The blood pounded in his ears, and his feet were clammy and cold. His saliva secreted at an abnormal rate. He tried to swallow, choked, and coughed. Then his stomach shuddered and contracted with a violent, painful, convulsive reflex and he was

173

suddenly, disastrously nauseated. After the first excruciating spasm, he heard McCoy's voice shouting.

"Hey! Use your sick-kits like I told you. Don't let that stuff get in the blowers." Dimly Libby realized that the admonishment included him. He fumbled for his cellulose bag just as a second temblor shook him, but he managed to fit the bag over his mouth before the eruption occurred. When it subsided, he became aware that he was floating near the overhead and facing the door. The chief Master-at-Arms slithered in the door and spoke to McCoy.

"How are you making out?"

"Well enough. Some of the boys missed their kits."

"Okay. Mop it up. You can use the starboard lock." He swam out.

McCoy touched Libby's arm. "Here, Pinkie, start catching them butterflies." He handed him a handful of cotton waste, then took another handful himself and neatly dabbed up a globule of the slimy filth that floated about the compartment. "Be sure your sick-kit is on tight. When you get sick, just stop and wait until it's over." Libby imitated him as best as he could. In a few minutes the room was free of the worst of the sickening debris. McCoy looked it over, and spoke:

"Now peel off them dirty duds, and change your kits. Three or four of you bring everything along to the starboard lock."

At the starboard spacelock, the kits were put in first, the inner door closed, and the outer opened. When the inner door was opened again the kits were gone—blown out into space by the escaping air. Pinkie addressed McCoy,

"Do we have to throw away our dirty clothes too?"

"Huh uh, we'll just give them a dose of vacuum. Take 'em into the lock and stop 'em to those hooks on the bulkheads. Tie 'em tight."

This time the lock was left closed for about five minutes. When the lock was opened the garments were bone dry—all the moisture boiled out by the vacuum of space. All that remained of the unpleasant rejecta was a sterile powdery residue. McCoy viewed them with approval. "They'll do. Take them back to the compartment. Then brush them—hard—in front of the exhaust blowers."

The next few days were an eternity of misery. Homesickness was forgotten in the all-engrossing wretchedness of space-sickness. The Captain granted fifteen minutes of mild acceleration for each of the nine meal periods, but the respite accentuated the agony. Libby would go to a meal, weak and ravenously hungry. The meal would stay down until free flight was resumed, then the sickness would hit him all over again.

On the fourth day he was seated against a bulkhead, enjoying the luxury of a few remaining minutes of weight while the last shift ate, when McCoy walked in and sat down beside him. The gunner's mate fitted a smoke filter over his face and lit a cigarette. He inhaled deeply and started to chat.

"How's it going, bud?"

"All right, I guess. This spacesickness— Say, McCoy, how do you ever get used to it?"

"You get over it in time. Your body acquires new reflexes, so they tell me. Once you learn to swallow without choking, you'll be all right. You even get so you like it. It's restful and relaxing. Four hours sleep is as good as ten."

Libby shook his head dolefully. "I don't think I'll ever get used to it."

"Yes, you will. You'd better anyway. This here asteroid won't have any surface gravity to speak of; the Chief Quartermaster says it won't run over two per cent Earth normal. That ain't enough to cure spacesickness. And there won't be any way to accelerate for meals either."

Libby shivered and held his head between his hands.

Locating one asteroid among a couple of thousand is not as easy as finding Trafalgar Square in London—especially against the star-crowded backdrop of the galaxy. You take off from Terra with its orbital speed of about nineteen miles per second. You attempt to settle into a composite conoid curve that will not only intersect the orbit of the tiny fast-moving body, but also accomplish an exact rendezvous. Asteroid HS-5388, 'Eighty-eight,' lay about two and two-tenths astronomical units out from the sun, a little more than two hundred million miles; when the transport took off it lay beyond the sun better than three hundred million miles. Captain Doyle instructed the navigator to plot the basic ellipsoid to tack in free flight around the sun through an elapsed distance of some three hundred and forty million miles. The principle involved is the same as used by a hunter to wing a duck in flight by 'leading' the bird in flight. But suppose that you face directly into the sun as you shoot; suppose the bird can not be seen from where you stand, and you have nothing to aim by but some old reports as to how it was flying when last seen?

On the ninth day of the passage Captain Doyle betook himself to the chart room and commenced punching keys on the ponderous integral calculator. Then he sent his orderly to present his compliments to the navigator and to ask him to come to the chartroom. A few minutes later a tall heavyset form swam through the door, steadied himself with a grabline and greeted the captain.

"Good morning, Skipper."

"Hello, Blackie." The Old Man looked up from where he was strapped into the integrator's saddle. "I've been checking your corrections for the meal time accelerations."

"It's a nuisance to have a bunch of ground-lubbers on board, sir."

"Yes, it is, but we have to give those boys a chance to eat, or they couldn't work when we got there. Now I want to decelerate starting about ten o'clock, ship's time. What's our eight o'clock speed and co-ordinates?"

The Navigator slipped a notebook out of his tunic. "Three hundred fifty-eight miles per second; course is right ascension fifteen hours, eight minutes, twenty-seven seconds, declination minus seven degrees, three minutes; solar distance one hundred and ninety-two million four hundred eighty thousand miles. Our radial position is twelve degrees above course, and almost dead on course in R.A. Do you want Sol's co-ordinates?"

"No, not now." The captain bent over the calculator, frowned and chewed the tip of his tongue as he worked the controls. "I want you to kill the acceleration about one million miles inside Eighty-eight's orbit. I hate to waste the fuel, but the belt is full of junk and this damned rock is so small that we will probably have to run a search curve. Use twenty hours on deceleration and commence changing course to port after eight hours. Use normal asymptotic approach. You should have her in a circular trajectory abreast of Eighty-eight, and paralleling her orbit by six o'clock tomorrow morning. I shall want to be called at three."

"Aye aye, sir."

"Let me see your figures when you get 'em. I'll send up the order book later."

The transport accelerated on schedule. Shortly after three the Captain entered the control room and blinked his eyes at the darkness. The sun was still concealed by the hull of the transport and the midnight blackness was broken only by the dim blue glow of the instrument dials, and the crack of light from under the chart hood. The Navigator turned at the familiar tread.

"Good morning, Captain."

"Morning, Blackie. In sight yet?"

"Not yet. We've picked out half a dozen rocks, but none of them checked."

"Any of them close?"

"Not uncomfortably. We've overtaken a little sand from time to time."

"That can't hurt us—not on a stern chase like this. If pilots would only realize that the asteroids flow in fixed directions at computable speeds nobody would come to grief out here." He stopped to light a cigarette. "People talk about space being dangerous. Sure, it used to be; but I don't know of a case in the past twenty years that couldn't be charged up to some fool's recklessness."

176

"You're right, Skipper. By the way, there's coffee under the chart hood."

"Thanks; I had a cup down below." He walked over by the lookouts at stereoscopes and radar tanks and peered up at the star-flecked blackness. Three cigarettes later the lookout nearest him called out.

"Light ho!"

"Where away?"

His mate read the exterior dials of the stereoscope. "Plus point two, abaft one point three, slight drift astern." He shifted to radar and added, "Range seven nine oh four three."

"Does that check?"

"Could be, Captain. What is her disk?" came the Navigator's muffled voice from under the hood. The first lookout hurriedly twisted the knobs of his instrument, but the Captain nudged him aside.

"I'll do this, son." He fitted his face to the double eye guards and surveyed a little silvery sphere, a tiny moon. Carefully he brought two illuminated cross-hairs up until they were exactly tangent to the upper and lower limbs of the disc. "Mark!"

The reading was noted and passed to the Navigator, who shortly ducked out from under the hood.

"That's our baby, Captain."

"Good."

"Shall I make a visual triangulation?"

"Let the watch officer do that. You go down and get some sleep. I'll ease her over until we get close enough to use the optical range finder."

"Thanks, I will."

Within a few minutes the word had spread around the ship that Eighty-eight had been sighted. Libby crowded into the starboard troop deck with a throng of excited mess mates and attempted to make out their future home from the view port. McCoy poured cold water on their excitement.

"By the time that rock shows up big enough to tell anything about it with your naked eye we'll all be at our grounding stations. She's only about a hundred miles thick, yuh know."

And so it was. Many hours later the ship's announcer shouted:

"All hands! Man your grounding stations. Close all air-tight doors. Stand by to cut blowers on signal."

McCoy forced them to lie down throughout the ensuing two hours. Short shocks of rocket blasts alternated with nauseating weightlessness. Then the blowers stopped and check valves clicked into their seats. The ship dropped free for a few moments—a final quick blast—five seconds of falling, and a short, light, grinding bump. A single bugle note came over the announcer, and the blowers took up their hum.

McCoy floated lightly to his feet and poised, swaying, on his toes. "All out, troops—this is the end of the line."

A short chunky lad, a little younger than most of them, awkwardly emulated him, and bounded toward the door, shouting as he went, "Come on, fellows! Let's go outside and explore!"

The Master-at-Arms squelched him. "Not so fast, kid. Aside from the fact that there is no air out there, go right ahead. You'll freeze to death, burn to death, and explode like a ripe tomato. Squad leader, detail six men to break out spacesuits. The rest of you stay here and stand by."

The working party returned shortly loaded down with a couple of dozen bulky packages. Libby let go the four he carried and watched them float gently to the deck. McCoy unzipped the envelope from one suit, and lectured them about it.

"This is a standard service type, general issue, Mark IV, Modification 2." He grasped the suit by the shoulders and shook it out so that it hung like a suit of long winter underwear with the helmet lolling helplessly between the shoulders of the garment. "It's self-sustaining for eight hours, having an oxygen supply for that period. It also has a nitrogen trim tank and a carbon-dioxide-water-vapor cartridge filter."

He droned on, repeating practically verbatim the description and instructions given in training regulations. McCoy knew these suits like his tongue knew the roof of his mouth; the knowledge had meant his life on more than one occasion.

"The suit is woven from glass fibre laminated with non-volatile asbestocellutite. The resulting fabric is flexible, very durable; and will turn all rays normal to solar space outside the orbit of Mercury. It is worn over your regular clothing, but notice the wire-braced accordion pleats at the major joints. They are so designed as to keep the internal volume of the suit nearly constant when the arms or legs are bent. Otherwise the gas pressure inside would tend to keep the suit blown up in an erect position, and movement while wearing the suit would be very fatiguing.

"The helmet is moulded from a transparent silicone, leaded and polarized against too great ray penetration. It may be equipped with external visors of any needed type. Orders are to wear not less than a number-two amber on this body. In addition, a lead plate covers the cranium and extends on down the back of the suit, completely covering the spinal column.

"The suit is equipped with two-way telephony. If your radio quits, as these have a habit of doing, you can talk by putting your helmets in contact. Any questions?"

"How do you eat and drink during the eight hours?"

"You don't stay in 'em any eight hours. You can carry sugar balls in a gadget in the helmet, but you boys will always

178

eat at the base. As for water, there's a nipple in the helmet near your mouth which you can reach by turning your head to the left. It's hooked to a built-in canteen. But don't drink any more water than you're wearing a suit than you have to. These suits ain't got any plumbing."

Suits were passed out to each lad, and McCoy illustrated how to don one. A suit was spread supine on the deck, the front zipper that stretched from neck to crotch was spread wide and one sat down inside this opening, whereupon the lower part was drawn on like long stockings. Then a wiggle into each sleeve and the heavy flexible gauntlets were smoothed and patted into place. Finally an awkward backward stretch of the neck with shoulders hunched enabled the helmet to be placed over the head.

Libby followed the motions of McCoy and stood up in his suit. He examined the zipper which controlled the suit's only opening. It was backed by two soft gaskets which would be pressed together by the zipper and sealed by internal air pressure. Inside the helmet a composition mouthpiece for exhalation led to the filter.

McCoy bustled around, inspecting them, tightening a belt here and there, instructing them in the use of the external controls. Satisfied, he reported to the conning room that his section had received basic instruction and was ready to disembark. Permission was received to take them out for thirty minutes acclimatization.

Six at a time, he escorted them through the air lock, and out on the surface of the planetoid. Libby blinked his eyes at the unaccustomed luster of sunshine on rock. Although the sun lay more than two hundred million miles away and bathed the little planet with radiation only one fifth as strong as that lavished on mother Earth, nevertheless the lack of atmosphere resulted in a glare that made him squint. He was glad to have the protection of his amber visor. Overhead the sun, shrunk to penny size, shone down from a dead black sky in which unwinking stars crowded each other and the very sun itself.

The voice of a mess mate sounded in Libby's earphones, "Jeepers! That horizon looks close. I'll bet it ain't more'n a mile away."

Libby looked out over the flat bare plain and subconsciously considered the matter. "It's less," he commented, "than a third of a mile away."

"What the hell do you know about it, Pinkie? And who asked you, anyhow?"

Libby answered defensively, "As a matter of fact, it's one thousand six hundred and seventy feet, figuring that my eyes are five feet three inches above ground level."

"Nuts. Pinkie, you are always trying to show off how much you think you know."

"Why, I am not," Libby protested. "If this body is a hundred miles thick and as round as it looks: why, naturally the horizon *has* to be just that far away."

"Says *who?*"

McCoy interrupted.

"Pipe down! Libby is a lot nearer right than you were."

"He is exactly right," put in a strange voice. "I had to look it up for the navigator before I left control."

"Is that so?"—McCoy's voice again—"If the Chief Quartermaster says you're right, Libby, you're right. How did you know?"

Libby flushed miserably. "I—I don't know. That's the only way it could be."

The gunner's mate and the quartermaster stared at him but dropped the subject.

By the end of the 'day' (ship's time, for Eighty-eight had a period of eight hours and thirteen minutes), work was well under way. The transport had grounded close by a low range of hills. The Captain selected a little bowl-shaped depression in the hills, some thousand feet long and half as broad, in which to establish a permanent camp. This was to be roofed over, sealed, and an atmosphere provided.

In the hill between the ship and the valley, quarters were to be excavated; dormitories, mess hall, officers' quarters, sick bay, recreation room, offices, store rooms, and so forth. A tunnel must be bored through the hill, connecting the sites of these rooms, and connecting with a ten foot airtight metal tube sealed to the ship's portside air-lock. Both the tube and tunnel were to be equipped with a continuous conveyor belt for passengers and freight.

Libby found himself assigned to the roofing detail. He helped a metalsmith struggle over the hill with a portable atomic heater, difficult to handle because of a mass of eight hundred pounds, but weighing here only sixteen pounds. The rest of the roofing detail were breaking out and preparing to move by hand the enormous translucent tent which was to be the 'sky' of the little valley.

The metalsmith located a landmark on the inner slope of the valley, set up his heater, and commenced cutting a deep horizontal groove or step in the rock. He kept it always at the same level by following a chalk mark drawn along the rock wall. Libby enquired how the job had been surveyed so quickly.

"Easy," he was answered, "two of the quartermasters went ahead with a transit, leveled it just fifty feet above the valley floor, and clamped a searchlight to it. Then one of 'em ran like hell around the rim, making chalk marks at the height at which the beam struck."

"Is this roof going to be just fifty feet high?"

"No, it will average maybe a hundred. It bellies up in the middle from the air pressure."

"Earth normal?"

"Half Earth normal."

Libby concentrated for an instant, then looked puzzled. "But look— This valley is a thousand feet long and better than five hundred wide. At half of fifteen pounds per square inch, and allowing for the arch of the roof, that's a load of one and an eighth billion pounds. What fabric can take that kind of a load?"

"Cobwebs."

"Cobwebs?"

"Yeah, cobwebs. Strongest stuff in the world, stronger than the best steel. Synthetic spider silk. This gauge we're using for the roof has a tensile strength of four thousand pounds a running inch."

Libby hesitated a second, then replied, "I see. With a rim about eighteen hundred thousand inches around, the maximum pull at the point of anchoring would be about six hundred and twenty-five pounds per inch. Plenty safe margin."

The metalsmith leaned on his tool and nodded. "Something like that. You're pretty quick at arithmetic, aren't you, bud?"

Libby looked startled. "I just like to get things straight."

They worked rapidly around the slope, cutting a clean smooth groove to which the 'cobweb' could be anchored and sealed. The white-hot lava spewed out of the discharge vent and ran slowly down the hillside. A brown vapor boiled off the surface of the molten rock, arose a few feet and sublimed almost at once in the vacuum to white powder which settled to the ground. The metalsmith pointed to the powder.

"That stuff 'ud cause silicosis if we let it stay there, and breathed it later."

"What do you do about it?"

"Just clean it out with the blowers of the air conditioning plant."

Libby took this opening to ask another question. "Mister—?"

"Johnson's my name. No mister necessary."

"Well, Johnson, where do we get the air for this whole valley, not to mention the tunnels? I figure we must need twenty-five million cubic feet or more. Do we manufacture it?"

"Naw, that's too much trouble. We brought it with us."

"On the transport?"

"Uh huh, at fifty atmospheres."

Libby considered this. "I see—that way it would go into a space eighty feet on a side."

"Matter of fact it's in three specially constructed holds—

giant air bottles. This transport carried air to Ganymede. I was in her then—a recruit, but in the air gang even then."

In three weeks the permanent camp was ready for occupancy and the transport cleared of its cargo. The storerooms bulged with tools and supplies. Captain Doyle had moved his administrative offices underground, signed over his command to his first officer, and given him permission to proceed on 'duty assigned'—in this case; return to Terra with a skeleton crew.

Libby watched them take off from a vantage point on the hillside. An overpowering homesickness took possession of him. Would he ever go home? He honestly believed at the time that he would swap the rest of his life for thirty minutes each with his mother and with Betty.

He started down the hill toward the tunnel lock. At least the transport carried letters to them, and with any luck the chaplain would be by soon with letters from Earth. But tomorrow and the days after that would be no fun. He had enjoyed being in the air gang, but tomorrow he went back to his squad. He did not relish that—the boys in his squad were all right, he guessed, but he just could not seem to fit in.

This company of the C.C.C. started on its bigger job; to pock-mark Eighty-eight with rocket tubes so that Captain Doyle could push this hundred-mile marble out of her orbit and herd her in to a new orbit between Earth and Mars, to be used as a space station—a refuge for ships in distress, a haven for life boats, a fueling stop, a naval outpost.

Libby was assigned to a heater in pit H-16. It was his business to carve out carefully calculated emplacements in which the blasting crew then set off the minute charges which accomplished the major part of the excavating. Two squads were assigned to H-16, under the general supervision of an elderly marine gunner. The gunner sat on the edge of the pit, handling the plans, and occasionally making calculations on a circular slide rule which hung from a lanyard around his neck.

Libby had just completed a tricky piece of cutting for a three-stage blast, and was waiting for the blasters, when his phones picked up the gunner's instructions concerning the size of the charge. He pressed his transmitter button.

"Mr. Larsen! You've made a mistake!"

"Who said that?"

"This is Libby. You've made a mistake in the charge. If you set off that charge, you'll blow this pit right out of the ground, and us with it."

Marine Gunner Larsen spun the dials on his slide rule before replying, "You're all het up over nothing, son. That charge is correct."

"No, I'm not, sir," Libby persisted, "you've multiplied where you should have divided."

182

"Have you had any experience at this sort of work?"

"No, sir."

Larsen addressed his next remark to the blasters. "Set the charge."

They started to comply. Libby gulped, and wiped his lips with his tongue. He knew what he had to do, but he was afraid. Two clumsy stiff-legged jumps placed him beside the blasters. He pushed between them and tore the electrodes from the detonator. A shadow passed over him as he worked, and Larsen floated down beside him. A hand grasped his arm.

"You shouldn't have done that, son. That's direct disobedience of orders. I'll have to report you." He commenced reconnecting the firing circuit.

Libby's ears burned with embarrassment, but he answered back with the courage of timidity at bay. "I had to do it, sir. You're still wrong."

Larsen paused and ran his eyes over the dogged face. "Well —it's a waste of time, but I don't like to make you stand by a charge you're afraid of. Let's go over the calculation together."

Captain Doyle sat at his ease in his quarters, his feet on his desk. He stared at a nearly empty glass tumbler.

"That's good beer, Blackie. Do you suppose we could brew some more when it's gone?"

"I don't know, Cap'n. Did we bring any yeast?"

"Find out, will you?" He turned to a massive man who occupied the third chair. "Well, Larsen, I'm glad it wasn't any worse than it was."

"What beats me, Captain, is how I could have made such a mistake. I worked it through twice. If it had been a nitro explosive, I'd have known off hand that I was wrong. If this kid hadn't had a hunch, I'd have set it off."

Captain Doyle clapped the old warrant officer on the shoulder. "Forget it, Larsen. You wouldn't have hurt anybody; that's why I require the pits to be evacuated even for small charges. These isotope explosives are tricky at best. Look what happened in pit A-9. Ten days' work shot with one charge, and the gunnery officer himself approved that one. But I want to see this boy. What did you say his name was?"

"Libby, A. J."

Doyle touched a button on his desk. A knock sounded at the door. A bellowed "Come in!" produced a stripling wearing the brassard of Corpsman Mate-of-the-Deck.

"Have Corpsman Libby report to me."

"Aye aye, sir."

Some few minutes later Libby was ushered into the Captain's cabin. He looked nervously around, and noted Larsen's presence, a fact that did not contribute to his peace of mind. He reported in a barely audible voice, "Corpsman Libby, sir."

The Captain looked him over. "Well, Libby, I hear that

you and Mr. Larsen had a difference of opinion this morning. Tell me about it."

"I—I didn't mean any harm, sir."

"Of course not. You're not in any trouble; you did us all a good turn this morning. Tell me, how did you know that the calculation was wrong? Had any mining experience?"

"No, sir. I just saw that he had worked it out wrong."

"But how?"

Libby shuffled uneasily. "Well, sir, it just seemed wrong— It didn't fit."

"Just a second, Captain. May I ask this young man a couple of questions?" It was Commander "Blackie" Rhodes who spoke.

"Certainly. Go ahead."

"Are you the lad they call 'Pinkie'?"

Libby blushed. "Yes, sir."

"I've heard some rumors about this boy." Rhodes pushed his big frame out of his chair, went over to a bookshelf, and removed a thick volume. He thumbed through it, then with open book before him, started to question Libby.

"What's the square root of ninety-five?"

"Nine and seven hundred forty-seven thousandths."

"What's the cube root?"

"Four and five hundred sixty-three thousandths."

"What's its logarithm?"

"Its what, sir?"

"Good Lord, can a boy get through school today without knowing?"

The boy's discomfort became more intense. "I didn't get much schooling, sir. My folks didn't accept the Covenant until Pappy died, and we had to."

"I see. A logarithm is a name for a power to which you raise a given number, called the base, to get the number whose logarithm it is. Is that clear?"

Libby thought hard. "I don't quite get it, sir."

"I'll try again. If you raise ten to the second power— square it—it gives one hundred. Therefore the logarithm of a hundred to the base ten is two. In the same fashion the logarithm of a thousand to the base ten is three. Now what is the logarithm of ninety-five?"

Libby puzzled for a moment. "I can't make it come out even. It's a fraction."

"That's okay."

"Then it's one and nine hundred seventy-eight thousandths —just about."

Rhodes turned to the Captain. "I guess that about proves it, sir."

Doyle nodded thoughtfully. "Yes, the lad seems to have

184

intuitive knowledge of arithmetical relationships. But let's see what else he has."

"I am afraid we'll have to send him back to Earth to find out properly."

Libby caught the gist of this last remark. "Please, sir, you aren't going to send me home? Maw 'ud be awful vexed with me."

"No, no, nothing of the sort. When your time is up, I want you to be checked over in the psychometrical laboratories. In the meantime I wouldn't part with you for a quarter's pay. I'd give up smoking first. But let's see what else you can do."

In the ensuing hour the Captain and the Navigator heard Libby: one, deduce the Pythagorean proposition; two, derive Newton's laws of motion and Kepler's laws of ballistics from a statement of the conditions in which they obtained; three, judge length, area, and volume by eye with no measurable error. He had jumped into the idea of relativity and non-rectilinear space-time continua, and was beginning to pour forth ideas faster than he could talk, when Doyle held up a hand.

"That's enough, son. You'll be getting a fever. You run along to bed now, and come see me in the morning. I'm taking you off field work."

"Yes, sir."

"By the way, what is your full name?"

"Andrew Jackson Libby, sir."

"No, your folks wouldn't have signed the Covenant. Good night."

"Good night, sir."

After he had gone, the two older men discussed their discovery.

"How do you size it up, Captain?"

"Well, he's a genius, of course—one of those wild talents that will show up once in a blue moon. I'll turn him loose among my books and see how he shapes up. Shouldn't wonder if he were a page-at-a-glance reader, too."

"It beats me what we turn up among these boys—and not a one of 'em any account back on Earth."

Doyle nodded. "That was the trouble with these kids. They didn't feel needed."

Eighty-eight swung some millions of miles further around the sun. The pock-marks on her face grew deeper, and were lined with durite, that strange close-packed laboratory product which (usually) would confine even atomic disintegration. Then Eighty-eight received a series of gentle pats, always on the side headed along her course. In a few weeks' time the rocket blasts had their effect and Eighty-eight was plunging in an orbit toward the sun.

When she reached her station one and three-tenths the distance from the sun of Earth's orbit, she would have to be coaxed by another series of pats into a circular orbit. Thereafter she was to be known as E-M3, Earth-Mars Space Station Spot Three.

Hundreds of millions of miles away two other C.C.C. companies were inducing two other planetoids to quit their age-old grooves and slide between Earth and Mars to land in the same orbit as Eighty-eight. One was due to ride this orbit one hundred and twenty degrees ahead of Eighty-eight, the other one hundred and twenty degrees behind. When E-M1, E-M2, and E-M3 were all on station no hard-pushed traveler of the spaceways on the Earth-Mars passage would ever again find himself far from land—or rescue.

During the months that Eighty-eight fell free toward the sun, Captain Doyle reduced the working hours of his crew and turned them to the comparatively light labor of building a hotel and converting the little roofed-in valley into a garden spot. The rock was broken down into soil, fertilizers applied, and cultures of anaerobic bacteria planted. Then plants, conditioned by thirty-odd generations of low gravity at Luna City, were set out and tenderly cared for. Except for the low gravity, Eighty-eight began to feel like home.

But when Eighty-eight approached a tangent to the hypothetical future orbit of E-M3, the company went back to maneuvering routine, watch on and watch off, with the Captain living on black coffee and catching catnaps in the plotting room.

Libby was assigned to the ballistic calculator, three tons of thinking metal that dominated the plotting room. He loved the big machine. The Chief Fire Controlman let him help adjust it and care for it. Libby subconsciously thought of it as a person—his own kind of person.

On the last day of the approach, the shocks were more frequent. Libby sat in the right-hand saddle of the calculator and droned out the predictions for the next salvo, while gloating over the accuracy with which the machine tracked. Captain Doyle fussed around nervously, occasionally stopping to peer over the Navigator's shoulder. Of course the figures were right, but what if it didn't work? No one had ever moved so large a mass before. Suppose it plunged on and on—and on. Nonsense! It couldn't. Still he would be glad when they were past the critical speed.

A marine orderly touched his elbow. "Helio from the Flagship, sir."

"Read it."

"Flag to Eighty-eight; private message, Captain Doyle; am lying off to watch you bring her in.—Kearney."

Doyle smiled. Nice of the old geezer. Once they were on

186

station, he would invite the Admiral to ground for dinner and show him the park.

Another salvo cut loose, heavier than any before. The room trembled violently. In a moment the reports of the surface observers commenced to trickle in. "Tube nine, clear!" "Tube ten, clear!"

But Libby's drone ceased.

Captain Doyle turned on him. "What's the matter, Libby? Asleep? Call the polar stations. I have to have a parrallax."

"Captain—" The boy's voice was low and shaking.

"Speak up, man!"

"Captain—the machine isn't tracking."

"Spiers!" The grizzled head of the Chief Fire Controlman appeared from behind the calculator.

"I'm already on it, sir. Let you know in a moment."

He ducked back again. After a couple of long minutes he reappeared. "Gyros tumbled. It's a twelve hour calibration job, at least."

The Captain said nothing, but turned away, and walked to the far end of the room. The Navigator followed him with his eyes. He returned, glanced at the chronometer, and spoke to the Navigator.

"Well, Blackie, if I don't have that firing data in seven minutes, we're sunk. Any suggestions?"

Rhodes shook his head without speaking.

Libby timidly raised his voice. "Captain—"

Doyle jerked around. "Yes?"

"The firing data is tube thirteen, seven point six three; tube twelve, six point nine oh; tube fourteen, six point eight nine."

Doyle studied his face. "You sure about that, son?"

"It *has* to be that, Captain."

Doyle stood perfectly still. This time he did not look at Rhodes but stared straight ahead. Then he took a long pull on his cigarette, glanced at the ash, and said in a steady voice,

"Apply the data. Fire on the bell."

Four hours later, Libby was still droning out firing data, his face grey, his eyes closed. Once he had fainted but when they revived him he was still muttering figures. From time to time the Captain and the Navigator relieved each other, but there was no relief for him.

The salvos grew closer together, but the shocks were lighter.

Following one faint salvo, Libby looked up, stared at the ceiling, and spoke.

"That's all, Captain."

"Call polar stations!"

The reports came back promptly, "Parallax constant, sidereal-solar rate constant."

The Captain relaxed into a chair. "Well, Blackie, we did

187

it—thanks to Libby!" Then he noticed a worried, thoughtful look spread over Libby's face. "What's the matter, man? Have we slipped up?"

"Captain, you know you said the other day that you wished you had Earth-normal gravity in the park?"

"Yes. What of it?"

"If that book on gravitation you lent me is straight dope, I think I know a way to accomplish it."

The Captain inspected him as if seeing him for the first time. "Libby, you have ceased to amaze me. Could you stop doing that sort of thing long enough to dine with the Admiral?"

"Gee, Captain, that would be swell!"

The audio circuit from Communications cut in.

"Helio from Flagship: 'Well, done, Eighty-eight.'"

Doyle smiled around at them all. "That's pleasant confirmation."

The audio brayed again.

"Helio from Flagship: 'Cancel last signal, stand by for correction.'"

A look of surprise and worry sprang into Doyle's face—then the audio continued:

"Helio from Flagship: 'Well done, E-M3.'"

Concerning Stories Never Written: Postscript

THIS aside is addressed primarily to you who have read the first two volumes of this series rather grandly titled "Future History." Volume One, *The Man Who Sold the Moon*,* is laid from right now until the closing years of this century and ends with mankind's first faltering steps toward space. Some of the stories are so close to the present time as already to be outdated by events—an occupational hazard I share with weather forecasters and fortune tellers. Volume Two, *The Green Hills of Earth*,† is concerned with the great days of exploration of the Solar System. All of the stories take place somewhere close around the year 2000 A.D. If you refer to the chart in the flyleaf of this volume, you will see that this second group of stories appears to cover about twenty-five years, but this appearance is a deceptive shortcoming of typography— printing the titles on the chart requires a certain minimum of space. Nor does the order matter materially—some of the stories overlap in time but concern different characters in differing scenes.

This present Volume Three starts about seventy-five years later than the end of the last story in Volume Two—and a great amount of "Future History" has taken place between the two volumes. *Green Hills* ended with the United States a leading power in a systemwide imperialism embracing all the habitable planets. But the very first page of the first story in this book finds the United States plunged in a new Dark Ages, no longer space minded, isolationist even with respect to this planet, and under a theocracy as absolute as that of Communism.

The effect on the reader could be a little like that which sometimes results from unskillful editing of magazine serials— the sort of thing in which one installment ends with the hero hanging by his heels over the snake pit while the sinister villain leers at him from above, only to have the next installment start with our hero walking up Fifth Avenue, debonair and undamaged.

I could plead the excuse that these stories were never meant to be a definitive history of the future (concerning which I know no more than you do), nor are they installments of a long serial (since each is intended to be entirely independent of all the others). They are just stories, meant to amuse and written to buy groceries.

* *Shasta Publishers, Chicago, 1950; New American Library, 1951.*
† *Shasta Publishers, Chicago, 1951; New American Library, 1952.*

Nevertheless, I think that you who are kind enough to buy this volume are entitled to more explanation as to the great hiatus between the second and the third volume. On the chart you will see three titles in parentheses between the last story in *Green Hills* and the first story in this book; these three stories, had they ever been written, would have covered the intervening three quarters of a century and might well have been an additional volume in this series.

The first of these unwritten stories, *The Sound of His Wings* starts shortly before *Logic of Empire* and continues for several years beyond the ending of *Logic;* it would have recounted the early life, rise as a television evangelist, and subsequent political career of the Reverend Nehemiah Scudder, the "First Prophet," President of the United States and destroyer of its Constitution, founder of the Theocracy.

The second story, *Eclipse,* parallels somewhat both the American Revolution and the break-up of colonialism taking place on this planet today, for it is concerned with the colonies on Mars and on Venus becoming self-sufficient and politically mature and breaking away from Mother Earth, followed by almost complete cessation of interplanetary travel. *Logic of Empire* suggests some of the forces that led to the breakdown. Interplanetary travel will be tremendously expensive at first; if the home planet is no longer in a position to exploit the colonies, trade and communication might dwindle almost to zero for a long period—indeed the infant nations might pass "Non-Intercourse Acts."

The Stone Pillow was intended to fill the gap between the establishment of the Theocracy and its overthrow in the Second American Revolution. It was to have been concerned with the slow build-up of a counter-revolutionary underground. It gets its name from the martyrs of the underground, those who rested their heads on pillows of stone—in or out of prison. These revolutionaries would be in much the same nearly hopeless position that anti-Communists have found themselves in these thirty years past in the U.S.S.R., but the story would have concerned itself with the superiority of the knife to the atom bomb under some circumstances and with the inadvisability of swatting mosquitoes with an axe.

These three stories will probably never be written. In the case of *Eclipse* I have dealt with the themes involved at greater length in two novels which were not bound by the Procrustean Bed of a fictional chart; it would be tedious for both you and me to deal with the same themes again. As for the other two stories, they both have the disadvantage of being "down beat" stories, their outcomes are necessarily not pleasant. I am not opposed to tragedy and have written quite a bit of it, but today we can find more than enough of it in the headlines. I don't want to write tragedy just now and I doubt if you want to read it. Perhaps in another and sunnier year we will both feel differently.

In any case, I feel that even Caruso, Cleopatra, or Santa Claus could overstay their welcomes; it may be that this pseudohistory has already taken more curtain calls than the applause justifies.

I am aware that the themes of the unwritten stories linking the second and this the third volume thus briefly stated above have not been elaborated sufficiently to lend conviction, particularly with reference to two notions; the idea that space travel, once apparently firmly established, could fall into disuse, and secondly the idea that the United States could lapse into a dictatorship of superstition. As for the first, consider the explorations of the Vikings a thousand years ago and the colonies they established in North America. Their labors were fruitless; Columbus and his successors had to do it all over again. Space travel in the near future is likely to be a marginal proposition at best, subsidized for military reasons. It could die out—then undergo a renascence through new techniques and through new economic and political pressures. I am not saying these things will happen, I do say they could happen.

As for the second notion, the idea that we could lose our freedom by succumbing to a wave of religious hysteria, I am sorry to say that I consider it possible. I hope that it is not probable. But there is a latent deep strain of religious fanaticism in this, our culture; it is rooted in our history and it has broken out many times in the past. It is with us now; there has been a sharp rise in strongly evangelical sects in this country in recent years, some of which hold beliefs theocratic in the extreme, anti-intellectual, anti-scientific, and anti-libertarian.

It is a truism that almost any sect, cult, or religion will legislate its creed into law if it acquires the political power to do so, and will follow it by suppressing opposition, subverting all education to seize early the minds of the young, and by killing, locking up, or driving underground all heretics. This is equally true whether the faith is Communism or Holy-Rollerism; indeed it is the bounden duty of the faithful to do so. The custodians of the True Faith cannot logically admit tolerance of heresy to be a virtue.

Nevertheless this business of legislating religious beliefs into law has never been more than sporadically successful in this country—Sunday closing laws here and there, birth control legislation in spots, the Prohibition experiment, temporary enclaves of theocracy such as Voliva's Zion, Smith's Nauvoo, a few others. The country is split up into such a variety of faiths and sects that a degree of uneasy tolerance now exists from expedient compromise; the minorities constitute a majority of opposition against each other.

Could it be otherwise here? Could any one sect obtain a working majority at the polls and take over the country? Perhaps not—but a combination of a dynamic evangelist, television, enough money, and modern techniques of advertising and propaganda might make Billy Sunday's efforts look like a corner store compared to Sears Roebuck. Throw in a depression for good measure, promise a material heaven here on earth, add a dash of anti-Semitism, anti-Catholicism, anti-Negroism, and a good large dose of anti-"furriners" in general and anti-intellectuals here at home and the result might be something quite frightening—particularly when one recalls that our voting system is such that a minority distributed as pluralities in enough states can constitute a working majority in Washington.

I imagined Nehemiah Scudder as a backwoods evangelist who combined some of the features of John Calvin, Savonarola, Judge Rutherford and Huey Long. His influence was not national until after the death of Mrs. Rachel Biggs, an early convert who had the single virtue of being the widow of an extremely wealthy man who shared none of her religious myopia—she left Brother Scudder several millions of dollars with which to establish a television station. Shortly thereafter he teamed up with an ex-Senator from his home state; they placed their affairs in the hands of a major advertising agency and were on their way to fame and fortune. Presently they needed stormtroopers; they revived the Ku Klux Klan in everything but the name—sheets, passwords, grips and all. It was a "good gimmick" once and still served. Blood at the polls and blood in the streets, but Scudder won the election. The next election was never held.

Impossible? Remember the Klan in the 'Twenties—and how far it got without even a dynamic leader. Remember Karl Marx and note how close that unscientific piece of nonsense called *Das Kapital* has come to smothering out all freedom of thought on half a planet, without—mind you—the emotional advantage of calling it a religion. The capacity of the human mind for swallowing nonsense and spewing it forth in violent and repressive action has never yet been plumbed.

No, I probably never will write the story of Nehemiah Scudder; I dislike him too thoroughly. But I hope that you will go along with me in the idea that he *could* happen, for the sake of the stories which follow. Whether you believe in the possibility of the postulates of these stories or not, I hope that you will enjoy them—at my age it would be very inconvenient to have to go back to working for a living.

ROBERT A. HEINLEIN

Colorado Springs, Colorado